TALES FROM TALIFAR

THE SCARRED KING I

EXILE

Rose Foreman and Josh Foreman

Breath of Life Development

P.O. Box 2357

Woodinville, WA 98072-2357

Visit us at www.breathoflifedev.com

ISBN paperback 978-1-942926-03-0

    ebook 978-1-942926-06-1

    audio 978-1-942926-07-8

Library of Congress Control Number: 2019900053

Cover art and design by Josh Foreman

Printed in the United States

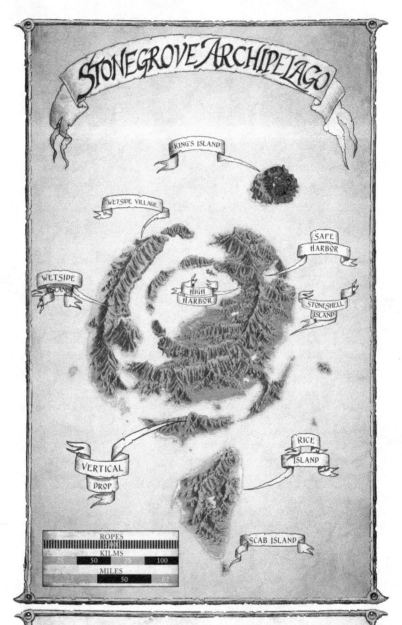

A SEA PREDATOR SHALL NOT HESITATE TO KILL ANY OUTSIDERS.
FAILURE TO FULFILL ONE'S DUTY COULD LEAD TO OUR DISCOVERY
AND ANNIHILATION.

~BOOK OF PROTOCOL OF THE SEA PREDATORS

2,500 years After the Crash

Ten-year-old Bowmark stared at two lifeless bodies on the beach: their skin ashen and gray, their fingers and toes long and webbed, the place on their faces where they should have had noses, flat and smooth. They must be adolescents older than him. And what were the small slits like porpoise's nostrils gaping on their foreheads?

He could not tear his gaze away from where the crabs and gulls ate at their eyes and picked pieces off their faces. Revolted, Bowmark waved them away until the scavengers retreated beyond Father and his entourage.

The local fishermen had likely contributed to the damage with their scaling knives based on the long gaping wounds. The crust of black sand stuck to parts of their bodies indicated a struggle; one that he tried not to imagine.

Flies rose and fell in haphazard clouds. He held his breath to avoid inhaling any.

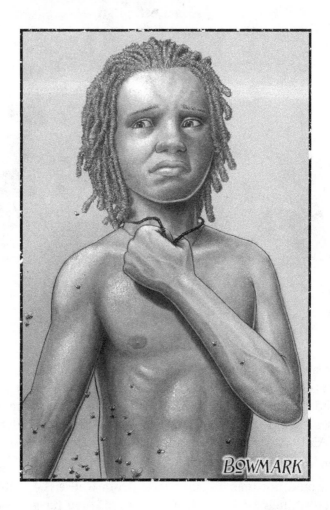

Bowmark's breakfast threatened to rise. He must not vomit. The king's son must not show weakness, not in front of the forty villagers, not in front of the servants and nobles that came to investigate, and definitely not in front of Father.

He glanced at Father who was examining a gray man half out of the surf. The body had been decapitated. Father's lips tightened to a thin line. He was famous for being inscrutable, but Bowmark could read this easily. His throat tightened. Father was furious. *At me?* Bowmark clutched his Giver's Hand medallion. What should he do? He stood, his feet rooted to the black sand as the smell of decay combined with the buzzing of the flies to make his stomach hurt.

The physician RunsFast moved forward and knelt by the strange people. She inspected closely but did not touch. "My King, these might be the children of the beheaded man. I guess their ages to be thirteen and fifteen. They were stabbed to death, as he was. They did not drown."

The surf gently touched Father's heels, as if timid about approaching the king. Overhead, gulls screamed at the people who had stolen their meal.

FATHER

Father left the adult body and strode closer to the dead adolescents. The sea had darkened the bottom hand-width of his long, official, indigo skirt. White triangular-shell designs stood out starkly on the fabric. The steel Giver's Hand medallion on his chest glinted in the early sunlight and the opal embedded on the palm cast a small round rainbow on the sheened copper skin of his forearm. He pulled back his tightly-coiled red hair and slipped off the loose hair tie.

WalkForward, a servant with the golden skin, golden-brown eyes, and straight black hair shared by the commoners, darted from the crowd of attendants waiting at the waterline by the canoes. He reached to redo the hair tie, but Father waved him away and redid the tie himself. The servant plucked at his knee-length brown skirt and briefly touched his wooden Giver's Hand medallion as he backed away a few steps into the surf.

Bowmark's curiosity overcame his revulsion and he stepped closer to these odd people. The corpses, a boy and a girl, had a bit of hair after all: tiny coarse tufts at the corners of their mouths. Both nobles and commoners of Bowmark's people had smooth skin and no body hair except on their scalps and eyebrows. He touched the corner of his mouth.

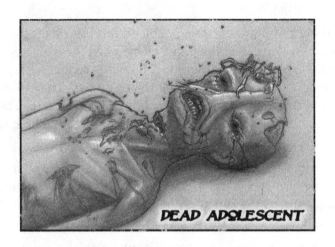

DEAD ADOLESCENT

Then he stretched out his fingers and compared them to that of the adolescents. Since their fingers were curled, he could not see if they had fingernails like his. Their skin did not have the sheen his did. They were barely taller than him, but then, even at age ten, he was taller than most children and even some thirteen-year-olds.

One of the children he was glad to be taller than, his second cousin RaiseHim, walked up to the dead youth with a crooked stick in his hands and poked the boy.

Father surged forward, grabbed RaiseHim by the shoulder, and shoved him into the surf. Everyone stared at them.

The boy's father, the tax collector murmured "Grant me pardon." and waded into the surf. He slapped his son on the head several times.

Bowmark looked away from RaiseHim's scowl. RaiseHim did not get along with his father or with Bowmark. So far as Bowmark knew, RaiseHim did not get along with anybody. He hoped RaiseHim's canoe would trail behind so he would not need to listen to the two of them argue. They would not fight here, not in front of the villagers, but once they were at sea, RaiseHim and his father would lose control. RaiseHim would yell until his father hit him.

Rather than watch the predictable drama, Bowmark examined the small village. Bamboo houses perched on volcanic cliffs above the narrow beach littered with fishing canoes, nets, and at the farthest end, racks of drying fish. The fish dripped oils on the dried seaweed and rice-straw fires beneath them. The fish oils sizzled, flamed, and transformed into drifting black smoke that wandered away from the nobles.

The villagers, commoners all, stood around the fish racks with furrowed faces and studied the nobles and servants who had interrupted the judgment circuit to sail in and investigate the invasion. The surf drowned out their whispers.

Bowmark tried to direct his attention to the dead youths' toes, but his gaze, against his will, kept returning to their ravaged heads. He swallowed again, closed his eyes, and turned away. Nobles and attendants moved around him.

When he opened his eyes, he finally saw the gray man's head spiked on an upright paddle barely an arm's length away.

He ran to the surf and vomited.

The maid ThreadTangle rushed to him, dipped a cloth in the ocean, and wiped his face and mouth. A strong desire for Mother washed over him. She had stayed behind at the Bamboo Palace when Father and he had sailed to WetSide.

Embarrassed, he waved ThreadTangle away. He hoped he looked as unconcerned as Father when he dismissed her, even if he had just vomited and shamed himself in front of everyone.

To avoid the eyes of the retinue, he turned away to study the islands in view. Far on the horizon rose the island of StoneShell, the largest in StoneGrove, where Bowmark's family resided. To the north of StoneShell stood King's Island, bristling with the Royal Forest and upon which a live volcano issued a thin stream of smoke. Smoke might mean lava was flowing.

ThreadTangle looked over where Bowmark's gaze was fixed. She whispered, "Don't worry. If it erupts today or tomorrow, you're still too young. They won't hold a proving."

Proving. Tears overflowed Bowmark's eyes. He vomited again. The maid cleaned him again, moisture welling in her own golden-brown eyes.

Bowmark stared at his feet. He had showed weakness, showed the fear he was not allowed to have.

RaiseHim splashed up to him and whispered in his ear, "You're a little girl," before the tax collector pulled his son to their canoe.

Bowmark swallowed bile. RaiseHim wasn't afraid. He didn't tremble every time the volcano prepared to erupt and open the time of proving. He wasn't the presumed who was destined to walk onto the Disc.

ThreadTangle bent over to murmur, "Compassion for these strangers—whatever they are—is not bad." The soothing aroma of coconut oil in her hair drifted by Bowmark's nose. He rubbed his eyes. If only he could be as bold as his hateful cousin.

The protocol officer limped up to Father. The woman's red hair had faded to a gray that matched her eyes. Her brown, spotted skin had more wrinkles than the mountains surrounding them. She also wore the long light skirt instead of the knee-length heavy skirts everyone else wore. Swinging her hand in a broad gesture that included the villagers, she leaned in close. "My King, these villagers should be rewarded for killing the enemy."

Father pointed to the adolescents with his elbow. "These people are not our enemy."

The protocol officer sidled in closer. "If they had lived, they might have carried word of us to our—"

"No."

Enemy. The people that plagued Bowmark's nightmares. The people that caused Father to spar every morning. The reason fishermen were not allowed past the islands of StoneGrove, but must fish between the islands lest they be captured and tortured into revealing the location of the last of the Bowmark's people, the Sea Predators. The enemy tribe, the Southils, liked to skin people alive, especially Sea Predators.

Every time Bowmark asked what the Southils looked like, he was told only that they wore three line tattoos under one eye. He had not been told there existed people with gray skin and noses on their foreheads.

Turning away from the Protocol officer, Father raised his voice, "Bring three of the extra sails and their lines."

Three of the manservants broke away from the crowd, racing to the closest end of the beach where the outrigger canoes had been pulled up under the shade of coconut palms.

A black seadog tied to the prow of the smallest canoe lunged to the end of its rope. The quills along its back rose and fell as it bugled.

The servants filled their arms with canvas and raced back to lay the sails at Father's feet.

"Prepare them for burial."

The protocol officer blurted, "My King! They aren't Sea Predators. Why would we honor them as our own?"

The servants froze, all eyes on Father. Without a word he glared at them and the slight thrust of his chin set them back into action. They laid the white sails on the black sand beside the bodies and then dragged the corpses into the centers of the canvas. The protocol officer moved as though to protest again but Father's cold eyes fixed on her and the old woman shied back to silence.

A few villagers came forward bearing rocks, laid them beside the strangers and scurried back to the watchful line.

Bowmark stepped behind Father. Perhaps if Father didn't see him, then he wouldn't be angry at him for showing weakness.

The gulls screamed and flapped away. In the distance, monkeys and bigfa birds hooted as though nothing momentous had happened here.

While servants wrapped and tied the bodies, the villagers around the fish racks stepped aside to let an old man through. He had gray streaks in his black hair and wore a faded brown skirt. His bare feet dented the coarse sand as he approached Father, bearing in his hands a large circular object that looked like a leather clam. The closer he got to Father, the slower he moved and the more he trembled until finally he knelt and averted his gaze as he extended the strange object. "What have we to do with books? The enemy brought this. We give it to you."

Father took the proffered artifact, unlatched a hook, hinged it open, and turned the thick, waxed pages. The protocol officer eyed the book as though it were a snake poised to strike.

Though most of the Sea Predators learned to read at least a few words, the islands of StoneGrove had few books. The Temple held the two Holy Books. The protocol officer carried the Protocol. The Records of the Kings rested under dust in the treasury room. The language tutor consulted a dictionary with five languages. The royals kept tax records, wrote a few letters to each other, and wrote out petitions to the king on paper made of banana fiber and bamboo leaves or on thin, scraped leather from pig hides.

This strange round book was larger than the two Holy Books combined and was made of thicker paper than the Sea Predators used.

The sun cast deep shadows under the brows of the villagers as they stared at Father. He clapped the tome shut and removed a bit of seaweed clinging to the cover. "This is a book of maps." He turned to Bowmark and thrust the book into his hands.

Bowmark gripped the volume and gulped. What was he supposed to do with this?

Father turned to his servants. "Place the strangers in my canoe."

Some of the servants eyed each other before jumping to follow his orders. Three carried each of the bodies and laid them on the trampoline, a net-like grid of ropes strung between the spars of the outrigger to carry cargo. ThrowPebbles carried the severed head. The servants' feet splashed in the surf.

While the servants were busy, the kingdom's tax collector approached the huddled villagers. He would want to collect taxes on the salvage from the strangers' shipwreck.

The only sounds were the splashing, the grind of the surf, and the squeals of ocean hawks.

Bowmark trailed behind the servants returning to the canoes. Black sand gritted under his bare feet. Sweat filmed his skin, and he squeezed the heavy book to his chest to keep it from slipping.

Although he could easily climb into a canoe by himself, SunGlare automatically lifted him. How was he going to convince them that he wasn't a toddler, and hadn't been a toddler for a long time, if he threw up every time he saw a dead body?

The prow of the outrigger scraped against the sand as servants shoved the red and black canoe into the surf and then splashed aboard themselves. Five more canoes followed Bowmark's.

Men tugged on lines and the triangular, indigo sails caught the rising breeze and belled out into a tight curve. The waves sparkled in the sunlight and slapped the canoe and its outrigger as the smell of decay blew away on the clean wind.

Bowmark hugged the book against his chest and shivered, staring at the wrapped bodies. Father moved to sit beside him and laid a hand on his shoulder. Even if the question made Father angry, Bowmark needed to know. He stuttered, "W-what are they?"

Father's deep voice held sorrow, not anger. "They are humans, as you and I are."

A maid reaching for a calabash of water bumped Bowmark's back. She cringed at the scowl from the protocol officer, but Father only glanced mildly at her.

Father squeezed Bowmark's shoulder. "We Sea Predators are born with red hair or black hair. Some of us have copper skin, and some of us have golden skin. Whether we have black hair or red hair, we are all Sea Predators as well as human. In the Records of the Kings I have read about the gray-skinned humans. People who have gray skin are called seafolks. The ancestors changed the shape of many humans and animals. Humans in our age come in a variety of colors and sizes in the wider world. Every one of them has the capacity for good or evil. Just like Sea Predators, common or noble." He looked up.

The servants who had been leaning in to listen hastily returned to their work.

Bowmark glanced back at the canoe holding RaiseHim and his father, the tax collector. They wouldn't like Father's words that implied the commoners were as good as nobles.

Although Father and Bowmark were pure-blooded nobles, Grandfather's first wife had been a daughter of the first commoner to achieve royalty by proving on the Disc. After she died, he had married a red-haired noblewoman who became Bowmark's grandmother, but the family still seemed tainted to some of the nobles.

The sailors tacked against the wind, slowing the outrigger canoe to keep on course. The flapping sail swung to a new position and its shade crossed Bowmark and Father.

Bowmark rubbed his lips with his wrist. "Are those gray people Sea Predators?"

"No. But neither are they our enemies." Father gently tugged the book out of Bowmark's arms and laid the tome flat on his lap. His fingers brushed the brown cover. "This is not the Sea Predator alphabet nor the Sea Predator language. You are learning Common, which is the language of the wider world. You can read this."

Bowmark stared at the embossed strange lines and curves he could not read. He had no idea what this strange book said. This much he knew: The Sea Predators had been hiding in StoneGrove from the Southils for two hundred years. On the other side of the ocean lived Southils and other people whose names were long forgotten. People spoke Common or South there, so Father forced Bowmark to learn those languages. If his tutor had not had permission to cane him, Bowmark would not have learned any of those useless languages.

He opened the book and stared at the first and largest letters. Slowly the shapes acquired meaning. His voice quivered, "A—at. Luh. Ss. Atlas. Uh. Of. The—the. Sea. Folk. Fam—fam ih. Family. Bree. See? Breezy?" He stopped, having run out of breath. Reading was hard.

"I think the family name is Breecee." Father squeezed Bowmark's shoulder. "Breathe, son. You cannot think if you do not breathe." He stroked Bowmark's hair. "I think Atlas must be the name for a book of maps." He pointed to the page on the right which was half filled with words in straight lines. Twisty lines filled the rest.

Father tapped the pages. "Son, I am giving you an important job. You will read this Atlas."

Bowmark gaped. There were hundreds of pages. Considering how long he took to read the first seven words, reading the rest of the book could take years.

Father continued. "I want you to find where the Southils live. Also, we need to find out if StoneGrove is marked in here. We need to know if we have been discovered."

Bowmark shivered at the thought of the Southils invading their islands. He gripped his Giver's Hand medallion. His throat squeaked and he coughed to cover the sound. As the king's son and presumed he must not be weak. He must not, or the Southils might kill them all. He swallowed, and then sniffed. "I will, Father."

He flipped a few pages to a drawing of people in outrigger canoes with rectangular sails rather than the triangle sails of the

Sea Predators. He tried to remember to breathe as he sounded out each syllable. "The Hahn of the Longboats are a fractious people, seldom willing to trade. When they are willing, they trade dried fish, fresh fruit, and coconuts for steel needles and steel pots. Father, what does fractious mean?"

Father dipped his head and whispered, "Like RaiseHim."

They exchanged smiles. Bowmark flipped to another page with an illustration of a creature with a long tail, holding its body in the position a bird does when walking. The word under the drawing was rumsha. "What kind of animal is this?"

Father studied the page and the words on the opposite page. "This is a non-human person. There are many kinds of non-human people in the wide world. The only non-human person I've ever met was a shlak. Someday I would like to see a varon seacastle floating on the ocean."

Bowmark's brain ignited. "Do all these people want to kill us?"

"So far as I know, only the Southils and their allies want to destroy us. All the other people of the world don't care whether we are slaughtered or left to live."

Bowmark ran his fingers along a sentence. "I will tell you everything I learn."

"I am pleased." Father gazed toward still far-off StoneShell. He shouted to the servants, "Furl the sail."

Bowmark grinned. Father was pleased! As the band around Bowmark's throat loosened, he vowed to himself that he would read as much as he needed to find what Father wanted to know. Bowmark would protect his people.

As Father's orders were followed, all the outriggers in the entourage slowed to drift and bob on the surface of the ocean.

Father stood and raised his hands. "May Giver grant these innocent people rest- as He deals our enemies death and destruction." He lowered his hands. They had not brought any priests with them. Who would say the Holy Words?

"Bury them," Father said.

Silently, sailors picked up the bodies from the trampoline and slid them into the blue water. The bundles sank rapidly, the white sail wrappings disappearing in the deep. Then one sailor muttered, "The fish feed us, then we feed the fish."

Father settled on the thwart, the board that served as brace and seat, next to Bowmark. He stared into the distance. No one said a word, holy or not, as servants reset the sail, and the canoe plowed through the sea toward Muntee Holm, an uninhabited island, to stay the night before heading for StoneShell. Bowmark had been looking forward to exploring the tiny uninhabited islet, but now he wanted to simply go home.

THUS THE ROYALTY WERE TASKED THE RESPONSIBILITY TO GOVERN. RULE AND GUIDE THE COMMONER. AND THE COMMONER TO GRATEFULLY PROVIDE LOYALTY. SUSTENANCE AND OBEDIENCE TO THE ROYALTY.

~BOOK OF PROTOCOL OF THE SEA PREDATORS

The sun lolled overhead. Bowmark's canoe did not sail into Safe Harbor, the bay of the Bamboo Palace, but rather floated into the tiny High Harbor bay on the other side of the island of StoneShell. Four fishermen's canoes bobbed near the narrow beach. Nets covered the water-smoothed black boulders.

Before Bowmark could step into the surf, SunGlare caught him and playfully swung him to the white sand. Blue crabs scuttled aside. Father waded in along with his servants and noble functionaries. The Atlas stayed behind with the men guarding the canoes.

Bowmark skipped up the steps carved into the basalt cliff and brushed aside vines spangled with red blossoms. Behind him servants carried bundles of fabric, poles, and equipment up the long winding path that cut across the massive cliff face that separated the harbor from the village above.

Halfway up Bowmark stopped skipping. The climb was arduous, and he marveled at the local fishermen who hiked it every day. A cool breeze refreshed the party as it blew in the noon rain clouds. When Bowmark reached the top of the stairs, he stopped, panting. Bamboo houses raised waist-high on stilts filled a wide indentation on the mountainside as did fields of orange rice and sharp-leaved yellowfruit. The majority of the houses clustered around a cleared field close to the top of the cliff-side stairs. The stench of pig manure thickened the air.

"Don't wrinkle your nose like that," Father said as he joined Bowmark on the field covered with the stubble of cut podvines and strewn rice straw. "Pig manure feeds the plants that feed us."

Pig manure fed the podvines? Maybe he wouldn't ever eat pods again.

Father strode to the far end of the field where the villagers of High Harbor had set up trestles with stiffened mats crowded with clay pots of food. There he stopped to greet the village head. The servants erected an indigo canopy with the royal design of paired triangular shells and assembled Father's portable throne and canopy in the center of the field.

The tax collector puffed as he climbed the last stair step and flopped onto the bench beside Bowmark. "I hate that climb. Why can't the dirt-eaters come to the palace?"

RaiseHim joined his father. "This place stinks!"

The village did stink. Enough to make Bowmark's eyes water. On top of the manure, there were the cesspools near the homes. The people of the village had no chambermaids to carry the waste far away as was done at the palace. But Bowmark would ignore the smell in accordance with Father's correction—and to spite RaiseHim.

Four men dragged out log drums and beat on them with exuberance. Flute players joined them. Men and women filed onto the field, and, in separate lines, clapped and stamped to the beat. The noon rain began and soon plastered everyone's skirts to their thighs. Mud and straw splashed the dancers' calves.

The villagers walked in from the fields or emerged from the houses fronted by large verandas. Small children danced on the verandas, their foot stamps and hip waggles a little behind the beat of the song their mothers were singing:

We welcome you, O King.

We welcome your justice.

We welcome your eyes.

We rejoice at being seen.

Braziers filled with sweet oils were set on bamboo legs by each pole of the canopy and lit, suffusing the air with aromatic smoke that masked the smell of manure. The wind shifted, further clearing the air.

The only commoner guard, NineToes, climbed up onto a veranda and danced with a little girl and two boys. He swooped up one of the boys and tickled him. The boy's screams of delight rang across the field.

A toddler tried to join in the dance on the field, but he slipped and fell. His mouth opened wide, revealing four baby teeth, as he cried and rubbed straw on his wispy hair. His mother scooped him up and tucked his head under her chin.

Homesickness tightened Bowmark's throat. He had been excited to travel this morning to WetSide with Father, but now he wanted to curl up in Mother's lap and feel her stroking his back the way the commoner mother was soothing her baby. But he was too big to fit on Mother's shrinking lap. *Please let there be a sister growing in Mother's belly.*

With a final *bang, bang!* of the drums, the dance ended. As though choreographed, the noon rain also ended. The clouds rolled away, leaving blue sky over blue sea and shining green jungle clinging to the steep sides of the mountainous island. Immediately, the fallen rain rose as steam to rejoin the sky. Father seated himself upon his portable throne and held the Orb of Justice in his right hand.

FATHER AND MOTHER

The protocol officer took her place beside the throne and called out in a reedy voice, "Let all who seek justice come forward."

Two warriors with obsidian tipped spears moved to their places on either side of the throne while the servants and nobles formed a knot on the main path through the village. The villagers sat on the steaming field of podvine stubble and straw.

Bowmark stepped to the front of the crowd as two men walked to the edge of the canopy and knelt. When Father waved them forward, they crawled on their knees to the base of the throne.

The protocol officer held up a palm fiber paper and perused the sheet. "This letter says there is a dispute about land between CatchaBird and StandUp." She lowered the letter to peer at the two men. "CatchaBird, tell your side of the dispute."

CatchaBird rose and held his Giver's Hand medallion. "May Giver deal me disaster and death if I do not speak the truth." He rudely pointed to the kneeling man with his hand while respectfully staring at Father's feet. "StandUp breached the wall around my field. All the water drained out onto his field."

StandUp interrupted. "CatchaBird had built the wall and footpath on my property. I was trying to restore the original boundary. The breach was accidental."

CatchaBird yelled, "Yet I was the one forced to repair the breach. You lie when you say I stole your land. You stole mine when you moved the boundary stone."

The protocol officer cut her gaze to a guard who stepped forward and leveled his spear. The farmers stopped arguing and pressed their faces to the ground again. "Speak only when I give you permission. StandUp, calmly tell us your side."

StandUp gripped his medallion and swore. "My King, my wife has recently given birth. I have many children. Should I let them starve while a footpath that grows nothing stands on my encroached field?"

Bowmark lost interest as StandUp argued that a man had a duty to feed his family, no matter what. These judgment ceremonies could take two or three candles. Bowmark could never focus on them for more than half a candle. Far more interesting were the children playing tag around the back of the canopy.

So long as they did not disrupt work or endanger anybody, the young of StoneGrove could play wherever they wished. The adults watched the argument and ignored the boys and girls racing among their ranks and around the king's entourage.

A child in a short black skirt brushed against Bowmark as he evaded the catcher. When the catcher ran by, Bowmark joined the chase. The boys ran, laughing, to the other side of the field and turned in a wide arc.

Bowmark stopped near a canopy pole when the Protocol Officer called, "Hear the judgment of My King."

Father kept his face expressionless as he announced, "StandUp has stolen CatchaBird's labor. We Sea Predators do not allow slavery or stolen labor within our lands." As he continued speaking his judgment, Bowmark rejoined the chase.

Father extended the Orb of Justice. CatchaBird and StandUp kissed the iron orb and backed away.

Another boy, this one in a brown skirt, ran by Bowmark.

Bowmark chased him down the field, and on the turn, tapped him between his shoulder blades. They skidded to a stop and reversed, the commoner boy now chasing Bowmark. They raced around the back of the canopy, arms swinging, feet kicking up clods of mud. When Bowmark rounded the back left pole, his big toe caught on a loop of podvine. He fell flat on his chest.

The chaser tripped over Bowmark and crashed into a brazier.

Boy and brazier rolled along the dirt as burning oil splashed onto his shoulder, neck and jaw. He screamed.

Shivers ran up Bowmark's spine. Adults stared, aghast, a long heartbeat before rising and rushing to the screaming child.

NineToes stripped off his skirt and threw it on the boy's neck and burning hair. The maidservant Nightfall dumped a calabash of water over the boy's head.

NineToes dabbed his wet skirt over the boy's hair and neck as the child screamed and kicked.

Bowmark rose and covered his mouth. A royal guard, FlyHigh, grabbed him from behind and pulled him away.

The guard lifted Bowmark's chin and asked, "Are you hurt?"

"No." Bowmark twisted his chin out of FlyHigh's hand. "Is he going to die?"

FlyHigh looked over at the huddle of people around the boy. "I can't say."

A kneeling villager talked to Father and the protocol officer, pointing here and there.

The court physician, RunsFast, bent over the child and slipped some dried bitefinger fish liver into the boy's mouth. The boy's flailing hand struck the physician in the face and tore off the ribbon that held back her reddish-brown hair. RunsFast seized the boy's fist and murmured, "Let me help you." She reached into her basket and pulled out a bottle of gray powder that she sprinkled on blistered, bleeding skin.

The screams reduced to whimpers.

RaiseHim trotted up to Bowmark and said, "I saw you trip him on purpose."

Some of the adults standing around the burned child turned to stare at the two royal children.

Bowmark stammered, "N--No." Why was RaiseHim lying about him? He backed up until he hit FlyHigh's knees.

NineToes retrieved his skirt and buckled the thick brown fabric around himself. Then he picked up the burned boy and carried him to a bamboo house farther into the village. The door slid open before him and he ducked to enter the darkness within.

Bowmark's feet could not move from his spot between FlyHigh and the canopy. The Protocol Officer moved from a group of villagers to Father and whispered in his ear. Father nodded slowly. His towering shadow fell across Bowmark as he approached. Bowmark looked up at Father's expressionless face.

"Kneel, son," Father said.

Bowmark gulped and knelt.

Father announced, "You have hurt one of my subjects. You have also removed his labor from his family."

"I didn't mean to."

"I am certain you did not mean to. I am not judging intent. I am judging result."

Bowmark bit his lower lip to keep it from quivering. Behind Father, RaiseHim smirked. NineToes returned to the canopy and studied the two youngsters.

"This is my judgment: Bowmark shall live with Sunrise's family and do Sunrise's chores until such time as Sunrise can

work again. I shall pay for all treatment that Sunrise requires."
Father bent and extended the Orb of Justice toward Bowmark's
mouth.

He stared into Father's blue-gray eyes. Father was going to
make him stay at High Harbor and not let him go home. At that
moment, all he wanted was to go home and hide from the stares
of the villagers. "But I didn't mean to hurt him."

"Kiss the Orb."

THE ORB OF JUSTICE

Kissing the Orb meant accepting the judgment. One did not
argue with Father. One only obeyed. Bowmark had seen other
sons argue with their fathers, but he had never been allowed to
argue with his. He blinked out a few tears and slowly kissed the
Giver's Hand engraved on the Orb. The cold iron chilled his lips.

Father stepped back and commanded, "FallDown, you retrieve the book. Nightfall, you will find the language tutor when we reach Safe Harbor and tell him to go to High Harbor. RunsFast, you stay here and attend Sunrise until I send for you. NineToes, I believe this is your village?"

NineToes averted his eyes. "Truth, My King."

"You will continue the presumed's training and ensure that no one harms him."

"My King, no one here would even think about harming him."

"Then your job should be easy." Father turned and watched his servants dismantle the canopy and throne.

Bowmark shivered. He hugged himself as he sat back on his heels. Father was leaving him and wouldn't even look at him. He must not be weak, but, oh, how weak he felt inside. He swallowed tears.

NineToes gripped his shoulder and murmured in his ear, "It won't be so bad. You'll see. Come on, let's go to your new home."

Bowmark nodded weakly.

NineToes chuckled. He led Bowmark to the bamboo house and sprang lightly to the waist-high veranda. He ducked into the central room crowded with people. Bowmark followed, using the steps.

At first, he could make out only dark shapes, but as his eyes adjusted the shadows resolved into the burnt boy sleeping in a hammock and a crowd of people staring at him.

Bandages covered the side of the boy's face, neck, and shoulder. Father had called him Sunrise. At one end of the hammock stood a stout man wearing a mud-brown skirt. A waxed wooden Giver's Hand medallion hung on a leather string on his wide chest and tangled in his long black hair.

At the other end of the hammock a round woman wore a tunic and skirt of faded blue with pale pink embroidered vines and sewn-on shell beads. Her shaved head gleamed in the light of the tiny oil lamp hanging on a bamboo post. She stroked Sunrise's black hair with trembling hands.

Tiny hands punched Bowmark's chest. He fell on his rear and stared at the little girl, maybe six years old, who had shoved him. Since he was much taller than her, he resembled a goliath beetle facing off an ant: an angry ant with sharp mandibles.

"You hurt my brother!" she shouted. Bowmark revised her age upward two years. She waved her fists.

He opened his mouth to say that he hadn't meant to hurt him, but her father reached down a huge hand, seized her thin arm and pulled her away. His voice was a bass rumble. "MoonGleam, behave yourself. It was an accident." The father's golden-brown eyes turned to Bowmark. "You don't need to look so frightened. We're not angry at you."

"I'm angry!" shouted MoonGleam.

Bowmark stared at her big, golden eyes, her tiny nose, her shining black hair braided in a coil on her head, and her pinched lips. She was the cutest girl he had ever seen.

The man rumbled, "Didn't you hear me say it was an accident? It will be no accident if I swat your bottom."

MoonGleam grabbed her buttocks and ran screaming from the room.

Bowmark stared after her. "I—I—I'm sorry."

NineToes ducked out of the room. After taking turns squeezing the mother's shoulder, some of the adults followed NineToes, making the light from the doorway flicker. Other adults entered, their bare feet nearly silent on the grass mats set on the bamboo floor.

Bowmark didn't know who any of them were. If only he could go home. Bowmark jumped when the broad hand of the father engulfed his shoulder.

Sunrise's father said, "You may call us Mom and Dad if you wish while you live here. Tomorrow is soon enough for me to introduce you to the joys of slopping hogs and shoveling out pens. Are you hungry, My Presumed?"

He didn't know if he was hungry or not. He knew his stomach hurt.

NineToes re-entered the room, holding the Atlas. "Presumed, My King has given you more instructions. You are to entertain Sunrise and distract him from his pain."

"How do I do that?"

NineToes shrugged both shoulders. "I don't know. Maybe you could read him the Atlas." He handed the massive book to Bowmark.

The bamboo posts creaked as Sunrise woke and turned to his side. "What is that?" Sunrise pointed with his elbow. He winced, as though moving his jaw hurt.

Bowmark hauled the book over to the hammock and propped the heavy Atlas against his chest. "This is a book about where people live and what they have to trade." He opened to a page he had studied in the outrigger canoe during their trip to High Harbor. "This is a person who isn't human."

The cloths on Sunrise's face, neck, and shoulder smelled of medicine and burnt hair. Sunrise's breath also smelled of medicine as he tilted closer. His Giver's Hand pendant that slid across his chest was made of crudely carved wood, now burnt. Instead of the blazing opal Bowmark's held, Sunrise's had a small cowrie shell attached with bronze wire. Sunrise weakly grabbed the book's cover. "That's a person? But it has a tail. And ears that stick up. What's a human?"

"You are. So am I."

"I thought I was a commoner."

"You're a commoner human. And because we live on StoneGrove we're also Sea Predators." Bowmark's arms ached from holding up the heavy book.

"Is this a commoner or a noble?"

"I don't know." Was he supposed to know?

The parents leaned over Bowmark to stare at the page. The father murmured, "How strange. I've never seen anything like this."

"Can I hold the book?" asked Sunrise.

Bowmark gladly relinquished the Atlas, placing it gently in crook of Sunrise's unburnt left arm. Sunrise winced and hissed, but he did not let go of the huge book.

The adults clustered around the hammock to stare at the picture of the person who wasn't a human.

"This is wonderful," Sunrise said. "What do all these lines mean?"

His mind blanked for a moment before Bowmark remembered what Father had said. "This is a map. It shows where these people who aren't human live."

After another wince, Sunrise grinned. "I want to go there."

A sharp intake of breath from several of the adults brought their heads up to see what was wrong.

"Please, Presumed. Don't pay attention to what he said. My son's mind is muddled by all the medication. He didn't mean what he said." Sunrise's plump mother bit her lips.

Why were they so nervous? Ah, he had spoken treason. The boys' eyes met. "I understand," said Bowmark. "Don't worry."

The tension eased and adults resumed their hushed conversations. Eventually all the guests left, and Sunrise drifted back to sleep. The mother—Mom—trundled over and gently pulled Bowmark against her pillowy hip and belly, stroking his red hair. "Welcome to our little family, son. This can't be easy for you." Bowmark stood numbly, his arms squeezed to his sides. He had never wanted Mother more.

Mom released him and turned to rummage through an old wooden box, then produced a hammock for him. "It's been a long day for you. I'll set you up next to Sunrise."

Tiny Moongleam pattered up and stood beside Bowmark and together they watched Mom attach the worn hammock to wall and ceiling beam. Moongleam whispered, "I still hate you for hurting Sunrise. Someday I'm going to kill you. With a knife. When you're asleep."

Bowmark twitched.

Mom said, "I heard that. Go outside and stay outside until you can apologize to the presumed."

"Mom! It's dark outside!"

"Truth."

"What if a kratchnak eats me?"

"Kratchnaks only eat bad children." Mom spread out the hammock, checking for holes and spiders. "Are you a bad child?" Are you going to keep blaming the presumed for an accident?"

Moongleam's lower lip trembled. "I'm sorry, Presumed." She sidled closer to Bowmark and whispered even lower, "But I don't mean it."

To teach him quick reflexes, Father sometimes ordered guards to attack Bowmark at unexpected times. Bowmark touched his throat. Unless she stabbed him in the eye, he could easily fight her off.

Mom said, "Let's all lie down and sleep."

Father refused to look at him. Mother slammed the doors of the Bamboo Palace in Bowmark's face and no one would answer when he pled to be let in. He startled awake, sweating and crying softly in the dark strange house. A sucking weight threatened to pull his bones into the ground. *A Sea Predator is brave.* The words evaporated in his mind like the noon rains.

Why would Father be so unjust? He knew that the accident wasn't Bowmark's fault. He knew that RaiseHim was a liar. RaiseHim's father might hit him in anger, but at least RaiseHim was allowed to argue with his father. At least RaiseHim was not banished from his home.

Rage at the injustice alternated with fear of the unknown roiling in Bowmark's head until he fell back into fitful sleep.

The next morning, Bowmark woke to the smell of boiling rice and the whimpering of Sunrise. Dad gently scooped his son up and deposited him on the floor in front of the eating mat. Bowmark slipped out of his hammock and sat beside him. Sunrise leaned on him.

In the cool morning air, RunsFast slid the door aside and entered with a glass cup filled with murky water. After watching the boys for a moment, she handed to cup to Bowmark. "Help him drink this if you please, Presumed. Tiny sips. This will ease his pain."

Then she gave a nutshell box to Mom. "This is bitefinger fish liver. Not until noon should you mix this with water and cane sugar. If you give him too much too soon, not only will his pain end, but so will his breathing."

"Ah," breathed Mom. "You royals don't play around, do you? Will this work better than boiled willow bark?"

"Truth." RunsFast peeled off the blood and serum-soaked bandages, dabbed an oil over the blisters and raw muscle, and wrapped clean bandages over the burns.

Sea Predators are brave. Sea Predators don't cry. Bowmark held the cup to Sunrise's lips and gave him tiny sips. Sunrise relaxed. Bowmark then gave him little bites of mashed rice.

Moongleam watched him as she ate more rice than she should have been able to hold. Then she collected the dirty banana leaf parts that had held the rice to throw into the cookfire behind the house. "I think I won't stab you after all."

Sunrise and Bowmark caught each other's glances. After a brief struggle not to, they both laughed.

NineToes darkened the doorway. "Is the presumed ready for training?"

"Not yet," Dad said. "Unless you mean training to muck out pig pens."

NineToes grinned. "That was My King's judgment."

Dad picked up Sunrise and placed him in his hammock. Sunrise instantly fell asleep. "Let's go, Presumed."

The two men and Bowmark walked up the hill to the row of sheds that housed the village pigs. Bowmark took shallow breaths, trying to inhale as little of the miasma of pig manure as possible.

Dad said, "You're worried about living here, aren't you? You're afraid that everybody will hate you."

Bowmark looked away.

"Don't worry. Even Moongleam will stop being angry at you in a few days. She's more excitable than the rest of the village together, but eventually she sees reason. Give it time to let us get used to you. You'll soon be one of us."

Bowmark hoped so. It looked like his stay would be long.

EVERY KING MUST PROVE WORTHY TO LEAD, IMMUNE TO PAIN.
CAPABLE OF BATTLE, WILLING TO SACRIFICE AND TO KILL.

~BOOK OF PROTOCOL OF THE SEA PREDATORS

The boar howled and charged. Bowmark threw down his shovel and ran for the bamboo fence. He vaulted over as the hot breath and tusk of the boar grazed his calf. His heart beat wildly. Too close. He lay on the gritty ground. The boar growled and beat its tusks on the fence and lashed its long, barbed tail. The fence shook under the animal's blows.

"Stop that!" Sunrise shouted. He cracked a bamboo pole against the boar's head.

The boar backed up. The quills on its back and neck rose and radiated like an explosion.

MoonGleam's laughter rang out.

Sunrise held the pole with his left hand in a threatening pose over the boar from the other side of the fence. "MoonGleam, that wasn't nice opening the gate before Bowmark was done. I'm going to tell Dad, and he's going to swat you."

"Ohhhh!" squealed MoonGleam. Waving her hands above her head, she ran along the terrace wall toward home.

"It was an accident." Bowmark stayed on the ground.

"It was not." Sunrise dropped the pole. "I saw her lift the latch."

Bowmark's breath raised a little ash. He jerked his head up to keep from inhaling the spiky motes of rock ash and laid his forehead on his fists. The ground called to him to stay down. "She didn't mean to harm me."

"Would you still be saying that if your butt was bleeding? You let her get away with everything."

"She's just having fun."

Sunrise scoffed. "She's a pest."

Bowmark rubbed his eye and watched the boar stamping within his pen. They would need to force the boar back to the other side of the corral so he could finish mucking out the pig pen.

Sunrise sat by Bowmark's head. He palpated his bandaged shoulder and winced. It had been three months since the accident, but the burns had been severe. "I think I tore the skin." White scars formed a web over glistening pink skin on his jaw, neck, and shoulder. His pungent lotion nearly overcame the smell of pigs.

"Maybe it's too soon for you to get out of the hammock."

A troupe of monkeys bounded up the path between pigsties, scaled the fence, and leaped on the thatched roof of the pig shelter. They tumbled over each other as they crowded the edge of the roof to look into the pig's trough.

Sunrise pitched a rock at them, and they scampered away. "I'm so tired of lying in the hammock. Listening to Sunset cry is shoving me into insanity."

"Me, I'm just tired."

Sunrise snickered. "I used to call the nobles lazy butts."

"Some of us are, but only after we're too old for proving."

"Not My King."

"No, not Father." Bowmark groaned and rose to his hands and knees. Sitting back on his haunches, he studied the boar still gnashing its tusks at him and flaring its quills. Sea Predators used those quills as tiny arrows for tiny birds, sewing and tattoo needles, as well as fancy fasteners on ornamental skirts and robes. He idly wondered why seadogs and pigs had the same quills.

A red, yellow, and black weaver bird landed on the bamboo fence, flicked its tail several times, chirruped, and then flew off just before a green and purple gliding lizard landed on the same spot. The thin layer of volcanic ash on the fence puffed away. Ash grayed the roofs, leaves, and paths of High Harbor. Fortunately, the noon rains washed off each day's layer of volcanic dust.

Sunrise stood and extended a hand to Bowmark to help him stand. "Come on. Help me catch Sparkles. She's walking funny."

Bowmark trudged after Sunrise. "Why do you name your piglets? You're just going to eat them."

"Not this litter. In two weeks they become weaners and Dad is going to auction them in the market at Mid Village. They're going to make us rich." Sunrise arrived at the sow's farrowing shed. He placed his hand on the gate, tensed his muscles to vault over, and then stopped, perhaps considering his healing skin. He opened the gate and stepped through.

Bowmark latched the gate behind them and helped Sunrise corner the squealing piglet.

Sunrise hauled up the squirming animal, waved the piglet's foot at Bowmark, and squeaked in a fake voice, "See? I have a rock in my trotter. Wouldn't you limp if you had a rock in your trotter?"

Bowmark smirked at his friend's silliness.

Sunrise pried out the wedged pebble. Piglets swirled around them like herrings around a shark.

Bowmark laughed at their manic movements.

"Dad's been breeding this new line of fast-growing pigs for twelve years. People are lining up to buy his fatty pigs at auction."

"Maybe I should buy some for the palace."

Sunrise's grin faded. "Who would bid against you? The palace could offer next to nothing and we would be forced to take it."

Bowmark sighed. Most of the villagers of High Harbor still watched him with wary eyes.

Sunrise looked past him. "Uh-oh, here comes NineToes."

Bowmark thought fast. "I need to look busy. Let me hold Sparkle." The piglet was transferred. The sparse, limp baby quills on its back twitched.

NineToes strode up to the fence and leaned on the top rail with his forearms. "Presumed, it's time to run the cliff steps."

"I need to finish mucking the boar's stall."

NineToes grinned and drawled, "You should have mucked faster. It's time for the run. I found a boy who will wrestle with you after the run. And then you need to practice knife-throwing for a candle."

Sunrise said, "I need Bowmark to—"

"Excuse me?" interrupted NineToes.

Sunrise tried again. "Please, Sir. I need the presumed to read me another page from the Atlas."

NineToes pushed back from the fence. "After the training. You can wait a candle and a half. It's still morning!"

Bowmark tried to keep the whine out of his words. "I ran the cliff three times yesterday."

"Then running it four times today should be easy."

If he said another word, he would do the run with left-handed staff drills and extra backflips. Bowmark let himself out of the pig pen.

Sunrise chuckled. "Now I call royals busy butts."

NineToes spun to point at him in warning, but Sunrise had already ducked inside the shed.

Bowmark jogged behind NineToes to the top of the steep stairs that switchbacked from High Harbor to the far-below bay where fishermen's canoes rose and dropped on sea swells. The guard hopped down the carved stairs and called back, "Aren't you glad half of this is easy?"

Bowmark's legs were not as long as NineToes', so neither down nor up the stairs was easy. When they reached the shore, he sat on the bottom tread, breathing in the reek of rotting seaweed. NineToes strolled over to ClamDigger who sat on a boulder, hunched over a damaged net. They clapped hands together and chatted as though NineToes weren't giving Bowmark a chance to rest before they ran back up the stairs.

Too soon, the men clapped hands again and NineToes returned to prod Bowmark up. At this angle, the winding path seemed to reach all the way to the blue sky. "Shall we rest a little longer so that you'll have the strength to practice archery while we run?"

Bowmark bolted up. "No need for more rest! No need for arrows!" His bare feet slapped the porous stone as he ran and jumped up the winding path. He still couldn't hit targets while both running and shooting.

They had jogged back up to High Harbor, ignored the rest bench at the top of the stairs, and continued all the way through and up to the watershed ridge of the island. At the summit, Bowmark flopped onto the bench for weary walkers while NineToes paused and looked toward the eastern side of StoneShell Island, toward the Bamboo Palace. From this vantage point they could see both the western side of the island where they had just come from as well as the eastern side, where the palace lay hidden in jungle. The path they were on connected to the two sides of the island.

NineToes tensed. "Wait a moment."

Bowmark gladly waited as the guard took a few steps on the path that wound down towards the palace. A red-haired man was toiling up the path. A few steps closer and Bowmark recognized the royal guard CrunchIt, coming for the weekly report from NineToes. Two days early.

Bowmark's pounding heart gradually slowed. He couldn't hear clearly what the guards were saying to each other over his pounding heart. So instead he looked west to study High Harbor. Farmers moved among their terraced fields. A silver thread of water arced from a distant mountain to splash into the dammed pond where people gathered buckets of water for their chores and crops. Pigs howled and grunted. Cluckers moved in the shade under the raised houses. From this height he could easily see Sunrise slowly carrying a bucket of pig manure to his dad's field of yellowfruit. Bowmark should be helping him. His friend had not yet entirely recovered from his burns.

High Harbor still stank, yet the odor had somehow grown less obnoxious.

MoonGleam leaped up from behind a tea shrub and startled Sunrise into dropping his bucket of manure. Sunrise's scolding tone, if not his words, carried across the field of bead seeds between the bench and him. Mom stumped out of the house with Sunset on her shoulder, the sun glistening on her shaved head. She chuckled. Bowmark laughed as MoonGleam scampered into the jungle.

MOONGLEAM

He startled when the shadows of NineToes and CrunchIt fell over him. NineToes said, "We're going to King's Island."

Bowmark's breath stopped. His mouth wobbled before he stuttered, "I'm too young to prove."

"Not you." CrunchIt sounded angry. "Someone challenged My King."

Father! Bowmark could not stand.

NineToes' face darkened. He grabbed Bowmark's arm and jerked Bowmark to his feet. "Who?" NineToes demanded. "Who dares to challenge the best king StoneGrove has ever had?" He dragged Bowmark down the path.

Bowmark didn't know. How could he know? But NineToes wasn't asking him.

CrunchIt jogged and caught up with them. "It's the descendants of Straightback. GreatJoy said he has already fasted the three days, which is why there's no delay. If GreatJoy is killed, HillMount will challenge and start the three-day fast. If HillMount loses, MoonChase will challenge."

Suddenly NineToes elbowed CrunchIt in the face, knocking him down. Bowmark jumped away as NineToes whipped out a knife and stood over CrunchIt pointing the blade like an accusing finger. "You knew this and you couldn't warn me? You couldn't warn *My King*?"

CrunchIt held his nose, ignoring the trickle of blood, and stretched out an empty hand in front of him. "I found out the same time My King did. I'm as angry as you are."

"I doubt it. All those men used to be guards. You know them. You know who stuck the donbi spider in my hammock."

Bowmark stared. The donbi spider's bite could kill.

CrunchIt propped himself on his elbows. "I didn't know that happened. How do you know someone put it there?"

NineToes teeth gritted. "It was stuck there with sap!"

CrunchIt's eye's widened. "When?"

"The night I defeated My King in a wrestling match."

"Ohh," breathed CrunchIt. "Is that why you don't win anymore?"

Hand over his mouth, Bowmark took another step back. Did all the guards deliberately lose to Father?

"I make My King work for the win, but truth, that's why I make sure I lose."

"Hot lava." CrunchIt sat up. "Fumes and ashes. Why didn't you tell someone?"

"Doesn't my black hair remind you that I'm the only commoner to guard My King? Should I have told a royal or noble that someone doesn't want a commoner in the royal guard? Are you going to look me in the face and tell me you didn't know?"

"I *didn't* know." CrunchIt offered his hand. NineToes huffed, then took it and helped him to his feet. CrunchIt brushed ash from his indigo skirt and pulled a twig from his dark red dreadlocks. "I thought we were friends."

"I thought so, too."

"Then stop spearing me with your anger. I didn't come here to assassinate the presumed. We have a job to do. We need to get the presumed to King's Island before My King steps on the Disc."

NineToes took a deep breath. "Truth. We need to hurry." The three of them set off, rushing down the steep stairs.

Father's going to step onto the Disc! Bowmark skittered down the trail, raising a gray cloud of ash. The guards' feet thumped behind him. He slid, tripped, and rolled until he hit a ledge that formed a natural step in the steep path. He was trained to roll with a fall, but panic pulled all memory of the maneuver from him. His knees and elbows stung. Blood oozed into his scratches.

CrunchIt picked him up and swung him around onto his back. He interlaced his fingers to make a seat for Bowmark. The guards jogged down the path between fields as farmers stood, holding dripping weeds, and watched them descend the long path to Safe Harbor. Each step jolted Bowmark's vision. Father was going to step on the Disc. Once you were king you weren't supposed to need to ever go back on the Disc.

Why would anyone hate Father enough to challenge him? "Why?" he whispered, swallowed, and tried again. "Why would GreatJoy challenge My King?"

The guards' pace slowed enough for them to be able to speak. NineToes said, "Many nobles hate My King because he is a great man."

CrunchIt interrupted, "The boy is only ten."

"He's old enough to know what his father is fighting for. My King lowered taxes so the commoners could breathe. He let me, a commoner, join the guard. He speaks respectfully to commoners. But the fish that broke the net was when he treated those weird gray people with the respect owed to Sea Predators."

Bowmark stared at NineToes' golden brown eyes. Why *wouldn't* Father treat the commoners with respect? They treated *him* with respect.

CrunchIt shifted Bowmark on his back. "Not all nobles, nor all royals, feel that way about his treatment of the commoners. Especially not the ones related to the Commoner King."

NineToes spat. "Commoner King! That was three generations ago. The royals have never gotten over that."

CrunchIt huffed. "Despite being a commoner, he won by the protocol. He ruled by the protocol. No one challenged him during his rule. Furthermore, he *became* a royal when he won."

NineToes looked straight ahead. "But what did you just call him?"

"The Com—" CrunchIt shifted Bowmark again. "Please stop being angry at me. I'm innocent."

After a long silence, NineToes said, "I'm sorry." He pulled Bowmark off CrunchIt's back and swung him onto his own back. They resumed jogging down the trail in silence.

It was late afternoon when they bypassed the Bamboo Palace and headed to the beach of Safe Harbor. Streams of people, mostly nobles, flooded the shore. Nets lay in piles on the beach as fishermen filled their outrigger canoes with people instead of fish. One man waited by an empty canoe. He waved at the guards and called, "I have your weapons here already. Hurry."

NineToes muttered, "They couldn't wait for the presumed to get back?" The three jogged to the canoe. Once Bowmark had been helped in, the men pushed the canoe past the surf and climbed in. All of them, even Bowmark, picked up paddles and stroked.

All around them people raised triangular lateen sails. The fisherman in Bowmark's canoe raised his sail, caught the wind, and soon rounded the northern tip of StoneShell to skip across the open sea to King's Island, less than ninety ropes distant. Bowmark was used to seeing the conical landmark obscured by haze, but as they sailed nearer its dense black solidity became more real.

He shivered. GreatJoy intended to kill Father. He had seen GreatJoy at feasts carrying his baby girl. Although HillMount had retired from the guard, he came around the palace every few weeks to help with training. HillMount had taught him how to juggle. Bowmark could not think who MoonChase was. Why did lowering taxes make them want to kill Father?

NineToes moved up to the thwart to sit beside Bowmark. He placed a hand on Bowmark's back. "I'm sorry. I didn't mean to frighten you. I saw My King prove. He'll easily defeat these challengers."

Bowmark must not show weakness. "How do you know?" he asked in a firm voice.

NineToes patted him. "The current flows like this. First of all, My King is a great fighter."

"You let him win."

NineToes cleared his throat. "Please don't tell My King that. Listen, even if I didn't let him win, he would still win most of the time. It was almost an accident the one time I defeated him. Secondly, the Protocol gives all the advantage to the ruling king. The challenger must fast for three days before the fight. The challenger is not allowed to take a single weapon to the Disc. The ruling king is allowed to eat and to carry four weapons."

Bowmark thought about that. His muscles loosened. Beyond the lone, volcanic mountain of King's Island, clouds plumed up from the steam made by molten lava dripping into the ocean. "Is that true for the presumed as well? Will it be as easy for me to prove?" Giver grant him a way to not be so afraid when the volcano erupted after he turned seventeen.

NineToes studied the shore they were approaching. "I'm sorry. The rules are entirely different for a presumed."

He was a Sea Predator, and Sea Predators are brave. Bowmark did not ask what the different rules were. Eventually, he would be taught all the Protocol. In a few years, on his adult name day, he would swear to obey the Protocol. In another few years he would be old enough to prove on the Disc.

He did not want to ask, but the question burst from him anyway. "What will happen to My Queen if My King loses?" *And me?*

CrunchIt leaned over them. "The Protocol is clear. The families of kings and challengers are not to be harmed. Anybody who tries to harm either one is considered a traitor and burned. My Queen and you would need to move out of the palace to your lands. But *you* would remain presumed. The winner becomes a designate, and since there isn't a king to train him for the next five years, the protocol officer stands in as ruling king and trainer. Unless there's another challenge. Then the designate fights with the same rules as with a ruling king."

The complexities of the intricate Protocol washed over Bowmark. No wonder the book of Protocol was so thick. Rising dread scraped his heart.

A brisk wind delivered the canoe to the single beach of King's Island. The rest of the island was fortressed by black lava cliffs. Bowmark and the armed guards joined the hundreds of people climbing on the opposite side of the canyon where a split in the crust once had formed a channel for the molten lava to flow to a cliff, and from there fall into the sea. This old channel had since filled with jungle and cut paths and steps.

They climbed through dense forest, through a border of burned trees, over the lip of the old caldera, and onto a boulder-strewn plain split by the newer deep crevice through which a river of molten rock poured. Heat pressed against them. The ground growled. The smell of poisonous gases and melted rock stung their noses.

Men finished setting up blocks on either side of the narrowest point in the canyon. Twenty strides below, the lava flowed through like a sleepy snake. The people sorted themselves, the commoners on one side, royals and nobles on the other.

Father stood like a stone formation beside Mother, one hand on her shoulder, the other holding a spear. Guards surrounded them. Bowmark ran to them and threw his arms around Mother's big belly. Laying his head on her, he studied Father's grim face. Was he still young enough to hug him?

Sixty strong men pulled ropes tied to the four-strides-wide bronze Disc, sliding it over logs until it straddled the ravine. The Disk was patterned after a shield urchin: a slight dome with spines radiating from the edge. The device balanced precariously, strapped with bronze clasps to a single massive ironwood log. The engraved portraits of prior kings on the surface of the Disc disappeared into glare from the setting sun. All that could be seen clearly were the long horizontal ironwood spikes. On one end of the support log a bar held the Disc upright. A hammer blow could unseat the tipping rod, allowing the Disc to rotate, dumping anyone on it into the lava. The final, brutal option if the rules weren't followed precisely.

THE DISC

Father murmured, "Today, you become a man early. You shall see what being a Sea Predator means."

Why wouldn't Father look at him? Mother stroked Bowmark's hair.

The guards moved to allow NineToes and CrunchIt into their circle. Another circle of guards closer to the Disc surrounded GreatJoy, who also stared only at the Disc.

The protocol officer stood between both groups, as did the priests. With a clang, the Disc fell into place. The bronze circle was suspended high enough to keep from burning or melting, but close enough to fry those upon it like fish in a pan if they took too long. The priests held up the two Holy Books and prayed. The protocol officer opened the Protocol and read aloud the rules for the challenge, her scratching voice echoing through the wasteland. Another priest tied cords with blood red feathers around father's arms. An array of weapons was unrolled from a large leather sheet. Father stooped and examined the weapons. Besides the spear he already held, he added two small bronze throwing knives to his belt, then a large curved obsidian knife.

Mother pushed Bowmark a short distance away. "Stand straight. Stand straight and show us that you're the son of a king."

How? He straightened, but he held onto her arm.

Barefooted, GreatJoy walked onto the heating Disc.

Wearing leather sandals securely strapped to his feet and ankles, Father strode onto the Disc, spear and obsidian knife at the ready.

Bowmark's heart pounded so hard, the noise of it covered whatever GreatJoy shouted. Hatred marked the man's face.

Father abruptly stepped forward and thrust the spear toward GreatJoy's chest.

The large man slipped aside and grabbed the spear.

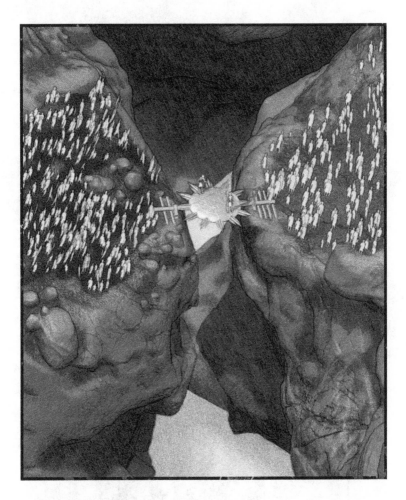

Father pulled back on the spear yanking GreatJoy toward him, spun, and slashed his knife across the unbalanced man's neck. Blood sprayed. GreatJoy dropped the spear and clapped his hand over the severed artery, but he was too late. Bellowing turned to gurgling as the man dropped to his knees.

Bowmark gasped.

Father kicked GreatJoy in the face.

The man fell back, and then went limp with his head hanging over the edge of the Disc. Some royal women screamed. The commoners and many noble men cheered.

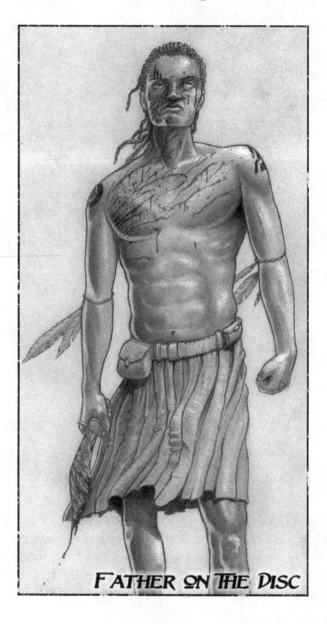

FATHER ON THE DISC

Father strode off the Disc, nodded at the men tending the supports, and headed toward Mother and Bowmark.

"That was fast," CrunchIt said. "I'm glad he didn't prolong this."

An attendant knocked the tipping rod out of its niche. The weight of GreatJoy's body tilted the Disc until his corpse slid off and fell onto the lava. Greasy, black smoke rose. Other attendants rotated a crank that pulled a chain which righted the Disc so it could be removed from the gap before the heat damaged it.

Father strode past Mother and into the crowd of royals. Everyone fell back from him until he stood in front of HillMount. The two men locked eyes. Father said, "Do you have something to say to me?"

Only the growling of the volcano continued as silence settled on the crowds of people straining to see past each other.

HillMount looked from side to side. GreatJoy's blood still dripped from the king's face and chest. His ominous glare withered all it crossed. HillMount's gaze dropped; he kneeled; and then he lay prostrate. "My King."

Father turned and scanned the crowd until he found MoonChase. "Do *you* have something to say?"

MoonChase's wife screamed. The man glanced in her direction before kneeling. Slowly he stretched out on the hot ground. "My King."

"We're done." With an expressionless face Father returned to Mother and Bowmark. "Leave us," he commanded the guard. The men pulled back. With light touches, he directed Mother and Bowmark toward the physician's tent. Bowmark swallowed and swallowed, but his gorge continued to rise.

RunsFast hurried to hang metal and bamboo wind chimes from the edges of the tent. Oil lamps pushed back the twilight. Pinging and clonking accompanied Father's steps as he ducked into the shelter. Bowmark ran in and vomited in a corner.

"Oh, my son." Mother handed him a gourd of water. She handed another gourd to Father as he sat on a banana leaf mat.

Father sipped and dropped the gourd. He trembled and groped for Mother. She eased into his arms.

Bowmark stared. He had shown weakness again, and now, what was Father doing?

Father clutched Mother, buried his face in her neck, and moaned. Then he visibly restrained himself and pulled back.

The physician RunsFast poked her head into the tent. "My King, are there injuries?"

Father shook his head. "No. Only after-fight shudders."

Bowmark threw up again.

RunsFast entered the tent. "I have medicine that might help the boy."

Father grabbed the physician's arm. "If you tell anyone about his weakness, I shall kill you."

Father had killed a man faster than it takes to club a fish to death. And now he was threatening to kill a woman? Sea Predators were only allowed to kill on the Disc over flowing lava or on obstacle courses. Bowmark gagged.

"As well you should," RunsFast replied, unperturbed. "There are only three sentences in the Protocol that rule physicians. We are to treat all alike. We are to do no harm. We are to tell no one what we have seen or heard."

Father released the woman's arm. "Grant me pardon."

"Granted, My King." RunsFast rummaged through a basket until she pulled out a small bag. She gave a tiny, pungent ball to Bowmark. "Suck on this."

Ashamed, Bowmark tried to blink back tears as he sucked on the medicine. He moved away from the acidic odor of his vomit.

RunsFast poured a jar of sand over the mess, then pulled a wet washcloth from her bag, handing it to the king. "For the blood on your face." Then she retreated from the tent.

Father's face struggled through a variety of expressions as he stared at Bowmark. He closed his eyes. "He won't—"

"He will," Mother said as fast as a snake and as fierce.

Father said, "I don't know what to do. I named him presumed too soon."

"Who else would you have appointed to presumed?" She gently took the cloth and blotted the blood from Father's face and chest.

They were talking about him, but Bowmark could not understand what they were saying. Hunched over the pain in his stomach, he drank more water, trying to remove the taste of vomit from his mouth.

Father whispered "It hurts how much I love him. And, burn me, it may not be a Sea Predator goal, but I want him happy."

Mother took Father's hand. "I understand."

"I want him to have what happiness he can have before . . . ."

Before what? Bowmark sucked harder on the physician's medicine.

Father knuckled his eyes. "I've decided. Bowmark is happy in High Harbor. I shall have him alternate living with us and in High Harbor a week at a time. Living with commoners will teach him what we stupid, stupid, *stupid* royals refuse to see."

Mother glanced at the fabric of the tent where the wind chimes clonked on the other side to cover their conversation. "Shh."

Father stroked Mother's belly and looked sad.

Bowmark's heart raced. He would be allowed home!

Mother held Father's hand in place where a ripple stretched her tunic. "You worry too much. I gave birth to Bowmark and survived. I'll survive this one, too."

What were they talking about? His mouth refused to form the question. CrunchIt's first wife had died while giving birth to little WanderOff, but Bowmark had never understood why. Was Mother sick?

Father tried to smile. "Of course you will."

Mother beckoned Bowmark to them and he wrapped his arms around her neck. She hummed a soothing song that reminded him of when he fit on her lap. She stroked his hair and kissed him gently on the forehead.

Father breathed in deeply, stood and helped Mother up. "If we don't go out soon, the people will think I've been injured."

They emerged from the tent. The people who had been sitting near the lip of the canyon and watching the tent cheered. They were a mass of silhouettes in the gathering dark of evening. Against custom, Father held Mother's hand as his small family began the trek back to the beach.

KING'S ISLAND

ROPES

KILMS
5 10 15 20 25

MILES
5 10 15

BAMBOO
PALACE

SAFE
HARBOR

HIGH
HARBOR

BOYHOOD ENDS WHEN DANGER BEGINS.
—SEA PREDATOR PROVERB

Maybe he could ask his commoner mom. Bowmark left Sunrise with the Atlas when Mom picked up a bucket and left to get water for the evening. Bowmark picked up another pail and caught up with her. The sun cast their shadows far over the fields as they neared the pond. Someone had built a pier of sorts that swayed under their feet as they walked. At the end the pond was deep enough for them to scoop water up without mud swirling into the containers. Mom grunted as she stood.

After putting on their woven head rings, they positioned the buckets of water on their heads and began the walk to their house. Bowmark had to hold the bucket with his hands to keep it on, while Mom strolled along effortlessly and rolled grass against her hip, forming temporary rope. Bowmark wondered if her shaved head helped her balance the bucket. Halfway home, Mom asked, "What did you want to talk about?"

How did she know? "My Queen said something I don't understand."

Mom gave a throaty chuckle. "And you think I will?"

"You've had babies."

"Ah. That I have. Listen, you can ask me anything. I don't promise to always answer, but you can always ask."

Bowmark chewed on his lips a moment. "My Queen said she gave birth to me and survived. And she will survive this one, too."

Mom said gently, "Since she has given birth before, she should do fine with this one. You don't need to worry."

"My King is worried."

"Son, fathers always worry."

"TripOver isn't worried."

Mom took a deep breath through her nose. "It is true that royal and noble women are more likely to have problems giving birth than commoner women. That's probably why commoners outnumber royals to such a degree. That, and royals sometimes come down with coughlung, but commoners don't."

"Will I come down with coughlung?"

"Most of you don't. I don't think you will, either."

"Sunrise says if all the royals married commoners, then all the babies would be healthy. I think it had something to do with breeding pigs."

Mom turned up one corner of her mouth. "Sunrise is clever, but he's not always smart. What he doesn't seem to be aware of is how many nobles are afraid of us. They think we want to kill them all."

Bowmark's bucket tilted and slopped water onto his shoulders. "*Do* commoners want to kill the royals?"

"Maybe a few do. I don't know. The way the wind blows for me is somebody needs to collect taxes and rule StoneGrove. Why not let the redheads do it? Let them stab each other and learn how to defend us from the enemy." She chuckled. "And here I was afraid you were going to ask me where babies come from."

"I already know. They come from mothers." Bowmark repositioned the heavy bucket of water on the red hair that allowed him to rule.

Mom slowed as they neared the house. "You started out worried about My Queen. Now you're worried about a hundred new things. Listen, don't worry. Giver has My Queen in His hand. He has you in His hand. Truth?"

"I think so."

She tugged one of his dreadlocks with her chubby fingers. "Just be a ten-year-old today."

When they entered their bamboo home, Sunrise shouted, "Look! I found a picture of a shlak."

A small rock dislodged under Sunrise's hand. It tumbled and whacked Bowmark in the forehead. Sunrise looked over his shoulder and down the cliff. "Grant me pardon."

Bowmark clutched the cliff and closed his eyes. His entire body focused on that point of pain. He should have climbed beside Sunrise instead of behind him. A warm trickle worked its way down the bridge of his nose. "Granted."

Sunrise shifted his foot. Smaller rocks bounced off Bowmark's scalp.

Bowmark slowly crabbed sideways until he cleared Sunrise's rockfall zone. Together they crept up the cliff, their fingers and toes probing for cracks and holds. They reached the edge and pulled themselves over.

SUNRISE AND BOWMARK

As Bowmark rolled onto his back and gingerly touched the swelling on his forehead, Sunrise jumped up, threw down his coil of grass rope, and pranced around the high spot. Only one other mountain rose higher on StoneShell. "I can see King's Island."

Bowmark didn't want to see King's Island. He didn't want to remember Father's face set in a snarl as he slashed GreatJoy's throat. The spurt of blood. The stench of burnt flesh.

"And I can see the cloud over WetSide." Sunrise moved to the other side of Bowmark. "Is that Fire Island or a cloud?"

Bowmark sat up. "I can't tell either." He pointed. "I think Fire Island is due north."

"I want to visit all the islands. I want to see the world."

Bowmark sighed. "If kings aren't allowed into the world, what makes you think pig farmers are?"

"I'm going to become a fisherman, and when nobody's looking, I'm going to sail to Akinda and Utali."

"They're on separate sides of the world."

"So then. I'm going to sail over all the world."

"You know why we can't do that."

"Maybe the Southils have forgotten about us."

Bowmark groaned. His gaze swept over blue ocean meeting blue sky. Green jungle stretched away under them. "You're talking treason. You know the penalty for treason."

"You want to see the world, don't you?"

Bowmark looked into his friend's eyes. "No."

Sunrise swung his arms above his head. "Why not?"

Bowmark shrugged one shoulder and stepped to the cliff edge to look straight down. A tiny figure moved along the base of the cliff. "Oh, no. MoonGleam is following us. She's going to get hurt."

Sunrise stood beside him. "That pest." He picked up a pebble. "If I drop this on her head, she'll back off."

Bowmark grabbed his wrist. "Don't."

"Stop me."

Bowmark jerked him away from the cliff edge. They pushed at each other and feinted grabbing holds. Bowmark hooked his foot around Sunrise's calf and knocked him to the ground with a move called Undertow. NineToes had only started to teach Sunrise how to wrestle whereas Bowmark had already spent years in wrestling lessons. Even though he was careful not to stretch or touch Sunrise's burnt shoulder, Bowmark soon had him pinned in Heavy Crab.

Sunrise tapped the ground, and they rolled away from each other, breathing hard. Sunrise laughed. "Tomorrow I'll defeat you."

Bowmark shook his head. "I'm sure."

Sunrise returned to the cliff edge. "I think I see . . . truth, NineToes is looking for you."

"He'd better find me. He told me he's going to make me stay in Mid Village instead of here if I keep hiding from him."

Sunrise uncoiled his rope and tied one end to a crabcrawl tree. Its multiple elevated roots anchored the tree firmly on the ridge. One after the other, they rappelled as far as the rope would reach, halfway down the face of the cliff. There, the climbing was a little easier, and they descended. Going down was always harder than going up, and so their descent over half the distance took the same amount of time.

MoonGleam reversed her climb as they rappelled past her. When she neared the ground she leaped onto Bowmark, nearly unbalancing him and then falling off.

He turned and crouched. "Get on my back. I'll give you a ride."

"No," Sunrise said. "Make the pest walk."

She squealed and jumped on Bowmark. Her little arms wrapped around his neck, strangling him. He rose and staggered from her weight. She seemed to be growing faster than he was. MoonGleam giggled as the boys walked down the trail that led to High Harbor.

A mossy fallen log lay over the creek they needed to cross. Sunrise cartwheeled across. Then he flipped and crashed into NineToes who had just come around a bend in the path.

Bowmark hesitated, then took one shaky step after another. The slime slipped under his feet sending him and MoonGleam into the creek.

They rose, drenched. Sunrise lay on the bank, laughing. Bowmark pulled MoonGleam to her feet. "Are you hurt?" She splashed water in his face and cackled.

"I think she's fine," said NineToes. The guard slid down the bank and boosted both children to the trail. After slipping backwards with frustrated grunts, he made it back to the trail. Mud coated his legs to the knees and his arms up to the elbows.

Bowmark's indigo skirt was now as mud-brown as Sunrise's.

MoonGleam's lip quivered. "Am I in trouble?"

NineToes said, "I wouldn't know. My business is with the presumed. So then, Presumed, are you ready to run the cliff stairs? Ah, I forgot." He turned to Sunrise. "I'm going to train you, too. Both of you, to the stairs."

Hadn't NineToes noticed his forehead was bleeding? Bowmark waved toward HawkFlight Cliff. "We just climbed HawkFlight."

"Good for you. I'll make a note that when you hide from me you train harder than when you train under my eye."

"No, please, don't tell My King I hide from you. I'm not hiding. Sunrise likes to explore, and I like to go with him." Bowmark's hands flopped to his sides. Surely NineToes would make him practice front and back flips on his runs now. Or hop on one foot. Or juggle while running. The guard was very creative when it came to punishing complaints.

Without a word, the children turned and walked back through jungle and by fields and homes to the top of the cliff stairs. NineToes trotted down the stairs as easily as a bird in flight. Bowmark followed NineToes, and Sunrise followed Bowmark.

At the bottom and without pause, NineToes spun and trotted up the stairs. Up, down, up, down, up.

NineToes stopped. The boys brushed past him to sit on the bench and pant. MoonGleam had been watching them, laughing every time one of them stumbled. Sunrise wasn't told to do the flips, but he still tried. Badly.

Moongleam stepped onto the bench. "Is that CrunchIt?"

No. Bowmark closed his eyes. *No. Not another challenge.* CrunchIt was three days early. Bowmark took deep breaths and recited to himself, Sea Predators are brave.

"Wait here." NineToes loped down the path that led to Safe Harbor and met with CrunchIt.

Bowmark sat on the bench and trembled. Sunrise sat beside him and, for once, said nothing. MoonGleam rubbed Bowmark's shoulder. He watched the two men toil up the path and tried to read their faces.

NineToes reached them. "Presumed, we're going to the palace."

"Can I come, too?" asked Sunrise.

"Why?" asked Bowmark.

"No," NineToes said to Sunrise. The boy drooped. NineToes' teeth flashed as he grinned at Bowmark. "Don't you want to be home when the baby is born?"

MoonGleam squealed.

"Oh!" Bowmark danced. "I hope Mother gives me a sister."

"You can have mine," muttered Sunrise. MoonGleam swatted his arm.

The guard said, "Wait here while I get the Atlas."

Bowmark could not wait. He skipped to CrunchIt and seized the noble guard's hand. "Will I get home before the baby's born?"

CrunchIt scratched his neck and tugged on his indigo warrior's skirt. "Probably. My Queen hasn't started yet. The midwives think she will soon, and so My King sent for you. Are you ready?"

"Let's go now."

CrunchIt laughed. "I can't rest for one moment?"

How many times had Father told him to take care of his people? Bowmark sobered. "You may rest."

The skin crinkled around CrunchIt's eyes. He pinched his nose. "I'd forgotten how bad High Harbor smells. I'm ready. Let's go." He turned and led the way down the steep path so that if Bowmark slipped, the presumed would crash into him and not a tree or lava outcrop. NineToes joined them, carrying the Atlas under one arm.

In the Bamboo Palace NineToes shoved Bowmark into the bathing room. "You're not seeing My Queen while you're covered in dirt."

He did itch all over, but Mother was having a baby and he needed to see her. NineToes pointed to the buckets of salt and fresh water. A maidservant brought in a clean skirt. Bowmark scrubbed quickly.

After dumping the bucket of fresh water over himself for the final rinse, he wrapped the clean skirt around himself, picked up the small gourd of coconut oil scented with plumeria, and stepped out into the birthing garden courtyard. The birthing hut had been set up in the center, but no one was inside. He settled onto a small stool set inside a dewdrop bush, one of the few places where he could be away from the gaze of people evaluating him. This garden smelled so much nicer than High Harbor.

Commoners often used hair oil, but they didn't need to the way the nobles did. Why? Why were commoners and nobles so different?

While he was rubbing oil on his scalp, footsteps neared him. He ducked and peered through the dewdrop leaves. Probably NineToes was looking for him so he could castigate him for not washing thoroughly enough. Itching in some delicate places reasserted itself and dirt still lined his fingernails. Maybe he hadn't washed enough.

It wasn't NineToes. RaiseHim's father and the protocol officer stopped and scanned the area, but they did not see Bowmark crouched nearby.

RaiseHim's father said, "Why won't you support us? He's slowly ruining us."

The protocol officer crossed her arms. "I don't like his policies either, but a civil war would ruin us quickly. How much in taxes can you collect from dead people? Until you can give me a way to help cause a change that won't result in war, don't talk to me."

"What if we do find a way?"

"We have the protocol. Find a way that doesn't violate the protocol, and then . . . maybe. Don't make me denounce you for treason."

They frowned at each other. Then they separated and walked in different directions.

Bowmark wiped a trickle of oil from his forehead. What was that about? Adults were so confusing. He had been away from Mother long enough, so he dismissed the conversation with a shrug.

He left the bush and nearly ran into NineToes. Together, they re-entered the palace and walked through several corridors to the weaving room where Mother sat on a stool and sorted threads on a loom.

Bowmark ran to hug Mother. A bump in her belly pushed against his arm.

She stroked his head. "Hello, My Heart. I missed you. Did you know that?"

The manservants and maids backed out of the weaving room leaving the two surrounded by looms and bolts of indigo cloth. A warm breeze flowed through the open windows, and silkwings fluttered in and out. Multicolored fabric embroidered with scenes of women dancing covered the walls made of bamboo and dried fish skin. A vase of red frangipani flowers perfumed the room.

Mother set her shuttle on a finished section of cloth and bent over Bowmark, hugging him back. "I want you to tell me all about your time in the village."

The bump under her skin retreated, and Bowmark kissed her belly where the bump had been. "I missed you every day, but I had a lot of fun in High Harbor. Can I have a sister? Sunrise has two, and I really like them."

"The child's name is Spearmark if it's a boy or ReachFor if it's a girl. Beyond the name, none of us are able to choose. We'll see what Giver grants us."

They both held their Giver's Hand medallions and sat on banana-leaf mats that covered the glass-block floor.

"Pigs stink more than you can believe. Ah, Mother, did Father tell you we found a shlak in the Atlas? They look like giant crabs, or starfish with crab legs. Oh, and I think I found the island where the Southils live. I need the tutor to help me read the words. The Atlas measures distance with something called kilms instead of strides and ropes. And Dad is selling piglets I think farmers here should buy. And SeeHerGo has pet monkeys she trained to speak! She's going to give me one when it's old enough. I need a present to give her. And I want a present to give Mom."

"I shall make that happen, My Heart." Mother gasped, grimaced, and clapped her hands on her lower back. "Bowmark, you need to go to the training yard and train for a while."

"I've been training. Can't I stay and talk to you?"

Mother breathed out, breathed in. "Later. Right now I need help to get to the birthing hut. Ohhhhh."

Bowmark raced into the hall. Nobody had told him that giving birth hurt. A maid pushed herself from the wall she had been leaning on. Bowmark called her, "ThreadTangle! ThreadTangle! My Queen needs you." She scurried past him and the hall suddenly filled with servants.

CrunchIt elbowed aside two servants and ran to Bowmark's side. He pulled Bowmark through the flow of servants to an empty hall and then to the training yard where Father wrestled with DigDeep. In a flurry of moves ending in Stone Drop, Father pinned DigDeep, who tapped the ground to surrender.

"My King," CrunchIt said.

Father stood, accepted a towel from a servant, and wiped his face and neck while looking up. "Son! Come here." He sat on one of the logs in the obstacle course and patted the wood beside him. "Have you seen your mother yet? She is most anxious to hear about your life in High Harbor."

CrunchIt nudged Bowmark forward. "My Queen has started birth."

"Ah." Father leaned back and blew out breath. The servant handed him a gourd of water.

CrunchIt, DigDeep, and the servant retreated to the far side of the yard. The two guards faced off in a wrestling stance. On the other side of the wall, a bird shrieked in terror.

Bowmark sat by Father.

"How long does it take to give birth?"

Father breathed deeply. "I think it is like fishing. Sometimes it will happen in a few heartbeats. Sometimes we wait for many candles."

The king leaned forward to press their foreheads together. He drank from the gourd and then offered the water to Bowmark.

Bowmark held the gourd in his lap and fiddled with the container. "Does giving birth hurt?"

Father made a face that came close to a smile. "Son, now comes one of the least pleasant parts of a marriage. We warriors like to think we're brave, but any one woman giving birth shows more courage than all the warriors on StoneShell together. If you hear your mother scream, remember that she screamed when she gave birth to you. After you were born, she sang over you. Don't be afraid."

Fear. Bowmark had almost forgotten the fear that constantly rode his back during the weeks with Sunrise. He was supposed to not fear this birth. He was supposed to not fear the Disc. "Father, what if—what if I don't win?"

Father's face went hard. "I and everyone here is trying to train you into the warrior you must be to win. You already have the intelligence, creativity, and compassion needed to rule. This is in your hands. If you fail, the Protocol dictates that I train the man who killed you. Don't let that happen."

Father stood. "CrunchIt, stop what you're doing and train the presumed in knife-fighting skills." He strode from the yard without looking back.

The servants slid shut the windows against the night-flying insects and lit sweet-smelling lamps. Bowmark sat in the corner of the paper-making room and stirred the rice with his chopsticks. He could not eat. Sighing, he set down his bowl, leaned back on the wall, and picked at the bandage over the knife wound on his hand. They should have let him keep training even after CrunchIt cut him. Though no one had given him an assignment, he should still be training, should never stop training until he proved on the Disc and became the designate. He pressed his hands on the floor and unrolled into a handstand. Wincing as the skin stretched his knife wound, he walked on his hands around the equipment.

The servants and their children all moved silently in the hall, stepping carefully so even their feet made no noise on the glass block floor. Every guest had departed. Each court functionary had returned to his home. The guards patrolled the perimeter between torches filled with incense and a fragrant fish oil that burned green.

Bowmark arched his back and stepped upright. He swished his hand through a tub of banana leaf fibers and water and ran his fingertips over some of the drying, stretched skins of fish and pigs.

A thin cry rose and fell. Bowmark darted to the door and held the jamb. The cry resumed in jerks and drew closer. He stepped into the hall.

ThreadTangle, wearing white ribbons of mourning tied around her neck, turned the corner. She held out a wriggling bundle of indigo cloth. "Do you want to meet your little brother, Spearmark?"

Her tears and the ribbons snared his attention. He automatically reached out his hands and received the bundle, but he could not shift his gaze from her wet face and reddened eyes. "What happened?"

"We are Sea Predators, and we are brave." Her voice broke.

Bowmark pulled the squirming bundle to his chest. "What?"

"My Queen . . ." She reached toward Bowmark, and then retreated. She stammered, "Your brother had a hard moment, but he's fine now."

Bowmark pushed back a fold of the cloth. Lamplight illuminated the dark face of a squint-eyed baby with tightly-coiled red hair capping his head. He opened a toothless mouth and cried.

ThreadTangle twisted her hands together and squeaked, "It's proper for babies to cry aloud. They haven't yet learned—"

"I want to see Mother, My Queen. Why are you wearing white ribbons?" Bowmark clutched his brother to his chest and dashed past the weeping maid and down the hall that led to the yard that held the temporary birthing hut. A grim-faced guard slid the door open for him.

Bowmark stepped onto a veranda and then into the inner garden of plumeria trees, sea grape, and jasmine. The stink of blood and musk overpowered the frail scents of flowers. Servants sat on the sand outside the hut with heads bowed. One of the women held a bowl of water on her lap. A rag, deep red with blood, hung over the lip. Her sob was quickly hushed. Most of the servants rose and shuffled back into the palace.

Bowmark's feet refused to move and his mouth refused to speak the questions screaming in his mind.

When only Bowmark, two servants, and the guard by the hut remained, the grim-faced guard in the hall slid the door shut. Bowmark looked up at a sky where clouds drifted across two of the moons, darkening the garden further. Tiny Spearmark wailed.

A muffled sound, like that of a hurt animal, came from the birthing hut. Bowmark waded through fear to the hut. Attempting to put command in his voice, Bowmark said, "My Queen needs to feed Spearmark."

The guard's eyes squeezed shut a moment. "A nurse is being sent for."

"I want to see My Queen."

"Not yet. My King is within."

"You're not allowed to keep me away from My King."

The guard bent and placed his hand on Bowmark's shoulder. "Tonight, I'm allowed." He took a shuddering breath. "My King will not want you to see him like this. Go to your sleeping room and await the nurse. Take care of your brother. That is what My King requires."

The sound of a hurt animal emerged from the hut again.

Blinking tears from his eyes, Bowmark stumbled onto the veranda and scratched on the door. When the guard slid the door open, he stepped into a hall filled with silent, slumped maids.

One of the maids approached Bowmark, gently pulled back the cloth to expose Spearmark's tiny fist, and tied a white ribbon on his wrist. She stirred the air with her forefinger, indicating that Bowmark should turn around. When he did, she tied the sacred number of three white ribbons around his neck, placed her hand on his back, escorted him to his sleeping room, hooked up the hammock, and set a lit lamp on the floor. The slow-moving servants left his door open and whispered in the hall.

Instead of climbing into his hammock, Bowmark sat in a corner and rocked. He rubbed his face on the baby's hair.

Spearmark stopped crying. His fist bumped Bowmark's nose. His tiny legs jerked back and forth. Then, like a candle blown out, he stopped moving.

Bowmark held him out to look at the baby's face. Instead of squinting, Spearmark's eyes and mouth grew slack. His face darkened.

Spearmark wasn't breathing!

"Help!" Bowmark leaped to his feet. Nobody came into the room. "Help! He isn't breathing."

Once, Bowmark had seen a drowned boy revived. He flipped Spearmark over and held him upside down. After patting his back, he laid his little brother on the floor and stroked his back. "Help!" He couldn't die. He mustn't die.

"Help!" Bowmark gently pressed on Spearmark's back.

The baby sneezed.

Bowmark snatched him up and clutched him to his chest as, finally, a maidservant stepped into his sleeping room. "He stopped breathing. Why didn't you help me?"

The maid's eyes widened. She leaped forward and pulled Spearmark from Bowmark's arms. As she unwrapped the baby, he cried. The maid relaxed. "Oh, little one, you frightened me."

She set him at her shoulder and patted his back. "He stopped breathing right after he was born, too. We'll need to keep a closer watch on him."

"I'll watch him," Bowmark said. "You weren't here when he needed you."

Tears spilled down the maid's face. She stuttered, "Presumed, I'll get the physician. And then I'll sleep right here next to you while you watch your brother. Please?" She hesitated before wrapping the baby and handing him back to Bowmark.

As she left, Bowmark retreated to the corner again and sat, rocking the baby and keeping careful watch of his face.

"Spearmark," he murmured, "I will always take care of you. Always."

A SON WITHOUT A MOTHER IS LIKE AN
ARROW WITHOUT A BOW.
~SEA PREDATOR PROVERB

The outrigger canoe rocked gently on the swells of the ocean. White ribbons fluttered from the masts of thirty canoes with furled sails. Father stood as stiff as a mast. Aching to hug him, Bowmark stood by his side. Maids crouched on the taut netting between the canoe and outrigger board. Between the women lay a still, white bundle.

Fishermen swam to the outrigger of the closest canoe and lashed its board to the outrigger of the king's canoe. A handler swam beside the fat, slow muntees pulling a barge of singers clad in white and directed them closer to the king'scanoe. One of the muntees nuzzled the prow of the priests' canoe.

Priests chanted words from the Holy Books. Bowmark heard them, but the words could not stay in his mind. The people in the flotilla sang a song to Giver. Everyone held their Giver's Hand medallion. Bowmark could not sing. His eyes felt scratchy. Being brave took every drop of his will.

Father's gaze fixed on nothing. Sometimes a slight frown creased his forehead and he turned his gaze on the bundle. He looked as though he did not know why he was there.

ThreadTangle shushed baby Spearmark in their crowded canoe. A nurse whose name Bowmark could not remember took the baby, sat on the thwart closest to the stern, and nursed Spearmark. Bowmark wanted to take care of his brother. Somehow. But he could not move.

Perhaps Father could not move either, for he stood and said nothing as the priests, protocol officer, and their assistants did everything, praying, directing the people to throw their flowers onto the ocean, sprinkling incense, and finally walking across one set of spars to the other. The maids spread white flower petals over the body and then helped the priests lift the bundle to the edge of the netting. They gently pushed Mother into the water.

She made such a small splash. As she sank, the white wrapping grew dimmer and dimmer until it was swallowed by the dark depths. A sprinkling of petals bobbed on the ripples that Mother left.

No one spoke as Father continued to stare into the distance. Sea birds circled the flotilla. The same fishermen who had lashed the canoes together slipped into the water, swam slowly to the outriggers, and untied them. They swam back to their canoes. Father stared into the distance as everyone stood, waiting for him to move.

Bowmark's nose itched, but he must not move until Father ended the vigil.

ThreadTangle whispered behind Father, "My King."

Father started. Looking confused, he scanned the crowd. He raised his hands and lowered them. He sat on the central thwart.

The people busied themselves, raising the sails and paddling when the canvas did not instantly billow in the wind. Bowmark sat, and now that he could scratch his nose, it no longer itched.

A guard said the words Bowmark did not want to hear. "The fish feed us, and then we feed the fish."

He would not think about that. He could not think about anything. Father did not speak. People in the other canoes murmured softly as they paddled back toward Safe Harbor, but silence ruled in Father's canoe.

The sun had moved a hand's width across the sky and then hid behind the clouds that brought the noon rain when they had reached close enough to see the individual trees that hid the palace from the enemy. Shouting drifted across the waves.

The guards stood and looked toward the first canoes to reach the shore.

Something rose among those canoes that Bowmark's eyes could not make sense of. Huge, banded orange and purple crab arms protruded from the waves and bumped outriggers as the canoes ran up onto the sand. The passengers boiled out of the canoes and ran the canoes to dry sand. There appeared to be two writhing, banded snakes that rose from the water to stand on their tails. Bowmark pressed against Father's leg. What were they?

The guard pointed with his spear. "Shlak." The paddlers adjusted the direction they stroked to move the canoe toward the shlak.

Now the shapes became body parts that Bowmark could understand. He had only seen a picture of one in the Atlas. The snakes were eyes on stalks. The long arms were armored limbs studded with bumps which were capped with purple sponges and other colorful underwater flora.

SHLAK

The mourners raced into the jungle. As Father's canoe bobbed over the waves near the shlak, guards that had remained at the palace ran out of the jungle, followed by the tutor with his dictionary and the scribe. They formed a semi-circle around the first person who wasn't a human that Bowmark had ever seen.

The prow of Father's canoe slid onto the sand. Before the paddlers could jump out to push the canoe all the way onto land, Father climbed out into waist deep water. He waded toward the shlak. "Come."

Bowmark splashed in. He waded in Father's wake, but the waves and undertow threatened to knock him down. He waded to where the water was shallower and walked parallel with Father.

Father waded up to the shlak and extended his hand. The shlak rose briefly to a height nearly twice that of Father and then dipped back under the water. Waves pushed and sucked on Father's waist. The shlak's arm, twice as long as Father was tall, but no thicker than Father's arm, stretched to his hand and extruded pulpy fingers that stroked his skin. Most of the shlak's body stayed underwater. Above the surface its stalked eyes twisted, its two front limbs motioned, and its many mouth parts vibrated with a buzz like the stridulating of crickets.

FATHER CONFRONTS THE SHLAK

CrunchIt splashed out to stand by Bowmark. "We should go to the palace, eat, and come back."

Bowmark pointed with his elbow. "I want to watch this." He glanced at the beach. Hundreds of people lined the beach and watched their rare visitor.

The shlak came every five or six years from undersea to trade with the Sea Predators and spoke in a pulse-and-silence code that spelled Common words.

"I understand, Presumed. I do. But we could eat, have a training session, bathe, eat again, and come back. They'll still be standing here. It takes a very long time to speak in code. People will be bringing food out to My King and the other people who belong here."

"I belong here."

"You do belong here," CrunchIt conceded, "But you don't need to be here the whole time. After a funeral, people need to rest. Your brother is going to the palace."

Spearmark did need to rest until the first moon came out.

CrunchIt bent and murmured in Bowmark's ear, "My King cannot attend the funeral meal. You must take his place."

Bowmark nodded. If Father needed him to eat and rest before coming back, he would.

The sun glowed like a golden ember on the horizon and then winked out.

He should have listened to CrunchIt and taken a longer nap. Bowmark's legs ached from standing in one place for candles. The guards had taken turns watching the negotiation between the shlak and Father. There was no one to take the turn of the presumed or king.

Servants stabbed holders into the sand and placed oil lamps on them. The daytime sounds of the jungle slowly gave way to nocturnal chirps and hoots.

Father, the tutor, and the scribe finally turned and waded ashore. The shlak submerged. Father lurched to the nearest canoe and sat on a gunwale. He placed his elbows on his knees and pressed his face into his hands. The tutor and scribe hovered around him for a while, and then they entered the canoe and sat on the thwarts. The guards repositioned themselves around the three.

Bowmark forced his stiff legs to walk to the canoe. He sat beside Father.

Everyone waited.

And waited.

Finally, the scribe said, "My King?"

"What?" Father snapped. He slapped his hands against his knees and glared at the man.

Bowmark started.

The scribe cringed. He spindled the paper he had been writing on. "Something must be done."

"Something must *always* be done."

By now the treasurer had drawn near. "My King."

Father stood. The wrath on his face frightened Bowmark. Slowly his face smoothed to his impassive mask. "Treasurer Candlelight, scour the kitchens for silver. Open the treasure room. Take . . . ." He scanned the guards. "Take Overcome with you. Don't touch the scrolls, books, or locked baskets. Pry the jewels from silver settings. Bring all the silver you find here by noon."

"My King, what do they want with our silver?"

"Do I care? They want our tarnishing silver and they're giving us nontarnishing gold, pearls, and diamonds. I would have preferred iron, but they don't have any this time."

The watching crowd expressed surprise and approval.

"The other matter?" asked the scribe.

"We will discuss the other matter later." Father grunted as he strode on stiff legs toward the palace, leaving everyone else scurrying to catch up with him.

Bowmark trotted behind him. He had never seen Father this curt before. Mother was gone and Father was transforming into something even more frightening than he had been before. Bowmark's stomach hurt.

Sea Predators are brave.

Father and his entourage crashed into the palace like a great wave. Servants and guards peeled away to perform their duties. Father rushed into his sleeping room, nearly slammed the door on Bowmark, and threw himself face-down on the mats.

Bowmark crawled into a corner, tucked his arms around his legs, shivered, and stared at Father. He should have gone into Spearmark's room where the nurse let him sleep next to his brother.

Father rolled over and gazed at Bowmark. His hoarse voice cracked. "Don't be so afraid."

"I can't help it."

Father sat up and leaned against a wall. "I'm drowning and my foot is caught in a net. We must not allow ourselves to be afraid. Fear won't let us find an answer."

Was it fear that made him unable to understand what Father was saying?

"We have a problem. You will need to deal with the problem. Your children will need to deal with the problem."

Bowmark squeaked, "Did the Southils find us?"

"No. I want time to think before I discuss this with the royals and nobles. Right now I can't see an answer."

What problem was so large *Father* couldn't see an answer?

"The shlak are not happy with us. They say our waste is polluting the ocean."

Bowmark frowned. "People are throwing their slops into the ocean?"

"Of course not. We need the manure to feed our crops. But sometimes we have rain so heavy the cesspools overflow."

This didn't seem like a thing kings should need to think about. Bowmark didn't want to think about it.

"But they live in the whole big ocean. How could a little bit of filth bother them? Can't they just swim away?"

"It is hard for us to understand, son. The truth is this; our islands are just the tops of mountains. Where the ocean begins, the rest of the mountain continues deep below the water. The Shlak live on the same mountain we do, and whatever runs off our land falls down onto theirs. They do not swim like fish or tearjaws. They walk and climb and build their homes on this mountain we call an island. They say our waste feeds the red algae that blooms, suffocating their gardens and sickening their livestock."

Bowmark gaped at the thought of a mountain under the ocean. "Can't we dig our cesspools deeper?"

Father shook his head slowly. "Then we pollute our own drinking water. I do not see a solution. The shlak inform us that if we continue to pollute their home, they will destroy all our canoes."

That was the problem. Bowmark rubbed his shins as he thought. "If we can't fish or collect seaweed, we'll starve to death."

"Long before we starve to death, we will start killing each other."

Bowmark did not want to know this. "How will I take care of Spearmark?"

Father rose, pulled his hammock from the wall, and shook it to toss out any hiding spiders. He hooked the ends on the hammock poles. "You'll find a way because you must. I will find a way because I must. Today was not a good day to haul this into my canoe. Maybe tomorrow I'll be able to think."

He rolled into the hammock, leaving the lamp burning. "Just tonight, do you want to sleep with me?"

Bowmark shot up. Truth. ThreadTangle could watch Spearmark tonight.

Father stretched out the hammock with one arm, leaving a space by his side for Bowmark to crawl into.

Finally, Bowmark could hug Father.

A GRATEFUL HEART GIVES HEALTH.
A JEALOUS HEART GIVES BONE-ROT.
SEA PREDATOR HOLY BOOKS

NineToes shrugged the backpack from his shoulders. His long black hair shone with sweat. "Presumed, let's rest here." They were on their way to High Harbor. He sat on a terrace wall that held up a rice field. A rare basket-needle pine tree cast shade and a refreshing, sharp scent over the path. A farmer balancing an enormous basket of yellowfruit on his head stepped around the guard and Bowmark and continued down the trail to Safe Harbor.

Bowmark chewed on his lip. "I must not rest. I need to be strong enough to protect Spearmark. He needs me."

"Put down your pack. The nurse and My King are taking fine care of your baby brother."

Who knew when the shlak would attack and then the Sea Predators would start killing each other? Bowmark unslung his pack and set his physical burden beside that of NineToes'. He trotted to a low branch of the old pine tree, leaped up, caught the limb, and did pull-ups.

"Presumed, sit down."

Bowmark released the branch and dropped. He sat where NineToes indicated. Trees whispered to themselves in a gentle breeze. When NineToes' gaze shifted to follow the flight of a shocking yellow lizard, Bowmark pressed his palms against the wall, lifted his rear from the stone and held his legs out straight. He drew his legs through his arms and rolled up to a handstand. His legs scissored in the air.

NineToes clapped. "Impressive. But not sitting."

Bowmark slowly rolled back into a sit. He clasped his hands over his head and pulled in static exercise.

"Fumes," NineToes swore, pulling on his pack and heading up the trail again. "You win. Let's go."

When they finally reached the flattest area in High Harbor, Bowmark slung his pack onto the bench at the head of the cliff stairs beside the familiar field now verdant with pigfeed grass. "Five times?"

"No, you're not running the stairs today."

Bowmark frowned up at NineToes. "I don't understand. You're always pushing me to train harder, and now you don't want me to train at all?"

NineToes retied the white ribbon that held back his black hair into a tail. He straightened the three white ribbons around his neck. "Of course I want you to train. But I know how hard to push you. You're pushing yourself past what growing bones can handle. You're going to cripple yourself."

"You don't know that."

"Did My King appoint me your trainer when you're away from Safe Harbor?"

Bowmark dropped his gaze. "Truth."

"So then. CrunchIt trains you at the palace. I train you up here. We're up here. That means you do what I tell you. You will go home to Dad and Mom and say hello. Then you will rest until it's time for your knife-juggling practice. Go."

"I don't want to rest."

"I don't care. Do you know what My King will do to me if I let you damage yourself?"

Bowmark's shoulders slumped. He didn't know what Father would do, but Father could slash a man's throat and kick him in the face. Father would do whatever he must, and so would Bowmark. He picked up his pack and trudged toward home until he noticed what he wasn't hearing.

Almost always, somebody on a break played the flute or sang. Children shouted while playing chase or leapfrog. Pigs howled or snorted. Children argued over whose turn it was to fetch water. Mothers called to their husbands.

Now, only the faint surf far below the cliff and the wind made a hushed sound. No children prowled the paths of High Harbor. The few farmers in the fields looked up, saw Bowmark or NineToes, and then walked behind bamboo houses or into the surrounding jungle. White ribbons hung in every doorway and window and from fruit tree branches. Bowmark fingered his white ribbons as he studied the silent, still village.

NineToes' face wrinkled. "What happened?"

"My Queen died."

"Truth. But this is more than mourning." Instead of following Bowmark to keep him in sight, NineToes ran up the hill to Dad and Mom's house, leaped onto the veranda and through the open door. A few moments later, he appeared in the doorway and gestured for Bowmark to come.

In the house, Bowmark's eyes adjusted to the dimness. Sunrise, his two sisters, and Dad and Mom all sat on the floor of the front room.

Mom stood and shuffled over to Bowmark. "Everyone else, please go away. I need Bowmark to help me."

Bowmark dropped his pack. *What?*

As the family and NineToes ducked out through the low doorway, the ribbons brushing their heads, Mom sat by Bowmark and stretched out her legs. She tugged Bowmark onto her lap. "I want you to help me cry."

Someone slid the door shut, darkening the room.

"Sea Predators are brave. We don't cry."

Her hands stroked his back. "I know that, My Heart, but sometimes this commoner Sea Predator needs to cry." She pressed him close.

At first, Bowmark stiffened, but then he relaxed into her soft warmth. It was true that commoners were not always as brave as royals.

Mom was much softer than Father. Her warm hand pressed his head against her breast. "Ohh," she crooned. "My Queen loved you so much. I miss My Queen. I miss her so much."

As if a dam broke, Bowmark sobbed. He tried to muffle his cries with her shoulder. She held him tighter, crooned and cried louder than he did, and kept telling him how wonderful My Queen had been.

Time passed. His cries subsided and he sniffed. Mom handed him a cloth and he wiped the tears and snot off his face. "Please don't tell NineToes I cried. He might tell My King."

"Shh. You only helped this commoner with commoner troubles, as any good presumed should. There is nothing to tell. Thank you for helping me."

BOWMARK AND MOM

Bowmark nearly cried again, but his eyes were so dry they ached.

"My Heart, I'm told you're commanded to rest." Mom pulled him down. "I know that a true Sea Predator like yourself will follow My King's commands. I set up your hammock. You don't need to rest for long."

His head felt empty and achy. Fatigue filled his limbs. He allowed Mom to lead him to his hammock and help him in.

Bowmark flailed awake from a dream that HillMount had killed Spearmark and was roasting him at a feast. His thrashing tipped the hammock and dumped him on the floor.

He rubbed his shoulder but was distracted from his pain by whispering just outside the door. A girl giggled. A different, tiny voice said, "Gimme mine!" and then three children were laughing out loud. Mom's voice boomed from the field. "I'm sure he's awake now. Go on in." The door slid open and MoonGleam burst into the room, ran around behind him and covered his eyes. "You get to guess!"

Bowmark heard Sunrise and a girl whisper as they entered. "Is that SeeHerGo?" he asked. Sunrise laughed. Something tickled Bowmark's nose. MoonGleam's hands came away from his eyes and he was confronted with the round fuzzy face of a juvenile monkey that was sniffing him. "Gimme mine!" the monkey piped and tapped Bowmark's cheek. All the children burst out laughing. The stiff muscles in his face melted into a smile he hadn't felt recently.

SeeHerGo held the monkey to Bowmark's shoulder and it hopped on, chittering and curious. It poked at Bowmark's hair and pulled on his Giver's Hand necklace.

"I thought they were too young to leave their mom."

SeeHerGo made a dismissive sound. "This one couldn't wait to get out and explore. And he already learned his first words. What will you name him?"

The monkey dangled around Bowmark's neck picking at the Giver's Hand medallion, one foot and its tail hanging onto Bowmark's hair. It tugged at the golden hand and squeaked. "Gimme gimme gimme mine!"

Its perfect tiny fingers—even smaller than Spearmark's—mesmerized Bowmark. He couldn't think of a name.

MoonGleam giggled. "I know his name! SnatchFast!" Sunrise laughed. "Truth! This is definitely SnatchFast."

SeeHerGo smiled gently. "That's a wonderful name, don't you think so, Bowmark?"

Still finding it difficult to focus, Bowmark nodded. Sunrise stroked SnatchFast and cooed. "We should teach him warrior shouts too."

Outside, a woman shouted angrily, "Pigfat! Pigfat!"

Bowmark jerked upright.

Then a man yelled, "Pigfat."

The door slid open. NineToes walked in. "Presumed, are you ready to eat?"

Bowmark handed SnatchFast to Sunrise and patted his swollen eyes. Maybe they wouldn't notice he had cried. He turned to SeeHerGo. "Thank you for this gift." He tried to recreate the kingly nod he saw Father give when presented with gifts. He walked out to the veranda where NineToes handed him a bowl of cold, unseasoned rice, the same food they had eaten at the funeral meal. His stomach hurt less than it had in days. Maybe he could eat this. Maybe SnatchFast would eat what he couldn't.

MoonGleam pattered up to him and dropped SnatchFast on Bowmark's head, giggling. Then, abruptly, she jumped off the veranda and chased after an adolescent girl twice her size. "Pigfat!"

The adolescent covered her head with her arms and ran up the path. At every house she passed, someone shouted at her, "Pigfat." Bowmark squinted in confusion. Wasn't that HideUnder? They had all played games with her on rest days. What had she done?

Sunrise leaped off the veranda, grabbed MoonGleam, and dragged her back to the house. She didn't stop struggling until Dad rumbled, "Behave yourself."

Bowmark looked from angry face to angry face. "What did HideUnder do? Why is everybody yelling 'pigfat' at her?"

Mom looked as though she would need Bowmark to help her cry again.

Sunrise tapped him on the shoulder. "Let's go up to the farrowing shed."

Had something happened to the fatty pig sow? Bowmark followed Sunrise higher up the slope to the pen and shed. SnatchFast hung onto Bowmark's dreadlocks as they walked. Farmers standing in the lane between pens moved out of sight.

No grunting, no howling greeted them. No boar battered the fence. No piglets thrust their noses through the bamboo bars.

Bowmark looked from empty pen to empty pen. "Did you sell all of them?"

Sunrise slumped against a fence. "HideUnder's family has been jealous of my family for a long time. Their pigs stay skinny or die. Then you moved in with us."

"Why would they be jealous of me moving in with you?"

"It doesn't matter. The night before the market, they stole all the piglets, the sow, and the boar. They cooked and ate all they could. What they couldn't eat, they killed and threw over Old Head Cliff into the ocean."

Bowmark gaped.

Sunrise held his fists close to his side. "Twelve years of breeding gone. Dad spent a lot of money buying the best pigs. Now we're ruined."

"No, I'll make Father—My King come and judge them."

Sunrise gripped Bowmark's arm. "You won't. Dad said we're not going to ask for judgment." The glossy skin under the white scars on his jaw, neck, and shoulder flushed.

"Why? This isn't right!"

"I don't know why. Dad says we still need to live here when you're not here. We've always lived here. I don't know what he's talking about."

"I'll have My King send you new pigs."

"Dad said you would say that. I'm supposed to tell you that you're not doing that either."

"Why?"

"Dad told me to take you to Mount Fist and explore some of the lava tubes."

"I don't want to. I want to give you justice."

"Everybody hates HideUnder's family now. Dad said we need to accept that as justice enough. Besides, we commoners usually help each other when there's need. NineToes agreed."

Standing in the hot sun, surrounded by dust and silence, Bowmark thought. He absentmindedly stroked SnatchFast. He didn't want another lecture from NineToes.

Sunrise said, "Bowmark? I heard you saw a shlak. I wish I could see a shlak."

No, he didn't. Bowmark repressed a shiver as he imagined the threat of giant crabs invading the beaches and smashing all the canoes. He should not share the shlak threat with those who could do nothing about it. Instead, he twisted his neck to look up at Mount Fist's peak. "SnatchFast hasn't seen the lava tubes. Maybe we can find some obsidian. Let's go."

Sunrise walked beside him. "We don't need to look at King's Island."

He had hoped Sunrise had not noticed his fear of the island. The volcano on King's Island had stopped pumping out lava, which meant the time for challenges had passed, but he held many new fears now besides the threat of the shlak. What would happen if the people thought they could get away with stealing that which other people had worked hard for? What would happen if the Sea Predators ignored the Protocol and the legal times for killing listed therein? Would Father and Spearmark ever be safe from jealous people?

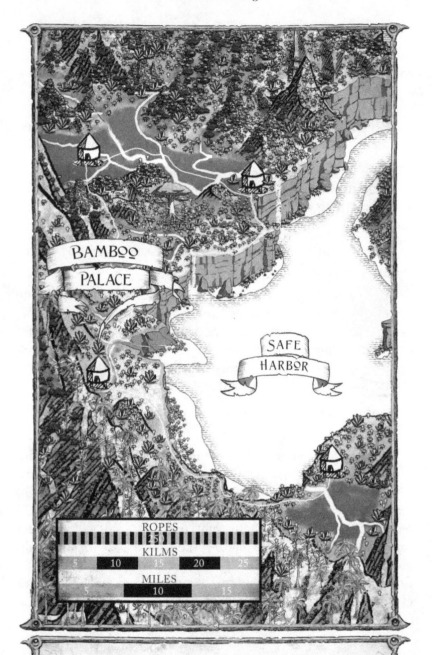

ORDER IS MAINTAINED THUSLY: ONE MAY NEVER KILL ANOTHER
UNLESS THE DEATH OCCURS ON THE DISC OR TRAINING GROUNDS.
~BOOK OF PROTOCOL OF THE SEA PREDATORS

Three years after Mother's death, Bowmark sat across the mat from RaiseHim, poked at his bowl of cut fruit with his chopsticks, and glared. RaiseHim glared back while brushing imaginary dirt from his new scallop shell patterned skirt. His cousin would find any pretense to insult Bowmark and his home. Bowmark's right eyebrow still hurt from yesterday's ceremonial scarring and tattooing of arrowheads, as did his shoulder now bearing the image of a spearhead. As most did, he had kept his birth name on his adult-name day.

RaiseHim's family had not bothered to come during yesterday's feast, claiming to be busy with some urgent matter on another island. But here they were today, eating in Father's sleeping room, pretending affection for Father's family.

Couldn't their fathers discern that RaiseHim and Bowmark hated each other?

With his usual calm voice, Father said, "I have received complaints about your rents."

RaiseHim's father fumbled his bowl of rice as he set it down. "Could we discuss this elsewhere?"

"The throne room is presently empty." Father rose and exited his sleeping room with RaiseHim's father following.

RaiseHim's mother hesitated, then picked up her little girl, ducked her head in farewell to the servant and the boys still eating, and said while exiting, "Come home when you're done eating."

The maidservant MorningMist reached over three-year-old Spearmark to gather his tiny bowls. SnatchFast was helping Spearmark finish his fruit. "Gimme mine! Fruit fruit!"

Spearmark joined his boisterous call. "Fruit fruit!" MorningMist chuckled at the monkey as she removed the bowls, rose and walked around the mat to RaiseHim's side.

As fast as a gecko's tongue, RaiseHim's foot shot out between the servant's feet.

MorningMist tripped. Her armful of bowls flew across the mat. One of the black-glass bowls clipped Bowmark's head; one grazed Spearmark's shoulder. She sprawled across the remains of the food, knocking over a jug of coconut milk.

Spearmark drew in breath, looking as though he was deciding whether or not to cry. SnatchFast darted out a window.

RaiseHim shouted, "Clean that up."

MorningMist whimpered, "I'm sorry, esteemed guest."

Bowmark shouted at RaiseHim, "You nearly hit Spearmark." He dove across the mat and knocked RaiseHim over. The two boys grappled a moment before RaiseHim broke free and sprinted into the hall.

He raced through the palace, past door after door, into the training yard with Bowmark close behind.

RaiseHim passed the wrestling mats and made it to the obstacle course before Bowmark tackled him by the uneven bars. They fell on the gritty sand. Bowmark grabbed RaiseHim's dreadlocks and pushed his face into the sand. Through clenched teeth Bowmark said, "You don't treat our servants like that."

RaiseHim flailed uselessly before he raised his face and spit out sand. "You won't always be bigger than me."

Bowmark was certain he would always be a few thumb-widths taller than RaiseHim, but RaiseHim was more ruggedly built. He kept his knee between his cousin's shoulders. "Don't mistreat our servants."

"You need to be shoved in hot lava. Your whole family does. You're too weak to be king. Your father is impoverishing the royals and nobles."

"Your father looks *very* well fed to me."

RaiseHim bucked. Bowmark stayed on him, scooted back, and wrenched his arms back. A knife hidden in RaiseHim's skirt pressed against Bowmark's knee.

A cold question pierced through Bowmark's rage. RaiseHim could have escaped through doors that were closer. Why had he chosen to run to the guard's training yard and obstacle course?

RaiseHim pulled a hand loose and seized the knife on his other side. Bowmark wrenched RaiseHim's wrist with Lobster Twist until he let go of the knife. RaiseHim spit out more sand. "I surrender."

Bowmark looked at the knife. Would his cousin have really knifed him? As with fights on the Disc set over flowing lava, any deaths in the obstacle course were legal. Bowmark swallowed to keep his meal down. He was four years away from being old enough to fight on the Disc when the volcano on King's Island erupted. What would Bowmark do when he was old enough to step on the Disc?

No. He would not believe RaiseHim was already planning to murder him. "Leave our servants and my brother alone."

The sound of footsteps brought his gaze to the doorway of the yard. Father and RaiseHim's father entered the yard and leaned against the wall with their arms crossed.

Bowmark resisted the urge to pound RaiseHim's face into the sand again. He slowly rose.

RaiseHim's father grunted and gave his son the look that always preceded a beating, then walked out of the yard. RaiseHim dragged after, shooting venomous glances at Bowmark and wiping sand off his scraped skin.

Father said nothing as he stood watching Bowmark.

A long moment passed before Bowmark could master his feelings enough to speak respectfully. "Why do you allow those people in our palace? Why do you feed them our food? Why do you keep putting RaiseHim and me in the same room?"

Father glanced down the empty hallway. "I am King of everybody on StoneGrove. I am king of people I don't like. I am king of people who don't like me. I swore to protect every one of them on my adult-name day. I swore that oath again when I became king. Did I hear you swear to protect all the Sea Predators on StoneGrove yesterday?"

Bowmark heaved out breath and swallowed bitterness. The thick ointment covering his arrowhead scars had been sweated away and now the wounds dribbled blood into his right eye. "Yes." Couldn't Father look at least a little angry about RaiseHim?

Father paused. "Part of the oath allows you to defend yourself. You seem to have done that well today. I am not clear, though, on whether or not RaiseHim attacked you."

Bowmark opened his mouth. He fingered the spot on his scalp that just now began to sting. "Spearmark was almost hurt."

Father gazed at the fruit pieces stuck in Bowmark's dreadlocks. "Are you telling me RaiseHim attacked Spearmark?"

"Uh. Uh. He was . . . . Not directly." Under Father's unflinching gaze, Bowmark stuttered, "He attacked the maid. Maybe not attacked." His words came faster. Father was not convinced. "But he tripped her on purpose. And when she fell bowls fell everywhere. One almost hit Spearmark. Uh, did, a little bit, on his shoulder." Bowmark ran out of breath.

Father unfolded his arms. "I did not find Spearmark lying in a puddle of blood. But we both know RaiseHim's real pain will come at the hands of his father tonight. This is how we differ. Listen to me. Fear will make men obey you. Love will make them follow you."

What did that have to do with RaiseHim tripping the maid?

"If you are to be king, you must learn to get along with everybody." Father left, no doubt going somewhere to get along with somebody.

Bowmark kicked the sand.

Bowmark re-entered the room they had been eating in. The grass mat that had absorbed the spills had been taken away, probably to be thrown on a compost heap. Where was Spearmark?

A manservant in the hallway walked by.

Bowmark popped out. "RockThrow, have you seen my little brother? I want to take him swimming."

Before the servant answered, SweetFruit ran down the hall. "Presumed! Our guest. The kitchen!"

Now what?

When she turned and ran toward the kitchen courtyard, Bowmark and the manservant chased after her. They spilled out into the sandy area surrounding the outdoor roofed-over kitchen.

RaiseHim stood defiantly holding SnatchFast. The tiny monkey squirmed, but RaiseHim squeezed his head and hind feet as he held him over a kettle of boiling water.

Bowmark skidded to a stop. "What are you doing?"

RaiseHim smirked. "Showing you what I'm going to do to you when I grow big enough to beat you." He released the monkey's head and thrust the hind feet toward the boiling water.

SnatchFast whipped around as one ear dipped into the boiling water and grabbed RaiseHim's arm. The monkey's sharp teeth sank into the boy's forearm.

RaiseHim shouted and flung his arm in a wide arc. The monkey released its hold, tumbled through the air, grabbed a dangling bit of thatch, and changed its trajectory to fly onto Bowmark. From his safe perch SnatchFast screamed at RaiseHim. "Gimme gimme gimme!"

RaiseHim slapped his hand over the bite wound and scowled at Bowmark. The servants knelt and looked away from them. Blood seeped between RaiseHim's fingers.

Bowmark did not trust himself to speak. He was not the one who was allowed to say who could come into the palace and who couldn't. He wasn't the one who could tell RaiseHim to go away and never come back.

SnatchFast pawed his scalded ear and whimpered.

The presumed was required to embody the Protocol. RaiseHim had a choice about whether or not he would step on the Disc. Bowmark had no choice about that. He had no choice about how he must treat RaiseHim with respect until RaiseHim attacked him.

RaiseHim said, "You wait." He walked around the frightened servants and did not turn his back to Bowmark until he ducked back inside the palace.

Bowmark unclenched his fists. He could do one thing. "RockThrow, follow him and remind him his mother wants him to go home. Remind him every few heartbeats until he leaves."

"I will, Presumed." The manservant jogged after the royal cousin.

Bowmark stroked SnatchFast. Maybe RaiseHim *would* try to murder him before he could step on the Disc. What had he done to make his cousin so angry at him?

What had he done that Giver had made him firstborn to a king?

OBSTACLES IN LIFE ARE GIFTS OF GROWTH
DISGUISED AS TRAGEDY.
                    -SEA PREDATOR HOLY BOOKS

Ten boys and two girls, all nobles near Bowmark's age of fifteen lined up on the beach and studied the obstacle course the guards had built that morning. Bowmark knew every finger-width and splinter of the obstacle course in the guards' courtyard in the palace. This was new.

Some of the contestants fidgeted with the knives hidden in the seams of their skirts or gingerly touched where a thin blade or awl hid in a dreadlock. Larger knives hung in sheaths from their waistbands. Bowmark willed himself to stillness and examined the new obstacle course.

The leftmost log in the disheveled pile of driftwood would fall and roll as soon as someone stepped on it. Some of the logs were set on end, rising up like poles to contain most of the other logs. How sturdily the upright logs were set in their pits he would not discover until he tested them.

The course curved into the jungle with a few guards lining the route. First the driftwood pile, then a crooked line of boulders wearing unstable rocks like hats, a cliff climb from the beach to the jungle, and likely a rope course in the jungle. The physician RunsFast sat on a nearby rock, kneading the medicine bag on her lap, fiddling with her reddish-brown hair that indicated a mixed heritage.

CrunchIt, with his coiled red hair cut short, paced in front of the adolescents and prodded them into an even line. "Do you see the glass ball out there?"

Everyone's head swiveled and nodded. They could see the netted ball floating just beyond the surf.

The royal guard brought all their gazes back by holding aloft a varon pearlescence knife, the only one in the nation of StoneGrove. The smooth, white curves of the knife gleamed with a rainbow effect in the sun.

Bowmark covered his mouth so no one could hear him snicker. He loved that knife. So did everyone else in the palace. The cooks aggravated the guards by sneaking the unbreakable blade that could not be dulled into the kitchen to cut bone and tough tendons.

CrunchIt grinned nastily and pointed at the course with the blade. "This knife can be yours. All you need to do is get through the obstacle course, reach the kapok tree while we beat you with sticks, retrieve a blade hanging from that branch, swim out to that float, cut the glass ball from its tether, and put it in my hands. The first one to bring me that ball wins the use of this knife for three weeks."

The oldest contestant let a small sound escape her lips.

"Do you have a problem?"

SpinFast shuddered. Her wide shoulders and right arm still bore the bruises from the last stick-fighting lesson. "No. But sir, are you giving us sticks to defend ourselves?"

"We are giving you nothing."

Bowmark blew out his breath as he thought of the thorns on that giant kapok tree towering over the rest of the jungle. Surely there must be a better way to celebrate his fifteenth birthday.

CrunchIt stopped in front of Bowmark. "Presumed, that may not be enough incentive for you. What are the consequences if you do not win this race?"

The same as they were every time he did not win. "I will need to run the obstacle course forward and backward while you throw rocks at me."

"For how long?"

"Three candles." Three that would feel like twelve. "That's right. What are the consequences for you, Rockfall?"

Rockfall squared his shoulders. "I will need to run from one end of the beach to the other for one candle."

"That's right. What are the consequences for you, RaiseHim?"

"There won't be any. I'm going to win and take that knife home."

The youngest boy groaned.

"Go!" CrunchIt shouted.

The contestants scrambled across the sand, elbows and feet flying. They leaped onto the pile of driftwood tree trunks. Bowmark bounced from one log to another, careful not to put his weight on any log for very long.

RaiseHim bumped into the youngest boy. The child spun away and landed awkwardly on the unbalanced log Bowmark had noted earlier. The log tipped and rolled away from the feet of the boy. He flung out his arms.

Bowmark swung around on an upright pole, swooped in, and grabbed the boy's outflung arm just before the child followed the log to the ground. As he pulled him in, his swinging weight tilted the pole and dropped Bowmark and the boy onto a root wad. The boy's knee struck a projecting root. He cried out and pushed Bowmark away before curling up.

The levered pole unset the entire pile. RaiseHim windmilled his arms as he wobbled on a shifting log. Bowmark leaped past him. Another boy's foot slipped and he fell, straddling the trunk.

Bowmark climbed to the highest part of the pile, snatched a marker rag from the apex, and stuffed the fabric into his waistband. RaiseHim pushed him. Bowmark turned his fall into a roll, scraped his back on the silvered wood, and jumped onto the closest log.

The end dipped under his feet. He raced up the log to where it teetered on a crossways branch, and then ran down as it thunked the other way. He swayed this way and that as he leap-stepped down an unsteady slope of thick branches. His feet plowed into a mound of sticks. He used his momentum to flip over the hazard onto the sand.

Turning back, he noted the physician RunsFast dealing with the boy and his bleeding knee. Good. He pulled sticks out of the mound and tossed them aside.

The second-youngest boy skittered down the slope, scrambled from the mound of sticks and ran to the line of boulders.

Bowmark uncovered a stick straighter and sturdier than most of the others and picked up his new weapon that was nearly as tall as him. Ironwood. It was old, but still quite strong. RaiseHim tackled him from behind. They rolled on the sand, tugging on the stick. Bowmark held on, pulled up his legs, and shoved on RaiseHim's chest. RaiseHim flew back onto the mound of sticks. As SpinFast skittered down the slope of driftwood she tripped and fell on RaiseHim.

Bowmark sprinted to the line of boulders. He pushed aside a rock that could tip and trap an ankle. Leaping from boulder to boulder, he knocked over unbalanced rocks, until he reached the rock formation called Old Man. That he scrambled up and over with practiced ease, as did all the children whether they were training or not. Two boulders later came a gap wider than could be leaped. If his feet touched the sand, he would need to start over at the beginning of the line. Using his stick to touch the sand instead of his hands, he cartwheeled over the space.

RaiseHim nearly vaulted onto him. Too much time had been wasted trying to make the rock course safer for the ones behind him.

One of the boys who had beat them to the rocks raced back on the sand to get the stick he had not thought of. Now in the lead, Bowmark jumped along the line with RaiseHim as his shadow. They jumped off the last boulder together.

A small pile of rocks lay beside the end of the rock course. They might be needed for something later in the obstacle course, like the sticks had been needed. Bowmark shoved his long stick into his waistband, positioning it along his spine. He kneeled and removed a small waterskin from his left belt satchel, making room for a fist-sized river rock.

SpinFast did the same as the rest of the contestants raced past them. RaiseHim shoved Bowmark aside and followed a line of stakes with orange flowers wrapped around them to the highest cliff on the beach. The jungle ran parallel to the beach, its edge undulating with the forest floor sometimes nearly at sea level, sometimes many strides higher.

After climbing the cliff, the contestants ran along the edge of the jungle to the start of the rope course.

RaiseHim threw his stick away and leaped to catch the single line strung along several trees. Each span of rope rose higher than the one before. RaiseHim lifted his feet so they wouldn't knock over the penalty poles placed on end under the line. Hand over hand, he swung away.

The next-youngest boy jumped, but he could not reach the rope. He turned to climb the tree trunk.

Bowmark snatched the boy and tossed him to the rope, close to where the line attached to the tree. Then Bowmark jumped and caught the rope in front of the boy. He swung like a monkey behind the line of boys in front of him, swaying easily around the bamboo lengths. He had learned a trick or two from studying SnatchFast's climbing techniques. Things would have been smooth, but every time he changed hands, the stick in his waistband smacked him on the back of his head.

The rope jerked when SpinFast grabbed hold of it. The boy directly in front of Bowmark kicked one of the penalty poles and knocked it over. He dropped to the ground and ran back to the beginning of the rope course. That left RaiseHim and three others in front of Bowmark, and four behind him.

Seventeen-to-twenty-year-old warrior trainees emerged from the jungle. They threw mud-coated pinecones at the contestants swinging along the rope. The pinecones did not hurt, much, but they did distract. The boy behind RaiseHim fell, rolled, and ran back to the start of the line as the older trainees jeered at him. The last rope challenge was for them to swing from a hanging rope down to a marked spot on the path. Two boys failed and fell in the lush foliage. They also ran back to the start.

As soon as Bowmark's feet touched the marked landing place, a guard attacked him with a staff. Bowmark jumped away from the first blow, pulled the ironwood stick from his waistband, and parried the next blow. The guard grinned and gestured toward the path.

Bowmark took two steps and spun to watch Rockfall swing onto the designated spot. Before the boy let go of the rope, Bowmark tossed him his stick. Rockfall barely blocked the guard's first attack and failed entirely for the second blow which smashed into his ribs.

Bowmark couldn't fight for all the boys, but he had given one a chance. He turned, ran toward the kapok tree, and passed a boy rubbing his shoulder where the guard had struck him. Since Bowmark had been the only one to think to bring a stick with him, the sound of contestants being hit followed him.

Still thinking about the kapok's thorny branches, he veered off the path to a wide-spread fig tree that wore a skirt of vines, mosses, and aerial roots. He climbed a strand to a branch of the fig tree, climbed a ladder of tree limbs, and stopped at five strides high. A cluster of vines and roots parted under his knife and dropped bit by bit as the cluster tore away from fellow-entangling vines. Bowmark slid down a separate cluster of aerial roots. The last contestant ran by, so now Bowmark lagged behind everybody.

One of the vines had grown too woody and stiff for use, so he unwound the rest of the vines and roots from the wood. He tied a knot near both ends of what he had left and wove the rock he had carried with him into one of the ends. He looped his makeshift rope and weight over his shoulder and hurtled up the path to the kapok tree.

This kapok tree was the largest on the island, spreading its massive roots wider than the palace grounds. All the boys had climbed the supporting buttresses, the folds of wood the tree had grown to support itself as it stretched higher and higher to tower over the rest of the jungle. The woody walls meandered sometimes merging, sometimes forking.

The contestants who had reached the trunk seemed stymied over how to climb to the branch that held their goal: the large knife hanging from a horizontal branch. Eight men holding hands could reach around the circumference of the tree. Above the narrow buttresses, climbing the tree would be almost like climbing a sheer cliff.

The jungle trembled. The volcano must be coughing again. Everyone still on the ground bent their knees, widened their stance, and scanned the swaying trees. The contestants clutched the buttresses. Monkeys screamed and eight-legged snakes groaned.

EIGHT-LEGGED SNAKE

Slowly, the tremor faded away. Dead leaves shaken loose drifted through the shafts of sunlight that pierced the canopy and then caught on lower boughs or settled on the dim ground.

After two breaths to wait and see if the ground would quake again, most of the contestants pulled out their knives and stabbed the tree to make pegs of the knife handles to pull themselves up by. RaiseHim sat on the buttress he had climbed and folded his arms. His gaze darted between the climbing adolescents and the hanging knife.

Bowmark held his Giver's Hand medallion a moment, grateful that Sunrise had shown him this trick. He bounded up the thin edge of the buttress to the boundary of buttress and trunk, positioning himself under the lowest branch. The goal knife dangled from a limb on the other side of the tree.

The ground jerked again, and two boys fell from the tree. Bowmark stretched to catch the nearest one, but he swished past the edge of his fingertips. The boy landed on his feet only long enough to push himself into a roll in the slopping valley between the tree support ridges. He rolled off the tree and flattened in front of a watching guard. The other boy tried the same but he wedged into a V made by two buttresses melding into one. He yelped and held still as a guard climbed to check on him.

Bowmark unrolled his loop of vines, swung the rock over his head to gain momentum, and then threw the rock and trailing vines over the lowest branch. When he pulled on the vines, the rock slid up to the branch where the limb attached to the tree, and then smoothly slid over. He caught the rock before it hit his head.

Two of the guards drifted over and watched him. Most of the other contestants continued to haul themselves up the trunk, bit by bit. The higher they reached, the more anxious Bowmark grew, fearing that another aftershock would knock them off and kill them. Protecting all the people he had sworn to protect was impossible.

He moved down the buttress until he stood under a fork in the branch. Again, he swung the vine, released the rock which sailed up and over the fork where he tugged, wedging the rock in the fork. After years of rope-climbing, he could climb almost as fast as a monkey. A few seconds later he swung his leg over the branch.

He stood and looped the rope over his shoulder again. Fortunately, the trunk and tree limbs at this level had aged enough for the thorns to have popped off the bark. He trotted toward the trunk where he stopped and studied the nearby branches. Then he crouched, swung his arms, and leaped to another branch. Like a frog, he jumped his way around the circumference of the kapok. He was now ten strides from the ground. A fall would break bones.

When he reached the correct limb, a girl, StarFall had already climbed onto the branch and crawled halfway to the knife. The branch was as thick as a fat man. There she clung, staring at younger bark which was a stride beyond her and still covered with a thick coat of flesh-piercing thorns.

"You can't reach it," Bowmark said. "Back up and let me try."

Unsurprisingly, StarFall did not relent. A boy crowded in between Bowmark and the trunk. He had to act. Bowmark ran forward and cartwheeled over StarFall, keeping his eyes on the prone girl and the branch. He landed a hand span from the thorns.

The branch vibrated. StarFall's knees slipped off the limb. Her arms wrapped around the branch as, wide-eyed, she kicked the air, trying to swing her leg over. The other boy, LookFor, backed against the trunk, his arms spread across the bark.

Bowmark dropped to straddle the branch next to StarFall. "Come on. I have you." His hand slid under the girl's armpit and he hauled on her arm, pulling until StarFall had wrapped both arms and legs around the bough and faced the trunk.

"There's no shame here. You got farther than all of us except me."

StarFall laid her forehead against the tree limb, sighed, and creeped toward LookFor.

Bowmark turned and studied the short but sharp thorns that could take out his eyes and shred his muscles. The thorns started as wide, round bumps and were topped by needle-thin points that faced straight out like the masts of canoes.

He dropped an end of the vine over both sides of the branch, then dropped off, grabbing an end in both hands. He swung himself back and forth under the branch until he had enough momentum to hop the vine forward. The braided aerial roots scraped across the thorns, popping the sharp points off but also tearing a bit in the process. Again and again he swung, hopped, swung, hopped.

THE KAPOK TREE

The contestants who had returned to the ground cried out.

On each swing, he edged closer to the blade that hung from the branch, tied to a grass rope. One last swing, and he grabbed the hanging obsidian blade with his knees.

Now what?

He hung like a banner, his hands gripping the ends of his fraying vine rope, his knees hanging onto the blade tied to the tree. This had seemed simpler when he was planning.

Now he thought of better plans. First, he could have wrapped the vines and roots around his bare feet until he had thick enough protection for him to walk over to the goal knife. Or he could have scraped off the sharp points with his rock as he crawled along the branch. Even using the stick he had foolishly discarded to scrape the branch could have provided an easier way to reach the knife. Somehow, he had managed to find the most difficult solution.

He released the goal blade, still dangling, and swung-hopped closer.

Hanging like a fruit, he considered the problem. He needed to cut the rope holding the blade. If he let go of one end of his vine to pull out a knife from his skirt, he would plummet to the ground, probably breaking his legs, possibly dying. Could he gnaw through the knife's rope, like a rat? Not before exhaustion made him fall.

He hitched himself up his vines until he had a loose end. Gasping, he grabbed the other end just above the rock and wrapped the loose end around his hand.

This was going to hurt. He let go his right hand. The pressure on his left hand doubled, grinding his bones together. He pulled up his knees and used them to grasp hold of the goal blade, and then sawed at the rope with a knife pulled from his skirt.

Once the goal knife was free, he was stuck again. The blade was far too large to fit in any of his satchels or hidden pockets, so he kept the blade between his knees. Next, he maneuvered himself around, unwound the end of the vines from his hand, and began the tedious process of swing-hopping himself back incrementally along the branch.

The boys below and one of the guards cheered him on.

RaiseHim shouted, "LookFor, cut his vines."

RAISEHIM

What? "No!" yelled Bowmark. He swung forward a few more thumb-widths.

"No!" cried StarFall. She flung himself upon RaiseHim.

RaiseHim threw the girl aside. "LookFor, you cut his vine or I'll make sure you wish you jumped on hot lava."

LookFor pattered along the branch to where Bowmark's rope of aerial roots and vines looped over the branch. Tears dripped off his face as he kneeled over the rope and pressed his knife against it.

A vine twanged apart.

He needed his knees. Bowmark released the goal blade and shinnied up the rope. He flung his arm over the branch as the obsidian blade bounced on the forest floor.

His makeshift rope parted and plummeted as he pulled himself over the tree limb.

LookFor backed away as his mouth trembled.

Bowmark growled. "Don't you ever do that again."

LookFor shook his head in jerks and threw himself onto his stomach.

Bowmark jumped over him, raced to the trunk, pulled out both his knives, and stabbed the trunk.

RaiseHim scooped up the goal blade and sprinted toward the path.

SpinFast intercepted him.

RaiseHim slashed her arm and shoved her aside. As he ran down the path, the other contestants chased after him past guards who stood with folded arms.

By the time Bowmark reached the base of the kapok tree, a guard was binding up the gash on SpinFast's arm. Bowmark sprinted along the path. When he arrived at the beach, all the contestants had swum beyond the surf. Bowmark dove in.

He swam under the surf as the turquoise sea swirled about him. Emerging into the smoother waves behind the surf for breath, he nearly collided with Rockfall treading water a body length from RaiseHim. Clinging to the glass float with one arm, RaiseHim slashed at any boy who approached with the other. Bowmark treaded water to watch and think.

RaiseHim ducked underwater to cut at the float's tether. Rockfall stroked toward him. RaiseHim popped back up and pointed the large obsidian blade at him. Rockfall backed away. HighKick plunged toward RaiseHim from behind.

RaiseHim spun and slashed toward HighKick.

Rockfall swam toward RaiseHim again.

RaiseHim kicked him in the head. The crunch of Rockfall's nose breaking rose over the sounds of splashing and surf.

Rockfall jerked back and fell limp. RaiseHim ducked under again and severed the tether, collecting the float.

Bowmark flipped Rockfall over, slung his arm over the unconscious boy's chest, and stroked one-armed toward the shore trailing behind the others. Bowmark and Rockfall tumbled through the surf until his feet found the sand. He hauled the limp boy through the crashing waves.

Everyone splashed onto the beach and raced toward the guard holding aloft the knife made of pearlescence. Boys tussled over the bit of tether trailing behind RaiseHim.

"Help me, HighKick," Bowmark called.

The boy hesitated, glanced at the other racers, and realized he could never get to RaiseHim before he returned the glass float to CrunchIt. Dejected, he ran back to help. He slung Rockfall's other arm over his shoulder and together they hauled the unconscious boy toward the physician.

RunsFast jogged toward them, her rusty-red straight hair working itself out of its tie. She gathered the boy into her arms. "I have him."

RaiseHim delivered the float and whooped. CrunchIt handed him the blade. RaiseHim leaped and waved the pearlescence knife over his head as the rest of the boys backed away from him.

"Dismissed!" shouted CrunchIt. All the boys except RaiseHim began their runs along the beach. Ululating, RaiseHim ran into the path through the jungle that led to his home.

Bowmark marched up to the guard. "Why didn't you punish RaiseHim? He injured two of my people, bullied LookFor, and nearly got me killed."

CrunchIt stooped to yell in Bowmark's face. "What he did was legal in the obstacle course. You keep wasting your time and energy trying to help warriors who should be taking care of themselves. What are you training for?"

Bowmark refused to back down. "We're training to fight a Southil invasion. How are we going to defeat them if we're fighting ourselves?"

"You fool! You learn how to form an army when you're a designate. What are you training for *now*?"

As if cosmically cued, the ground shook for a second. Both guard and Bowmark turned to look in the direction of King's Island. So many earthquakes so close together could mean the volcano would erupt soon, but no smoke marred the blue sky above the jungle. The driftwood pile collapsed into a tighter configuration.

The guard said, "It's a good thing you're still too young to prove. As long as you continue to sacrifice pragmatic victory for your naive heroic gestures you will *die*."

Bowmark briefly closed his eyes. If only he could stay too young forever. He grasped his Giver's Hand medallion and whispered, "Giver, please don't let the volcano erupt while I'm in age range. Please let me age out." That was an evil prayer. If Bowmark aged out, then Spearmark would become the presumed. How could he allow his sweet brother to go on the Disc?

The two faced each other again. CrunchIt repeated, "What are you training for *now*? What are all of you training for?"

Bowmark's throat tightened. "I don't want to kill anybody. Not even that pig's anus."

"Then you want to die."

"No, I don't want to die."

"Presumed, those are your only two choices."

"I don't—I don't—"

"You are choosing to become ash and smoke. And you're condemning me. Do you think My King won't pitch me onto the hot lava after you for failing to train you properly?"

Bowmark struggled to breathe. "He wouldn't. He hates the Disc."

"We *all* hate the Disc. That's the point. Why else is My King secure on his throne?" CrunchIt grabbed Bowmark's chin and wrenched his face up. "Listen to me. RaiseHim has caught the fish your net refuses to snare. His father makes sure of that with pitiless beatings. Why do you think he is so cruel? You need to be able to do anything, *anything*, to win. If he takes you out even before you get on the Disc, who do you think is going to win?"

Bowmark pulled his chin from the guard's fingers and backed a step. "You think RaiseHim will be the challenger."

"I *know* RaiseHim will be the challenger. Unless you take him out before the proving. Unless you *change*. If both of you end up on the Disc, RaiseHim will become My King and I will obey him like I obey all the Protocol. And. You'll. Be. Ash."

Bowmark's jaw was so tight his teeth hurt. "I will never be like RaiseHim!" A hot tear escaped his eye and he trembled.

CrunchIt shook his head in disgust. "And you consign your baby brother to death."

Bowmark squeezed his eyes closed. "Shut up. Shut up! SHUT UP!" his hand whipped out a knife and he charged at CrunchIt.

The guard clouted him on the temple. Bowmark staggered backward and fell on the pile of driftwood.

"You fool!" CrunchIt shouted. "Why would you do a frontal attack with a knife on someone who is bigger than you and has a longer reach? If you want to kill me, what weapons should you use? What weapons?"

Bowmark choked out. "Spears. Arrows. Rocks. Ranged weapons."

"What has My King uselessly tried to teach you about anger?"

Stifling a sob, Bowmark croaked, "If you get angry, you die."

"What did you just demonstrate?"

"If you get angry, you die." Anger still thrummed through his veins, but Bowmark tried to suppress the narrowed vision, the narrowed thinking.

"Run the course. Go!"

Bowmark turned and scrambled up the pile of wood.

Bowmark limped into the room. Today, the family was eating breakfast in the distribution room of the armory. A manservant followed him with a platter of hot redfish.

Father laid his chopsticks across his bowl of yellowfish. After Bowmark had settled onto the floor next to Spearmark and the servant had set the fish down and left, Father said, "I hear you had a rigorous day yesterday. I am pleased to hear SpinFast, LiftHim, TakesUp, and Rockfall are recovering well. SpinFast is proud of the scar she's going to show off."

What RaiseHim did was legal. Bowmark pulled off some crinkled fish skin. "Four trainees is too high a casualty rate. Somebody might die the next time."

With a calm that infuriated Bowmark, Father said, "It is too high. You will see it get worse, My Presumed."

Bowmark chewed on the fish skin and glowered.

Spearmark motioned with his chopsticks, flinging some seaweed. "I wish I had seen it. Some fishermen said I was supposed to help them fish instead. They threw me in the ocean and made me swim back."

Wait until they sail out of sight of land and throw you in. Bowmark stabbed a slice of yellowfruit. "Destroying ourselves before the Southils invade is not wise. Why don't you change that part of the Protocol?"

Father said, "That part, I cannot change. Is there anything else you would like to whine about?"

Bowmark stabbed another piece of fruit and broke his chopstick.

Father's only reaction was to raise one eyebrow.

Spearmark asked, "What can you change?"

Father picked up a bowl of fried chunknuts. "No king is allowed to change the rules about proving, challenges, ruling, and training. Also, I cannot totally dismiss a rule on the list of those that I am allowed to change. I am permitted to take out a 'not', effectively negating a rule. I am permitted to add a 'not', which might accomplish the same thing. Though it's not prohibited, none of the prior kings have added a sentence to the Protocol."

Spearmark blinked and returned to his bowl of seaweed-seasoned rice.

Bowmark licked his teeth. "Father, I will not whine. I want to ask a question."

"Ask."

"Have you thought about changing the rule that says royals can't marry commoners?"

"I have thought of changing a great many rules. Since I am permitted to change only one rule during my entire reign, I am still considering what to change that would benefit our people the most. That particular rule is not my highest priority."

The number of "royal-blessed" people with curly hair or less-dark hair proved that many royals weren't waiting for a rule change or marriage. Bowmark drank a cup of coconut milk. He would not shame MoonGleam like that. If only there was a royal girl who demonstrated even half the vibrancy of Sunrise's sister.

Rather than keep stepping on the hook, Bowmark tapped the back of his hand against Spearmark's hand. "Is there anything you want me to bring back from High Harbor?"

"Bobo, I want to go with you."

Bowmark looked at Father, who shook his head.

"Not this time. Maybe next time." Oh, to see Spearmark's face the first time he smelled pigs that weren't roasting on a spit.

"It's always next time."

"Actually," Father said, "Except within the palace, I want to keep you two apart."

A shiver ran up Bowmark's spine. Father feared losing two sons at the same time. How could it be that the best way to protect sweet Spearmark was by keeping the target painted on Bowmark's back far away from him? He rose from the floor. "I'll see you next week."

Bowmark plodded along the main path of High Harbor. SnatchFast clambered over his back and shoulders, hooting or occasionally making human words. Bowmark rewarded talking with dried fruit bits.

The farmers looked up from their work and returned to their chores without remark. NineToes' new wife weeded a rice paddy. The clack of sticks drew Bowmark around the communal hay shed. Four boys fought with staffs. NineToes moved among them correcting their stances. Nine people watched closely. Bowmark leaned against a wall.

ShellCrush was soundly beating Sunrise. Being five years older and much heavier gave ShellCrush an advantage. If his hands still hadn't hurt from yesterday's obstacle course, Bowmark would have joined in to defend Sunrise.

NineToes stopped in the middle of positioning Birdsong. "Dismissed."

Everyone looked in the direction he was looking, saw Bowmark watching them, and then scattered like cluckers running from a seadog instead of from Bowmark's gaze. Everyone except Sunrise and MoonGleam.

Sunrise laughed. "I think you showed up just in time. I was about to get my head broken."

MoonGleam picked up a dropped stick. "I haven't had a turn yet. I could fight Bowmark."

"No, you can't," NineToes said. "He's older than you and stronger."

"But you let Sunrise fight with ShellCrush."

"ShellCrush is his only competition. Both of you go home. I need to speak with the presumed."

Bowmark straightened. "Why did you dismiss the class? I could have waited."

NineToes gathered the sticks and leaned them against the shed. "I should have paid more attention to the sun. You weren't supposed to see that."

"See what?"

"See me training the commoners."

Bowmark sat on the dirt. "You *should* train the commoners. If the Southils invade, we're going to need every warrior possible."

NineToes made a wry face. "Not every royal or noble is as wise as you. Some of them are more afraid of commoners than they are of Southils."

"Why?" Commoners had abundant reasons to dislike royals, but why would royals fear commoners?

NineToes interlaced his fingers and studied them a moment. "They fear that if we learn to fight, we'll kill them."

Bowmark squirmed. "Are there commoner Sea Predators who will kill royal Sea Predators?"

"Nobody here." NineToes paused. "I can't speak for all thirty thousand of us. A lot of us would provide feasts if every royal sailed away, but I haven't heard of any plots against royals."

"Would you provide a feast if I sailed away?"

NineToes crouched and sat on his heels. He looked Bowmark directly in the face. "No, Presumed. I would miss you."

Bowmark relaxed. "My King says he wishes your wife had moved to the palace instead of you moving to High Harbor. He misses you."

"And I him. Someday, you'll discover how heavy an anchor a wife is."

Would he? Was there a royal girl who liked Bowmark more than she liked the thought of becoming a queen?

"I would be grateful if you kept this extra training a secret."

Already Bowmark must keep secret how he felt about MoonGleam. He kept as secret the shlak's threat under their feet even as the commoners grumbled about moving the cesspools farther inland and enlarging them. What was one more secret? "What you do when you're not training me is none of my concern."

"I give you thanks." He and Bowmark rose.

"So then. Staff fighting?" asked Bowmark.

"No. I'd rather you rest before we do some knife-throwing. Have you done log-rolling yet?"

A small troupe of monkeys ran between them, stirring up more fetid dust. SnatchFast dropped onto the last monkey and wrestled it playfully before bounding back up a fencepost and hopping onto his usual perch on Bowmark's shoulder. Why couldn't humans be born as agile? Bowmark quirked his eyebrows. "If I say no, is there a log in the harbor we will tow to the beach?"

"You are so intelligent. We might as well gain some use from the driftwood before we cut it into firewood."

Bowmark plodded down the path to Sunrise's home. He watched the farmers in the stair-stepped terraces, the cliff edges, the sea birds wheeling above a fisherman's canoe in the sparkling blue ocean, and, beyond a second row of houses, the rustling in jungle tree tops of monkeys, lizards, and bigfa birds. Sunrise and MoonGleam sat on the edge of the wide veranda, Sunrise with the Atlas on his lap. One corner of the house sagged. Bowmark and Sunrise needed to walk down to the bamboo forest and harvest some poles to rebuild that corner and the slumping veranda.

Wherever he looked, there was something that needed to be done: terrace-wall shoring up, crop harvesting, fish drying, house repairing, path repairing, water fetching, rice hulling, firewood gathering, egg finding, fruit picking and peeling, compost turning, mat weaving, and rope plaiting. If only these were the *only* things that needed to be done.

MoonGleam patted the floor beside her. "You look tired. Sit beside me."

He must not allow her to think—to think—Maybe she wasn't thinking the kind of thoughts he was. Bowmark trudged past her and past Sunrise to sit on his other side.

Sunrise flipped open the Atlas near the end. "I translated six more sentences this week."

Bowmark had already copied those sentences and worked through them with the tutor and his dictionary. Considering how slowly Bowmark had learned Common, the tutor would be astonished if he knew how fast Sunrise was learning.

Sunrise read the sentences in halting Common and then translated into Predator. "In the seas beyond northernmost

Akinda and Utali lies the something-covered land of Artika. Should you see any of the floating mountains of something that have broken away from Artika, and see upon them elaborate structures of something, flee and prepare for battle. The native inhabitants, known as kruli, eat or enslave the humans they capture. They plunder the ships of seafolks. One kruliss can kill dozens of humans at a time. It is said that it is better to die fighting the kruli than it is to be captured and taken north as a slave."

He set the book on his lap.

With her shining, black hair brushing the pages, MoonGleam examined the drawing of a kruliss on the opposite page. A bar the height of a seafolk indicated the six-limbed, furry kruliss stood twice as tall as a seafolk. "They eat people?"

Sunrise shrugged. "We eat pigs."

MoonGleam shoved him, and he collided with Bowmark. "Pigs aren't people." She pulled the picture of the monster closer to her. "Kruli are ugly."

"Not as ugly as majismontems. Those people are as big as kapok trees, have dozens of legs and smell like manure." Sunrise pulled the Atlas back and put his finger on a word in the text. "What does this word mean in Predator?"

"The tutor said we don't have that word. 'Ice' means water that is so cold that it becomes as hard as rock."

The siblings stared at Bowmark.

"That's what the dictionary said. I don't understand it either."

MoonGleam squished her lips to one side. "Do you remember two years ago when hard rain fell? It looked like white sand and disappeared almost instantly."

"I must have been inside the palace then. I never saw that."

Sunrise said, "If this is true, then the Kruli make cities out of hard water that floats on water! I want to see that hard water."

Of course Sunrise did. Bowmark leaned back and propped himself on stiff arms. "You want to see the Southils who are waiting for us to show up so they can finish slaughtering us. You want to see kruli who eat humans, majismontems who step on humans, and Warrior Women who gain strength with a magic stone."

MoonGleam said, "The magic stone makes them strong enough to fight men. I want to be that strong."

"That's just so you can beat me up," Sunrise said.

MoonGleam slapped Sunrise's arm. He bumped into Bowmark again.

Sunrise grinned. "I want to challenge a Warrior Woman to a wrestling match."

Bowmark sat up. "Wouldn't you be humiliated if you lost?"

"Not at all. Then I could demand a rematch." When MoonGleam punched him in the arm, he said, "Ow," and laughed. SnatchFast mimicked, "Ow Ow Ow Ow!"

MoonGleam leaned forward and her black hair fell across the side of her face as she gazed at her dirty feet, baring her neck and shoulder. Lovely neck and shoulder. Smooth skin. Kissable skin.

Bowmark clutched his Giver's Hand medallion and tore his gaze away from the soft skin that smelled of vanilla and coconut. He looked over the terraces, jungle, and ocean below them. "It's so beautiful here. Why would you want to leave?"

"Because I hate pig manure. How beautiful is that?"

What if the shlaks forced them to leave? How would they leave if the shlaks destroyed their canoes?

"Wake up, Bowmark." Sunrise waved a hand in front of his face. "What are you worried about now?"

Bowmark startled. "Do you know of anybody who wants to kill me?"

Sunrise scoffed. "Of course I do."

"Who?" Bowmark's stomach clenched.

"RaiseHim."

Bowmark punched him in the arm. "I meant *besides* RaiseHim."

"Ow. The two of you are going to squash me flatter than a majismontem could. How do you and RaiseHim handle seeing each other at feasts?"

"The Protocol says nobody is allowed to harm me during feasts or daily life."

"But he's allowed to kill you on an obstacle course run?"

How had the news about the obstacle course reached High Harbor before Bowmark did?

Sunrise asked, "What if he ignores the Protocol, doesn't challenge you or anything, and just kills you when you're not looking?"

"If he tries to kill or harm me, even if he fails, he would be thrown onto hot lava or a bonfire."

"What if he says it was an accident?"

"Hello, children," Dad rumbled. Mud coated his feet and hands. Behind him stretched a line of wet footprints to the field he had been weeding. He sat on the veranda, which creaked ominously, put his hands on his knees, and gazed pointedly at an empty bucket by his feet. "Why is there no water to wash myself before I enter the house and take the rest that some others of us here don't deserve?"

Bowmark pushed off the veranda and grabbed the bucket. "I'm sorry, Dad."

Dad's gaze moved to Sunrise. "Are you planning to sit there like a tick on a pig's rump?"

Sunrise and MoonGleam propelled themselves from the veranda, grabbed the rest of the buckets and chased Bowmark up to the pond. They pounded across the newly replaced, sturdier pier and, breathless, shoved the buckets into the water.

While the bucket filled, Bowmark splashed the water with his fingertips, chasing away the gathering boatmen insects. How could this much water become hard? And become a mountain? And then float? He pulled the full bucket out.

Small hands from behind toppled him into the pond. SnatchFast screeched and leapt off Bowmark's shoulder just in time.

Bowmark's head emerged from the water just as Sunrise flung shrieking MoonGleam into the pond. Then Sunrise jumped in, making a large, loud splash. SnatchFast chittered on the pier. Dad was waiting, so they didn't play but swam to the pier and filled their buckets again.

As they balanced the pails on their heads, Bowmark kept his gaze away from the wet tunic and skirt clinging to MoonGleam's body and forced himself to think about Sunrise's question. What if RaiseHim decided to ignore the Protocol and arranged for Bowmark to have an accident?

STUPIDITY AND LOVE ARE TWO SIDES OF THE SAME FIN.
~COMMONER SAYING

Sunrise shouted, "I'm getting off this island even if it kills me!" He crouched in the dust, his hands before him in a defensive posture. His obsidian-black hair escaped from its band and plastered against his sweaty brow, hiding the burn scars on the side of his face and neck. The dangling fuzzfruit vines cast stripes of sun and shade across his determined face.

Birds and lizards hopped through the massive surrounding trees and glided through the clearing the young men practiced in.

"You can't!" Bowmark wiped stinging sweat from his eyes. His eyebrows wrinkled as he considered his next move. His heart thudded, and sun glare obscured his vision.

"Why not?" Sunrise shifted his weight.

GLIDING LIZARD

Bowmark panted as he shoved back his dreadlocks. "I'll need you in my court when I'm king." He lunged. The two young men grappled briefly, and then broke apart.

Bowmark's tiny pet monkey bounced on a nearby log, screeching. "No no no!"

Sunrise stood, stepped back, and barked in laughter. "Me, in the court? That vein in the protocol officer's neck would burst. I can see it spraying across the nobles." His dirt-caked hands gestured widely.

Bowmark laughed and then stopped abruptly. GreatJoy's spray of blood still haunted his nightmares. The cold look in Father's eyes as he turned.

SnatchFast shouted, "Ah, ah, ah, ah, ah," in a parody of laughter.

"And Raisinbrain would turn three shades of purple," added Sunrise.

Bowmark choked on dust.

Sunrise threw himself at Bowmark and hit him squarely on the chest with his shoulder.

Bowmark toppled backward and fell outside the line scratched in the dirt. Boar Charge. The dumbest, most basic move. Sunrise was making a point.

"Giver of Sun and World!" Sunrise screamed. "In the lava again! When will you learn to stay focused?"

Bowmark shaded his eyes with his arm as he looked up at his best friend. "If RaiseHim ever hears you call him Raisinbrain, your life will be shorter than mine in the lava."

Sunrise shrugged. "He can't catch me if I'm sailing to Ironia." He reached for a gourd of water sitting in the shade of a ridgeleaf tree and guzzled, eyes closed, water trickling down his face and bare, golden chest.

He nudged away Bowmark's chittering pet as it attempted to lap at the rivulets. "Be gone, SnatchFast!" The monkey hopped onto the tree trunk and hissed.

The ground vibrated a few seconds. Bowmark tensed. He'd be seventeen in a month and old enough to prove. He could no longer pretend that he had time.

Bowmark wrestled with the despair that dragged his feet and weighted his arms. He had not slept the night he finally figured out that Father sent him to live in the village half-time because he expected him to lose. That was what Father had been talking about in the tent after GreatJoy's challenge. Father wanted him to have some happiness before that moment he stepped on the Disc and RaiseHim turned him into ash. The thought of sailing to Ironia pulled on his heart. Sneak away to live—and condemn whom to death?

Father should never have commanded Bowmark to read the Atlas to Sunrise. If his friend hadn't learned about Ironia, Akinda, and Utali, would Sunrise still chatter like a monkey about going to those places? He knew how dangerous his words were. Why did he persist in speaking treason?

A splash of water on his face roused Bowmark from his reverie. Sunrise stood over him, laughing, with another cup full of water poised over Bowmark's face.

Bowmark scrambled up, grabbed the cup, and gulped it dry. Then he tossed aside the cup and formally grasped both of Sunrise's forearms in a posture that meant he was about to bestow a vow.

Surprised, Sunrise took hold of Bowmark's forearms, golden-brown hands against copper-brown skin, and dropped to one knee to receive whatever vow the presumed would make.

Bowmark looked into his friend's golden-brown eyes. Who would protect the commoners and the royals? So far, Father's commands had kept the shlaks happy. Maybe. Could a shlak feel happy or sad? How would anyone know? Bowmark hauled his skittering thoughts back to the point at hand.

If he survived the proving—no. *When* he survived, passing from presumed to designate, he was going to change the protocol. People would be permitted to leave if they needed new land.

Bowmark cleared his throat, strengthened his grip, and announced, "When I am king, I shall give you three trees from the Royal Forest to use in building your outrigger so you can explore the world."

Sunrise jumped up with a grin. "So! Bowmark! So! That would be—" His grin disappeared. "That would be impossible. You have sworn to obey the Protocol."

"A king wrote the Protocol. This king is going to change it."

Sunrise studied the dusty ground for a few seconds. "Right. All the more reason for me to make sure you prove."

"You need to do something for me now."

Sunrise looked confused a moment. "Ah. What does My Presumed require?"

"Before the proving, you must break your arm or foot so you will be ineligible."

"What!" Sunrise released his hold. "No, no, no, no. Mom's paternal cousin broke his foot on a reef, and he took two miserable years to die from the results."

"Then accidentally chop off a toe or little finger. If you are chosen, I don't know what I will do."

"You worry too much."

In unison, they said, "That's the king's job," but Bowmark did not smile this time.

SnatchFast hooted. Overhead, a tern squealed. Underfoot, the ground shook once.

Sunrise folded his arms. "It won't happen. First of all, RaiseHim is going to volunteer. His side of the family hates your side of the family, especially you since you've been contaminated by us dirt-eaters."

Bowmark winced at the slur. Who did the nobles think grew and caught their food?

Sunrise continued without pause, "You practice six candles a day. He practices eight."

"He isn't forced to memorize the location of every cistern on the island and oversee the digging of every new cesspool."

"Second, if he doesn't volunteer, there are about a hundred of us eligible. The chances are one in a hundred, right? No, less. Even if the dice did roll my number, the protocol officer would reroll. There is no way she would let me on the throne."

"You just made an offensive assumption."

"Oh? How did I offend the presumed?"

"You assumed you would win."

Sunrise stooped to grab two staffs and tossed one to Bowmark. "Then prove to me I won't."

Their staffs cracked together.

Sunrise shook a large bamboo pole in the middle of the bamboo forest. Dead, yellow leaves fluttered around them and the tall lava pillars that stabbed the steep slope like daggers. Lizards twittered and a frog glided away from the pole. SnatchFast scampered up a different pole. "This one should work well." Sunrise hefted his machete, stepped back, and whacked the base of the bamboo which shivered and dropped more leaves.

A snake emitted a stench of fear and slithered away under the leaves. Bowmark let it go, for the reptile had no legs and was not venomous. Ah, but that spider creeping down the pole toward Sunrise was. Bowmark swung over Sunrise's head and cut the spider in two with his machete.

Sunrise ducked and yelled, "What are you doing?"

Bowmark showed him half the spider still adhered to his blade.

"Oh. I give you thanks. Next time, though, warn me."

The wind whispered through the leaves as Bowmark stepped back. He used a twig to scrape the spider off his machete. Instead of cutting down his own bamboo for repairing the house, he stopped and thought.

Tomorrow he was going back to Safe Harbor for his seventeenth birthday. After that, any time the volcano erupted, he would need to prove. Somehow, he had to find it in himself to kill RaiseHim. He would be doing StoneGrove a favor.

Still. He hated the butchery of pigs that the entire village had assigned to him as his chore for every feast, probably hoping to toughen him. He now knew the feel of a blade piercing through skin and muscle. He still fought the urge to vomit every time he killed a squealing pig. The first five he had ended up tormenting because he had not moved quick enough or hard enough.

Crackle, crackle, crackle, thump. Sunrise bent over the fallen pole and sliced away the branches.

But what if something happened to RaiseHim: a tearjaw, a fall off a cliff, a tree falling on him, a snake bite? Who in the pool of challengers would challenge Bowmark? He liked nearly all the boys in proving age.

He looked at Sunrise's back. His friend still refused to damage himself in some small way, even though the islands had a long history of young men having accidents with blades just before a proving.

Ah, brooding would not cut down these poles. He grabbed a stem and paused. Here was a machete. There was Sunrise's foot. A smaller blade would be better for cutting off one middle toe. A blade this large might shear off two or three toes. However, the amputation would not look suspicious. Boys often sliced into their feet when cutting bamboo.

Sunrise moved up the felled pole, chopping off the side branches. Bowmark crept up behind him. There was a moment with every step where Sunrise's foot angled away from his body. Bowmark slowly raised his machete. If he stabbed rather than slashed, he might be able to amputate only one toe.

"Gimme gimme gimme," the monkey screamed.

Sunrise looked up, startled, and pivoted. "What are you doing?"

Bowmark moved the machete to his side. "Nothing."

Sunrise's gaze flickered between Bowmark's face and the machete. "Jump in lava, you were going to cut me."

"No. I was just thinking."

Sunrise surged up, grabbed Bowmark's wrist, and shoved him against a lava pillar. "No! You're not thinking that. Not ever again. You could have crippled me for life. You could have killed me with an infection. Your blade still has spider blood on it!"

"I wouldn't—"

"You cut me and Dad would beat you. I'd never talk to you again. MoonGleam would kill you."

"I wasn't—"

"You were. I'm done. I'm taking my pole home." Still keeping his eye on Bowmark, Sunrise shouldered the thickest end of the bamboo and let the rest slide along the ground.

"I'm sorry. Truth, I was only thinking. I wouldn't have gone through with it."

Sunrise maneuvered the pole between two of the pillars.

Frantically, Bowmark chopped down a pole, shouldered it, and chased after Sunrise. He caught up to him at the edge of a ravine. "I'm sorry."

Sunrise scowled at him. "Isn't it enough that you burnt up my neck? Do you know how stupid you are?"

MoonGleam had mentioned his stupidity more than once, but Sunrise never had. "I only look stupid next to you. And MoonGleam. That's why I need you as my advisor."

Sunrise turned away from him. They continued their trek in silence for half a candle.

They stopped at a brook winding around tree roots and drank. Sunrise picked up his pole but did not move as he stared at his feet. "What I said back there wasn't fair."

Which part? Bowmark switched the pole to his other shoulder.

"You burning me was an accident. But listen, My Presumed, don't you ever try to hurt me again."

He was My Presumed and not Sunrise's friend Bowmark anymore. His throat tightened as he grasped his medallion. "May Giver deal me disaster and death if I ever hurt you again."

Sunrise nodded once and resumed the trek. Bowmark trailed slowly after. A quarter-candle later they emerged from forest and into fields and dragging the poles became easier.

MoonGleam skipped up to help Sunrise drag his pole. "MightyArm said he'll help us tomorrow." Neither boy said anything. She glanced from face to face. "What happened?"

Sunrise said grimly, "Nothing."

If Sunrise wasn't going to talk about their argument, Bowmark certainly wasn't. "Nothing."

"Something happened. Both of you are acting strangely." Neither replied. She shrugged. "I forgot. While I was watching for you, I saw RunsFast coming down that last hill before us."

Bowmark frowned. "RunsFast? I expected CrunchIt. Why so soon? I thought I had another day before I needed to leave." Sunrise might have eroded his reluctance to leave. He frowned some more. "Why RunsFast? Is someone in the village hurt?"

Sunrise said, "The only commoners RunsFast takes care of are those My King commands. If I'm not *hurt*, and My Presumed isn't *hurt*, she has no reason to be here."

"I don't know what you two are angry about, but I hope you'll stop before we reach home. Mom is making a good-bye feast. Dad is roasting the pig ShellCrush donated."

After crossing a few more fields, they dragged the poles alongside the veranda and laid them in the dust. The cluckers under the veranda complained. MoonGleam held up a bucket. "I have water for you."

Sunrise said, "RunsFast is here."

The woman was trudging up from where the trail to Safe Harbor and the cliff stairs met.

Mom emerged from the house with Sunset on one hip. A few other villagers came out onto their verandas as well and watched the physician toil toward the three. MoonGleam set the bucket down and whispered, "Something's not right."

Usually MoonGleam could tell what others were feeling candles before Bowmark could, but this time something about RunsFast's steps alarmed him. Bowmark straightened up.

The physician finally reached them. She laid his hand on Bowmark's shoulder. "Sea Predators are brave."

Through tear-filled eyes Bowmark watched MoonGleam climb up the bluff above Hidden Lake toward him. In this dry season, the lake should have been named Hidden Puddle. He wiped away his incriminating tears and wordlessly scooted aside to let MoonGleam sit beside him. Their legs dangled over the edge. The sun shone high and birds and lizards rode the thermals.

Over the shoulder of Bamboo Mountain could be seen the tip of King's Island which he had been staring at since noon.

"We didn't know where you had run. Sunrise is looking on HawkFlight. Dad is helping Sunset hunt through the boar huts and under the house." They watched a monkey troop gather at the edge of Hidden Lake and drink.

"Do you mind if I sit here?" She smelled of coconut, vanilla, and herself, an intoxicating scent he needed to wall himself away from.

He must not look at her or he would lose all composure. "I need to go back."

"CrunchIt said you can wait until late-afternoon. Right now, he and NineToes are entertaining the village with demonstrations. Mom is cooking to feed all of you before you return to the palace."

Bowmark drew up his legs and wrapped his arms around them. Giver, if only he could wrap his arms around her.

She whispered, "It's not fair."

No, it wasn't fair. Ah, wait, she meant about Father. He held back his retort to say neutrally, "My King has often said that I must never expect the world to be fair. Sea Predators are brave. Father won't show sorrow until the moment he collapses and—and dies. Maybe not even then."

After an uncomfortable silence, MoonGleam asked, "He has . . . years, hasn't he?"

Hadn't RunsFast told them? "Five, maybe seven years. Listen, no one must see me like this."

Her hand slid across his shoulder and settled on his neck.

His skin buzzed with desire everywhere their skin touched. She shouldn't have touched him. He couldn't—

"I wish I could go with you to your festival. It must be like stepping on poison snails to celebrate the day after you hear he has coughlung."

Bitterness broke the stranglehold sorrow had on him. "I'm going back to the palace, but I'm not going to the festival. I have no desire to celebrate becoming seventeen."

"Aren't you required to be there?"

"No. I'm required to step onto the Bronze Disc."

MoonGleam looked toward the clear air above the peak of King's Island. "It might be years before it erupts."

A sea eagle screamed overhead and a hot breeze blew the sweet scents of plumeria and hibiscus blossoms over them.

"I need to pray that it erupts soon." Bowmark slowly shrugged her hand off. *I can't let anyone know that Father expects me to die on the Disc.* "If My King can't—can't finish the five years of training the designate, then, ah, the protocol officer takes over. The protocol officer hates me."

"Why?"

So much he must not tell her. "Maybe because Sunrise dropped a spider in her rice during my last birthday festival."

"Oh! I'm going to pummel my brother." She flicked her hands out dramatically.

Good. Now she might stop asking questions that would lead to him saying out loud that it no longer mattered exactly when the volcano erupted. When Father grew too sick to rule, lava or no lava, Bowmark was stepping onto the Disc, even if it was over a pit of knives to make the ceremony proper.

In a nearby thinleaf shrub, some bigfa birds scuffled and squawked at each other. The leaves shook as the male birds thudded into each other, competing for females..

MoonGleam pitched a rock into the bush and the birds ran away in a cloud of dust and feathers. She touched Bowmark's shoulder with her fingertips. "May I give you the present I made for you?"

He hadn't even noticed the bag she wore slung over her shoulder and chest. Now he averted his eyes. He mustn't look at her chest. He stood up and turned away from her. Any moment now he might—

She stood up and pulled out folded royal fabric, indigo stamped with white, arrowhead-shaped spiral shell designs on it.

His hand brushed hers as he took the fabric and he sucked in breath. He took a step back to shake out the cloth: a new warrior's skirt, a little over knee-length, pleated, and lined with secret pockets in the waistband and seams. Many loops for a belt and pouches. "I could hide over ten knives in this. I give you thanks."

Pressing the skirt against his nose, he inhaled her scent. Time to think of something else besides her putting this on him—or taking it off. "Where did you get this fabric? It's only made in the palace."

"CrunchIt got it for me."

Thinking, Bowmark frowned. "How did you pay for this?"

"He said all he wanted in payment was a smile."

A shudder ran through Bowmark's core. "If CrunchIt has laid a hand on you, I'm going to kill him."

MoonGleam laughed. "You haven't been able to so far."

"I'll hire someone to kill him. Did he lay hands on you?" *The way I want to?*

MoonGleam laughed again. "What are you getting so upset about? Mom was standing right behind me. I smiled at him. Then Mom said, "Don't forget who your wife is." He made a strange face and said he had to find NineToes. Then he left."

Bowmark blew out breath he hadn't realized he was holding. CrunchIt had never acted dishonorably toward a woman before, either commoner or noble. Why had he leaped to such a conclusion? "So CrunchIt paid for it. I'll need to pay him back."

"I don't think you understand the idea of gifts."

"I don't like the idea of you owing anything to a royal or noble."

MoonGleam danced away to a crabcrawl tree and climbed up to sit on a projecting branch. She tossed a twig at him. "You worry too much."

He did. How do you not worry when you have a target on your back and a cousin like Raisehim? He must think he could win. Raisehim might slip or sneeze at a crucial time. Even if he only crippled Raisehim before he died, that could count as a win, for a cripple could not take the throne. Bowmark sniffed the skirt again. If only he could think even one day past proving. If only he could think about decades of MoonGleam teasing him.

"I don't know how to cheer you up." She swung her feet while looking at the mountain tip. "Let's run away."

Bowmark coughed. "Run away . . . where? There are enemies out there and enemies right here."

"The Atlas shows lots of places we could sail away to and live."

Say you'll go. Say you'll go. Bowmark squeezed his eyes shut. *Tell her you will.* "We'd be caught and killed for treason. Even if we weren't caught, what will your family do when their land is seized because they raised a traitor? What becomes of My King? Whom does he name as presumed?"

"You promised Sunrise some trees for a canoe so he can leave."

"Scorch, MoonGleam! He wasn't supposed to tell you that. We're trying to figure out if we can make him a fisherman. And maybe he'll go out in a storm. If he disappeared, maybe people would think he drowned, and not ran away. We haven't figured it out yet. If you and I suddenly disappear, what are people going to think?"

MoonGleam shrank away. "That you love me?"

The words hung between them. Bowmark crumpled the skirt. *I do love you.* "There's the burning protocol that I must not break." *Or else RaiseHim becomes king.*

"I don't care about the protocol."

I hate the Protocol. "We would be punished severely. If I lose my presumedship or even my life, who faces RaiseHim on the Disc? Sunrise? Rockfall? I'm the only one who has a chance to kill him." *A small chance.*

"Maybe CrunchIt would like to be king."

"He has children. He wouldn't risk his life like that. Don't forget I made a vow to protect Spearmark. And how can I leave My King after . . .?

MoonGleam's face pinched. "Bring My King. Bring all your family. Bring all my family."

Easier to wish the protocol away. "Your aunt and her family? Your three uncles and their families? Why don't we evacuate the entire island in our ninety canoes?"

MoonGleam hung her head.

Bowmark reached for her and then redirected his hand to the branch she was sitting on. "I'm sorry. We're talking nonsense because the truth is too hard right now." *Soon I'll be a killer or I'll be ash. Maybe both.*

"I want to be with you."

It's time to move to the palace and never come back. I can't handle this. "My Sister, don't. I can't. I—I can't. Stop tormenting me."

"My Sister? Truth? My Sister?"

"It must be. I won't shame you with a royal-blessed child."

"I want to help you."

"Then don't ask me to do what I must not do. I'm leaving now. Don't follow me."

She wept as he walked away. He did not. He must not or he might never stop.

KING'S
ISLAND

WE ARE STRONG NOT BECAUSE WE CLAIM TO BE
STRONG WITH WORDS. WE ARE STRONG BECAUSE WE PROVE.
EVERY DEATH ON THE DISC PROVIDES MORE PROOF.
                    —BOOK OF PROTOCOL OF THE SEA PREDATORS

Nearly a year later, five thousand islanders roared in anticipation on the rocky slope. The smells of molten rock, scented driftwood fires, his sweat, his fear, and the fragrant oil poured over his braided red hair overwhelmed Bowmark. He gripped his carved staff tightly and stood as still as befitted a presumed heir who waited only to prove himself to become designated king. He stared straight ahead as a priest tied ceremonial blood-red feathers around his elbows.

Bowmark glanced at the crowd arrayed around the Disc, many sitting or standing on large boulders. How many of them hoped he would die? Raisehim's family, for certain.

Had MoonGleam come? Likely. Sunrise stood among the other potential challengers on the other side of the ravine that the river of oozing lava flowed through. Staying away from MoonGleam had been the right choice. If Bowmark survived this, he would need to find a royal or noble to marry, someone to make his queen. Someday, perhaps, he would stop aching for MoonGleam. If he didn't survive, then he wouldn't need to handle his constant longing for her and he would have done the right thing for her.

Father stood in a long cape ornamented with feathers. Six-year-old Spearmark fidgeted under his gold embroidered tunic. Bowmark repressed a shiver. How could he protect Spearmark if he died?

The protocol officer held the Protocol book, thick banana fiber paper sheets bound with bronze wires. Her face had wrinkled into a scowl; but when did she not look angry?

THE PROTOCOL OFFICER

The priests in feathered and jeweled headdresses sang, and the nobles and royals stood proudly as sunlight glinted off their multitudinous jewelry of gold and ancient gems.

The cluster of young men on the other side of the ravine within proving age toe-bounced to the rhythm of the drums. Why were commoners included in the pool of potential challengers when almost none of them received the training royals did? Three of the young men, including RaiseHim, wore the same Royal Warrior tattoo that Bowmark wore, an ornate black spearhead on the left shoulder. If Bowmark survived—no, when!—the Orb of Justice would be tattooed on the other shoulder.

He must focus. Why couldn't he focus?

RaiseHim grinned at him and made a mock salute.

Bowmark gripped his staff tighter, and suddenly he felt nothing. Events were running to their conclusions, and he was simply riding along. No, he did feel one emotion, but remotely, or as though he were wrapped in kapok fluff. He missed Mother.

He reached up to touch his Giver's Hand medallion he had received with his tattoos—and brushed bare skin, for the reminder was not worn during the proving.

Bowmark bowed to let a priest place a crown of sweetvine on his head, glanced again at his father and brother and then far beyond them to the peaks of some of the other islands of StoneGrove. A true warrior would not be thinking of his mother at a time like this, but he could not work up any self-disgust. How had his feelings gone numb?

His monkey dashed to his little brother and hopped on, clinging to Spearmark's indigo skirt decorated with the customary shell design.

"Why?" Bowmark had asked his father years before. "Why does every king need to start his reign with a death? What's wrong with life?"

His father had replied with roughened words, "Shall we do as our enemies do? When there is a challenge for the kingdom, entire families of nobles die. Friends and supporters are killed. Kings must test their food and beds, and can never trust anyone. Our way, the people know the king can defend them against enemies. Only the challenger is killed. StoneGrove remains safe for nobles and commoners."

The sun pressed heat down on the ceremony and heat rose from the lava crust as Bowmark kissed the Orb of Justice. His sandals were removed by the protocol officer's assistant and thrown into the canyon to land on the sluggish lava far below. The twisted-grass sandals flashed into flame and collapsed into instant ash.

The drummers and singers stopped. The protocol officer stepped forward and handed the book to her apprentice who held it on his upraised hands. Facing the young men on the other side of the lava, the officer shouted, "Let the challenger step out!"

Many looked at RaiseHim who grinned wider but did not move. What was he doing? RaiseHim had trained his entire life to challenge.

The protocol officer shouted again, "Let the challenger step out!"

The young men shifted uneasily as RaiseHim stood his ground.

If no volunteer stepped out, the challenger would need to be chosen by dice. The Protocol Officer held up hands cupped together and shook them. She clapped them atop the book and peered at the ten-sided dice left on the book. "A challenger has been chosen. Number fifty-three, step out!"

RaiseHim crossed his arms and smirked at Bowmark as the young men glanced anxiously at each other. Was the chosen a friend, someone from their village, a cousin?

Sunrise stepped away from the group.

Bowmark's knees weakened. Not Sunrise! He had known. He had always known.

The protocol officer shouted, "Prepare the challenger!"

Sunrise looked as though he wanted to vomit as the priests on his side of the ravine attached feathers and removed his sandals and Giver's Hand medallion.

Bowmark frantically reviewed the Protocol and history to find a way to save Sunrise, save himself. Once, when his people lived on atoll islands, and the proving had been done over a pit of knives, both the challenger and presumed had tried to run away. They were caught and both hurled into the pit. Forty-two years after the settling of StoneShell, the chosen challenger refused to walk on the Disc. He had been thrown onto the lava, and another chosen.

Bowmark swallowed back acid. Once, no, twice, the challenger and presumed had fought bare handed the first candle mark and the ten candlemarks after with spears, and still neither had been killed or seriously injured. The Disc had been tilted and both dumped onto the lava. Two new challengers had been chosen. Once, both had been so injured that neither could attack each other again, and both had been dumped onto the molten rock.

The drumbeat resumed. Sulphurous air stung his nose and eyes.

Once, the presumed refused the challenger because he claimed that the protocol officer had been corrupted by bribery. After brief argument, the officer, presumed, challenger, and briber were thrown in, and two new challengers fought for the kingdom. In recorded history, anywhere from one to five deaths occurred per proving. One *only* became a designate after actively killing a challenger or presumed and remaining whole. Once the proving began, the ritual could not end until a proper killing had happened. Either he or Sunrise, or both, would die in the next quarter candle. Bowmark's wet palm slipped on the staff.

Sunrise kissed the Orb of Justice with trembling lips.

Bowmark's vision grew dark around the edges. Despite the sun and heated ground and sweat darkening his skirt, a chill spread through him.

Sunrise's sandals were thrown onto the lava. They flamed into black ash.

The protocol officer shouted, "Proceed to the proving Disc."

The watchers shouted and screamed.

Bowmark and his best friend handed the ceremonial staffs to the priests since the first candle mark required wrestling. They walked barefoot over the sharp pumice path and ignored the shredding of the thick soles of their feet. Hot air shimmered over them as they walked across the warming Bronze Disc and met in the middle, raising and clasping each other's hands.

They faced each other. Tears dripped off Bowmark's face. Sunrise's expression was grim but calm.

"Let the king prove his worthiness!" the officer shouted.

"Shoulder to shoulder," Sunrise murmured. The young men moved into position and pretended to shove against each other. Sunrise spoke into Bowmark's ear, "Giver! I should have heeded you." His foot slipped, and they repositioned. "So here's what we do. We fake wrestle this first mark. When we get the spears, I'll leave an opening. You strike me in the heart. I want it to be quick."

"I can't kill you." Bowmark's voice broke.

Sunrise pushed harder. "You must. If you don't, oof! RaiseHim will. Some dark night, or on a hunting trip."

"I can't."

"You need to. You care about us. We commoners know what RaiseHim cares about."

"We could die together."

"Don't. Waste. My. Death!"

Bowmark breathed through gritted teeth as they continued to grapple. His sweetvine wreath fell off. Their hands could not find purchase on their sweat-slicked arms and backs.

Horns blared. "The first stage has passed with no proof. Let the presumed and challenger receive their spears!"

The young men broke apart. The aides tossed ribbon wrapped spears tipped with sharp obsidian blades. The Bronze Disc was growing hotter. The air scorched their throats and dried their flowing tears.

They approached each other warily, feinting here, there, as they circled, careful to stay away from the edge. Sunrise jabbed once, twice, and on the third parry slipped under Bowmark's spear shaft to tear a red line down his forearm.

Sweat stung Bowmark's eyes. He blinked furiously and shook his head.

"Now," Sunrise said. He jabbed carelessly and did not resist when Bowmark knocked the spear aside.

Bowmark danced back, holding his spear before him with both hands.

"You missed your chance!" Sunrise hissed.

"I can't do it," Bowmark groaned.

Sunrise glanced at the lava, red and smoky, far below the rim of the ravine where they fought. "And I can't throw myself in the lava for you, Brother. I've been burnt, and I—I can't. Please." He panted. "Make it fast. Take care of my family." He feinted toward Bowmark's left.

Bowmark jumped out of the way. How could he throw accurately when his gritty, stinging eyes could barely see? Make it fast. Make it fast. How? His heel hit part way off the Disc. Somewhere, somebody screamed. The other foot missed completely.

He fell into a furnace blast, one leg hooking on an ironwood spike, the other furrowing on the point. One hand snagged a spike. He hung a moment by his knee and hand, sweat pouring off him. He swung far enough to grab another spike and slid his knee off. Sweat-slicked hands slid toward the points. He swung and flipped as he had practiced thousands of times, and landed on the Disc. He slipped and fell on his discarded spear. Heart thudding, he rolled, snatched the spear while Sunrise pretended to try to skewer him, and jumped up.

Then he looked into his best friend's eyes, and he nodded.

Sunrise pulled his spear back as though he were going to throw it.

Bowmark shoved his spear upward into his best friend's chest.

Sunrise gasped as he rose on his toes and dropped his spear. As he came down, a look of surprise covered his face and he staggered back a step. His hands grasped the spear shaft. He swayed.

Bowmark could not breathe. He let go the spear.

Sunrise staggered back another step.

SUNRISE
DIES

Too late, too slow, Bowmark reached for him.

Sunrise fell off the Disc, rolled over the spikes and dropped out of view.

Bowmark fell to his knees. The people shouted, but their shouts could not override the frantic cries of Sunrise's sisters, the screaming of Mom, the low wailing of Dad.

Bowmark sagged onto the hot Disc and begged Giver for death.

Someone reached under his arms and tried to pull him up. He neither resisted nor helped. Had Sunrise felt the lava? Had he felt his skin blacken and vaporize? Fire: the only thing Sunrise feared. Bowmark breathed through his mouth so he wouldn't smell the burnt flesh of his friend—and choked on black, greasy smoke.

Someone pulled on Bowmark again. Some of Father's words penetrated the roaring in Bowmark's brain. "Do not weep, Son, not in public. Stand, like a king! *Stand!*"

With Father's help, he rose, shaking, looking for a way to throw himself into the lava.

Father embraced him and spoke into Bowmark's ear, "Your throne is now secure. The people do not envy what a king must do to prove. They will remember that you do what you must, whatever the cost. Always, they will remember this day."

So would Bowmark. Father's words disappeared into the sucking whirlpool of his loss. Why was the sun still shining? Why did his lungs still draw air?

Father raised Bowmark's right hand and shouted loud enough for echoes. "Behold the proven designate! Behold your future king!"

The people shouted, the drummers pounded their logs, and the trumpeters blew on their conch shells.

Tomorrow was the investiture, then five more years of training, and then the assumption of the throne. Bowmark could not do it. Nobody could live with this kind of pain. His eyes stung. The smoke coated his tongue. *My friend, oh Giver, my friend!*

"Come, Son." Father guided him to the pumice stanchions and steps.

The Sea Predators waved streamers of red and black and purple.

"You must be strong until you reach the healer's hut."

Each step became an agony. Spearmark stared at Bowmark with scared, wide eyes. Sunrise's mother still screamed. The priests sang of victory in the strength of an arm, the speed of a foot, the clear sight of an eye. Servants lower down on the volcanic mountain set out food on banana leaf mats: roast pig and chunknuts, spiced fish, baked papaya and oilfruit, dried jellyfish, greens, and seaweed-wrapped rice. The people, with their streamers fluttering, moved toward the celebration banquet.

Gritting his teeth so that he would not whimper, Bowmark limped toward the physician's hut. The blood seeping from his lacerated feet showed only as slightly darker patches on the ropy ridges of solidified lava. The sense of being surrounded by kapok fluff returned. He walked. He breathed. He hurt. But nothing felt real. The people moved toward the feast as though the best person on the island had not just been murdered.

Father let go of him and turned to speak to his sister's husband, a man who chose to oversee the royal expenditures because he could sit all day and claim to be working. Spearmark clung to Father's legs and stared at Bowmark wobbling to the temporary hut adorned with red and brown striped banners. Bamboo wind chimes clonked at the corners.

Although he faltered, he did not fall, not until he had passed into the shade of woven grass mat walls. The healer caught him and laid him on a kapok-filled mattress. Bowmark's monkey crept in and sniffed his bloody arm.

"Hold this under your tongue," Physician RunsFast said as she unstopped a vial and extracted a thread of salted bitefinger-fish liver. Bowmark did, waiting for drowsiness to blunt his mind and pain as the physician washed his feet and rubbed a salve of aloe and sea snail toxin into the torn soles. Bowmark watched and waited for RunsFast to turn her back. If he ate a whole liver, he would stop breathing within minutes. His fingers twitched as he gauged whether or not he could reach the vial undetected.

"Before I tend to your burns, drink this."

Bowmark drank a mixture of sleep pollen and water and fuzzily wondered, "What burns?" Then he noticed his forearms, and . . .

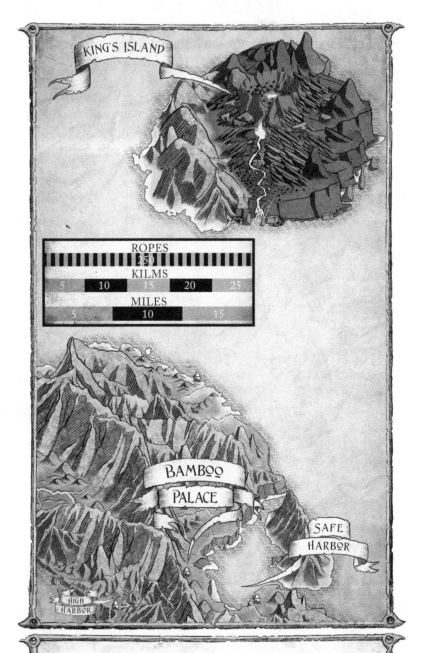

KING'S ISLAND

ROPES
250

KILMS
5   10   15   20   25

MILES
5   10   15

BAMBOO
PALACE

SAFE
HARBOR

HIGH
HARBOR

THE WORDS IN THIS BOOK. THE CUSTOMS AND LAWS CONTAINED
HEREIN. THESE ARE WHAT KEEP OUR PEOPLE FROM UTTER
ANNIHILATION. THOSE WHO WOULD SUBVERT THEM ARE THE ENEMY.
                     -BOOK OF PROTOCOL OF THE SEA PREDATORS

He opened his eyes as the physician, wearing a different tunic, unwrapped his arm and hand. He sat up abruptly. Most of the medicines had been put away. The sound of splashing drew his eyes to the entrance where rain dripped. "What? How long?"

"Easy, Designate. The sun hides straight up. There's yet plenty of time for you to reach the investiture. And if you choose to do the investiture the day after you arrive, you would not be the first to do so. Let me finish."

Bowmark watched numbly as the physician spread a pain killing ointment on his arm and shoulders. RunsFast swaddled Bowmark's feet in thick padding and strapped wooden soles to the padding. What had the healer given him that he would sleep half a day, all night, and half another day with absolutely no awareness? Sleep pollen alone never lasted so long.

"You should be able to reach the palace without tearing open any wounds, if you walk carefully and don't do anything stupid."

"Do—" His lip cracked, and his dry tongue rasped against his dry palate. "—anything stupid? *Yesterday* was stupid! The *protocol* is stupid! We need to change the bloody protocol before somebody else as decent and good as Sunrise is killed." He turned his face away. Do not show weakness. He must walk off the volcanic mountain, steer a royal sea chariot to Safe Harbor on StoneShell, and then walk to his palace without assistance to demonstrate his continued physical worthiness.

"Designate, if I may suggest, you should wait until you have healed completely before you make any decisions."

Bowmark stared at the rain. His heart had been torn apart. How did one heal from that?

Tomorrow, no, today the investiture, then five years of training under Father, then the assumption of the throne. First get to the chariot. Then investiture. Sunrise would laugh at the ceremony. No, he wouldn't. Sunrise was ash. Sunrise had two choices, and he chose ash.

SnatchFast cooed from one of the bamboo poles. Bowmark looked up at his pet but could not focus on him. The physician produced a piece of dried fruit and offered it to the monkey. "He's been by your side through it all."

That should give him an emotion, but he couldn't remember what. He couldn't feel anything except the void of despair swirling in him. Without another word, he forced himself to stand. Inhaling deeply to chase away the dizziness, he began the twenty-rope long trudge down the volcano to the chariot.

A boy, one he did not know, skittered over the lip of the caldera on the path to the beach, his blue skirt fading into the rain and cloud. The boy would tell of the designate's coming so the people would be prepared. Bowmark tried to empty his mind of thought as he placed his feet carefully on the gritty trail. Behind him, rain hissed into steam on the oozing lava. He climbed up and over the ridge that separated the lava field from the Royal Forest.

A step. The next step. Another step. First, not the investiture, first the chariot, the walk to the palace, the investiture, five years learning all the Sea Predator secrets, the throne. He slid on a slick of mud and ash. How could Sunrise be ash?

First, he passed the stumps of trees killed by the volcano and salvaged for their precious wood. Then he plunged into the shade of living trees. Spicewood permeated the air with its warm essence and canoewood trees towered over him, bundling the rain into gouts that splashed on him.

The physician passed him with her basket of medicines tucked under her rain cape and hat. The monkey hopped onto his neck. Bowmark did not touch the creature.

Reach the chariot.

Bowmark slogged on with rain slapping his bare back and legs, his sodden skirt clinging to his thighs. The crunching of black lava gave way to the slurping of gray mud as he hiked past hibiscus and candlenut trees. The trail widened to a path that divided fields of fatroot and sweet lumps, sugar grass and yellowfruit with its flesh-slicing leaves. He trudged across black sand, trying to ignore the pain tracing the furrow in his leg.

He fell into the sea chariot left for him on the beach that faced StoneShell Island, a crooked interruption of the horizon slightly darker than the rain. The shouts of people in outriggers—launched when the messenger boy announced the beginning of The King's Trek—arrived on gusts of wind. He dragged himself to the reins, and slapped them against the blue-gray, flexible shell of the fat muntee harnessed to the chariot. Its paddle-shaped fins stroked the water as the sea animal swam toward its pen and food. The broad, whiskered nose of the chariot beast furrowed the dimpled sea. Purple jellyfish and brown kelp drifted by.

Bowmark leaned his forearms on the carved edge of the black, red and indigo painted sea chariot, then yipped and straightened. The carvings of kelp, whales, and cowrie shells pressed like knives against his burnt arms. Bowmark took shallow breaths to keep from moaning. A king did not show weakness. *Burn the protocol!*

The island of StoneShell and flotilla of outriggers became clearer. The noise of the surf overrode that of the slackening rain. The chariot beast veered right around the jetty and toward the palace beach. Sunlight speared through breaking clouds.

Bowmark left the chariot beast to its keepers and trudged toward the palace.

When he reached the flooded fields of horn nuts and rice, a little girl, his first welcomer, held an armful of dripping flowers. He stretched out his hand to stroke her head and she flung the flowers at him. Bright petals of yellow and orange clung to his stomach and indigo skirt. She squealed with delight.

The closer he came to the palace, the thicker grew the crowds that cheered as they threw armloads of flowers over him. He searched the faces. Were any of the people from High Harbor? Child after child pressed in to be touched by him, and then splashed in puddles, whooping after his touch of blessing.

Surprise bumped his grief as hundreds of people multiplied into thousands and then many thousands surrounding the palace and dancing on the black and pink sand beach, standing knee-deep in the flooded fields, trampling the crops.

Had everyone in StoneGrove come? As yet he saw no one from High Harbor. No, there stood MightyArm, the fence-builder and neighbor to Sunrise's family. MightyArm stood like a rock amidst crashing waves, neither waving a wet streamer nor throwing flowers. Bowmark stopped briefly to look into the man's eyes which held a grief that matched his own. He looked away, mindful of Father's advice to never put your sorrow upon an innocent person. He turned his face away from MightyArm and pulled his lips back into what he hoped was a smile and moved through the crowd of children.

He walked like a puppet animated by duty and custom.

When he finally stumbled through the bronze-clad palace gates, servants escorted him into an antechamber and toweled off the water and flowers coating his skin. He managed to stand while they replaced his skirt with a purple tunic embroidered with gold and pearls. Then he dropped onto a floor pillow on the glass blocks. The physician redressed his feet.

Father entered, sat beside him, and offered him a bowl of pana fruit in nut milk.

SnatchFast deserted Bowmark's neck, grabbed a piece of fruit, and swung to the bamboo rafters.

Bowmark stared at the food and could not remember what he was supposed to do with the stuff.

Father said gently, "It's been four days of fasting. If you don't eat now, you will faint during the investiture. If you can't eat yet, we can delay the ceremony to tomorrow."

Bowmark chewed a slice of fruit but could not swallow. He set the bowl down and covered his face with his hands. "Father. I understand why we go through an ordeal to become king. If it weren't this hard, anyone with a knife and some friends could try to become king."

"Truth."

"But I swear to you, by Giver of all that is good. When I am king, I shall change the Protocol. The proving will still be hard, but no one after me will need to kill an innocent man."

"Son."

"Let the presumed go out to battle a tearjaw. Let him fight a boar blindfolded."

The king took hold of Bowmark's shoulders. "Tearjaws and boars are not our enemies."

Bowmark pressed his fists against the floor. "Neither was Sunrise!"

"Designate. Listen to me. Listen. I too am angry. Sunrise was a son of my heart. Everyone knows RaiseHim was poised to challenge. I don't know why he didn't. Look at me! Listen. I honor Sunrise for dying bravely to keep our people unified. Do not dishonor him by speaking before you have considered all your words will do. There are many things a designate or king must not say until he has been secure on his throne for many years. You are not listening." He gently shook him. "You must try to understand what I am telling you. When you are angry, the first thing you lose is your ability to think. The next thing you lose is your life."

Bowmark stared up at the bamboo and thatch roof.

Father continued. "I don't say you are wrong. But already a large number of nobles and royals are upset with your love for the commoner."

"Why should they care? Why should I care now that I'm designate?"

"That . . . is one of the things you will be learning the next five years. Be careful. Mouth closed, eyes open." Father touched his lips.

Bowmark wrapped his arms around his knees and looked into Father's gray eyes. "How did you feel when you proved?"

Father studied him as rain battered the roof and incense smoke curled in the thatch. Merry people singing passed in the hall. After several moments, Father glanced around the room, checking if all the servants had left, then leaned toward Bowmark. "I have not discussed my proving with you, as my father did not with me. Proving is something you never want to talk about. Talking means remembering." He shifted uncomfortably. "Mine was not a friend. I did not even know him. He was a commoner from WetSide, a fellow with high hopes." The king glanced away, then looked back with moisture in his eyes. "I had thought that investiture would be the most glorious day of my life. Instead, it was the most miserable."

Bowmark nodded.

As Father rose, he said huskily, "Eat. Rest. Investiture starts soon." He left and slid the door shut.

Bowmark hugged his knees tighter. He tried to think of nothing, but memory painted, over and over again, the obsidian point piercing Sunrise's chest, the surprise on his face, his fall off the Disc. He sipped some coconut milk and choked.

Time passed, and servants entered the room. They laid upon his shoulders a heavy red cloak of banana-leaf fiber embroidered with gold and pearls and brilliant bowfish scales. Upon his head they placed a circlet of gold wires entwined with gems from an ancient realm: rubies, sapphires, yellow diamonds, each bracketed by the talons of birds of prey. He put on the proffered gold and glass earrings. Armbands of shells were wrapped above his elbows. Patchouli-scented oil was rubbed on his neck.

Father appeared in the doorway. Still the dutiful puppet, Bowmark joined him to walk down the central hall to the throne room. Servants: HighFoot, MyTreasure, BirdSang, YellowFlower, TreeFell, LargeHand, TwigSnap, and others lined the hall, kneeling and grinning up at Bowmark and the king. Bowmark knew each one for he had always taken care to learn their names and families, but since he would never smile back at anyone again, he faced forward, intent only on . . . on what? On doing what he must until he died. Why hadn't he forced Sunrise to kill him instead?

One of the court maids, Greenleaf, rushed up to them and bowed deeply in apology. "Esteemed Royals, the protocol officer wishes to meet with you in the treasure room to discuss some details of the investiture."

"Plague take that woman," Father muttered. "Always fussing about something." Frowning, he followed the girl.

Bowmark walked with him. Sunrise used to beg to see the treasure room. He wasn't going to steal anything—he just wanted to see the riches. Since even Bowmark had never been allowed in, Sunrise never got his wish. Now he never would.

They entered the room and the maid slid the bronze-strapped door shut. Bowmark gazed at the ceremonial capes festooned with bigfa bird feathers and glass beads. He would wear one on his coronation day. The ostentatious capes hung on the wooden walls overlaid with strips of thin steel. The capes and carved boxes seemed to shift under the flickering yellow light of oil lamps. Inlaid mother-of-pearl in the boxes and gold beads piled in shallow baskets reflected a rich light. One basket held dozens of King's Vow coins, made of nacre carved in Father's likeness, set in a solid gold frame. Bowmark ached that Sunrise could not be here to see this.

Instead of Sunrise, here stood the protocol officer, and there, ClimbsHigh and KnifeSlash, men from the court. RaiseHim stood in the corner with his arms crossed. In the middle, little Spearmark jittered, staring agape at all the shiny regalia, monies, and boxes.

Why was Spearmark here when Bowmark had never been let in? And why were these other people here?

Father scanned the room, frowning.

RaiseHim displayed the same cocky grin he had shown Bowmark at the proving.

"You." Bowmark pointed rudely with his finger at his cousin, "I never want to see you again."

RaiseHim smirked. "Good. We have mutual desires."

"Hush!" the protocol officer snapped. She beckoned toward a paper she held. "My King and Designate, if you would look at this arrangement."

Father and Bowmark stepped toward the protocol officer. Sudden motion swirled around them.

RaiseHim grabbed Bowmark from behind and pressed a knife against his throat.

Bowmark stood still, moving only his eyes. The men of the court held knives against the throats of Father and Spearmark. He swallowed and felt the knife break skin even with that small movement.

Everyone stood watching each other, for several breaths.

Father said quietly, "Why do you break protocol, My Officer?"

The old woman held her hands out flat, a message to the men to do nothing. "I am doing this to save the protocol. You knew that your son did not have a proper kill, yet you raced to proclaim him designate before we could call for another challenger."

"They fought."

"It was a mockery. This son of yours mocks all the protocol. He promised that commoner an outrigger so he could leave StoneGrove."

Bowmark sucked in breath. The protocol officer had been spying on him?

The wizened woman looked at Bowmark with an intense hatred that shocked him.

Father coughed, holding as still as he could, but a dribble of blood ran down his neck.

The lower half of Spearmark's tunic darkened with urine. The boy whimpered, and ClimbsHigh cuffed him on the ear. Spearmark stopped crying, but his breathing grew ragged.

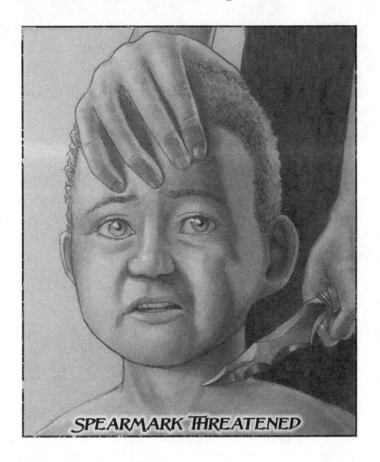

SPEARMARK THREATENED

The protocol officer returned her gaze to Father. "Were you aware of this?"

"No."

"Were you aware that your son plans to change the protocol as regards the proving?"

"Truth. I assumed he would change his mind, as I did, as my father did, as my grandfather did. As all kings have during their designancy."

"Were you aware that he intends to ruin our revenues by lowering the taxes on the commoners even more than you did?"

Father said, "It does not matter how many accusations you have. My Officer, stop and think. Safe Harbor is thronged with commoners right now. The designate is truly loved by the commoners. At best, we nobles are outnumbered six to one. Do you think they will tolerate what you plan here? I know my side of the royal family will not. Are you truly willing to start a civil war on StoneShell? Are you truly willing to spill the blood of thousands? Who will the protocol protect if we are slaughtering each other?"

Now Bowmark understood the purpose of Father's tiresome maxims, the irksome duties, the ridiculous disciplines. Father was not telling only the protocol officer to stop and think. He was reminding Bowmark.

Father and officer studied each other. Time slowed.

Think: all three of them were physically pinned down. If any struggled, all would die. That would be a benefit on Bowmark's part, but not for Father or Spearmark.

Think: RaiseHim. Ah. A plot. First, the friends fought, so that one threat would be killed, the kill deemed invalid, and then RaiseHim would challenge the weakened survivor. It was not *chance* that chose Sunrise.

The protocol officer said, "I do not want a war."

Bowmark's mind flashed back to that strange conversation he had heard in the birthing garden. Had they been planning the death of his family for *seven years*? The protocol officer had said then that she didn't want a civil war. Had she meant it?

Think: The protocol meant little to him, but it meant life itself to these conspirators. They were willing to kill on an island where a murder happened maybe twice or thrice a decade outside challenges and guard training. If he continued to threaten the Protocol, he continued to threaten them.

"I want—" The officer glanced at the other men.

Think: RaiseHim again. Sunrise's words struck Bowmark. "We commoners know what RaiseHim cares about. Do. Not. Waste. My. Death."

"I want to redo the proving," the protocol officer said.

Bowmark retorted, "And another innocent commoner will die." *No!* He had spoken without thinking. Around these murderers, he *must* think.

They didn't plan to kill another commoner, they planned to kill Bowmark.

The protocol officer glared at him.

Think: He needed to make an argument that fitted their interests. He needed a solution that didn't require him to slaughter another innocent commoner or to be slaughtered by RaiseHim.

Behind him, RaiseHim chuckled. "There's a reason they're called commoners. Two or three less makes no difference."

The knife pressed against Bowmark's stiffened neck and jaw. He blinked to clear his vision. First you lose the ability to think, then you lose your life.

Think: Even if RaiseHim became designate, it would be five years before he ruled.

Bowmark took a deliberate deep breath. "We can work this out."

"You will agree the kill was inadequate?" asked the protocol officer.

Everyone watched him. RaiseHim tightened his grip.

Why was it so hard to think? Anything to buy more time. "If you meet my conditions, I will . . . abdicate."

Everyone stood still. RaiseHim's breaths began to speed up. Suddenly he burst out, "NO! No abdicating! That was not the plan! You don't get to run away from this."

The protocol officer's steel gaze shut Raisehim's rant down.

Bowmark thought frantically. Conditions. What could he say that would save his family's lives and keep RaiseHim off the throne? His gaze fell on the Atlas on a shelf beside the officer.

Why was that here? Ah, for more accusations. And then he knew what to say.

The protocol officer shook her head. "Meet your conditions? Boy, we hold the knives."

Bowmark refused to let the insult anger him. He said quietly, "And I hold the hearts of the people of this island." He thought some more.

The protocol officer studied him with narrowed eyes. "What are these conditions?"

"I have three." Could he get away with three?

RaiseHim shifted behind him. His cousin's rage was palpable; the knife trembling against Bowmark's jugular. Bowmark guessed RaiseHim didn't care if there was a war. But he knew that the protocol officer wanted to avoid war at almost any cost. She simply wanted Bowmark's family away from the throne.

"One: you must vow to never again hurt my family or Sunrise's."

The officer considered. "That is a difficult vow to make unless My King likewise vows not to take revenge on any of us." She looked at Father.

Good. The protocol officer spoke truth when she said she did not want war. And yet, what had the woman thought would happen after pulling knives on the royal family? The anger of the protocol officer had made her stupid.

Father said, "I can so vow."

Could Father truly pretend this hadn't happened? Ah, he was buying time for Bowmark to think.

Bowmark said, "Two. StoneGrove is in trouble. Our farms crowd one upon another. Almost all our canoewood trees are gone, and the saplings we planted won't be useful for many years yet. The cisterns empty sooner every year. Once, angry neighbors could simply move away from each other. That is growing difficult. Every year our fishermen must sail farther to catch fewer fish. The birds number less and less as our people grow more and more. Our wastes leak into our water."

The protocol officer had forgotten about the shlak. Sunrise had seen a way for the Sea Predators to escape the increasingly crowded cage of StoneGrove.

RaiseHim quietly hissed a curse into Bowmark's ear.

Think: RaiseHim saw nothing but the chance to rule the cage and squeeze all he could from the commoners. The protocol officer was wiser, understanding the bigger picture.

Bowmark kept pushing. "If you look in that Atlas, you will see that the area marked Unknown is great. There may be more islands with resources that some of our people could move to. I need an outrigger and supplies that I may look for those islands."

"Leaving StoneGrove is treason," RaiseHim growled.

"This lying Atlas," the officer sneered as she grabbed the book and held it up. "Your maybe-islands are fantasies. The enemy is real. We have a reason for the prohibition. When the enemy catches you, you will reveal the presence of StoneGrove. The enemy will descend on us in numbers you cannot imagine." The woman hobbled closer to him.

Bowmark met her gaze. "I will never betray StoneGrove."

"Don't tell me what you will say when they peel off your skin one thumb-width at a time," the officer said, her face nearly touching Bowmark's.

"When I am released, I will vow to you that I will kill myself before I am captured." He couldn't breathe. *Back off, RaiseHim!*

"Perhaps you mean to go to the enemy and form an alliance." The officer backed up a step.

How do you reason with someone who so single-minded? "Never. I love StoneGrove. I promise to sail west only, to the great lands west of us. I will listen for news about the enemy. Somebody should. It has been over two hundred years since the last slaughter. How do we know the enemy still exists? Perhaps disease has taken all of them. Perhaps they have been slaughtered in turn by a people with no grudge against us. Perhaps the peoples of the western lands have weapons we can use to defeat the enemy. Who knows what advantages or knowledge I might return with?"

What did he need to say to make her listen to him? Bowmark panted. This plan would still let Raisehim legally murder someone. No way existed for him to prevent that. But if he could save his family, he might still—still what? Whatever he had just said fled his memory.

If he agreed to redo the proving, RaiseHim would kill him. Then RaiseHim would be king for decades. Bowmark would have wasted Sunrise's death.

The protocol officer's eyes widened, as though she had just come up with an idea. "How can we know that you would return from the west with "advantages" instead of the east with our enemy?"

"I will vow that also. Listen. My family would perish with everyone else if the enemy learns of us!"

The protocol officer mocked, "Vow upon vow you are promising us. But even an honorable man might say anything with a knife under his chin." She looked at the Atlas and hefted the tome. "I require physical proof. If you return with the greatest treasure from ten of the lands shown in here, I will believe you."

Bowmark swallowed and the knife pressed against his throat. Ten lands. Ten treasures. Giver preserve him. He glanced at Father. He had been granted a concession he thought he would not get. He was not in a position to press further. "I will so do."

The protocol officer smiled a crafty smile. "And the third?"

"When I return with proof of my honor, then I will be allowed to challenge the designate. And you will accept the result. No plots. No treason."

He held all their startled attention. To challenge a designate or king outside the regular proving times meant the challenger had to fast three days and go weaponless, while the well-fed designate started with their choice of four weapons. The conspirators looked at each other, and all grinned, except for RaiseHim.

His cousin must have felt the sure victory slipping away. He shouted, "This was not the plan! We agreed I would kill this pig's anus today! Not let him run away like a coward! This is what happens when women are allowed to interpret the protocol—"

SMACK!

The protocol officer silenced RaiseHim with a shockingly powerful blow to his ear. The impact caused his knife to graze Bowmark's collarbone.

Bowmark summoned all his willpower to resist the urge to break free and attack during the commotion. He knew his father and brother would be dead before he could help them. He could not get angry. He was close to closing a deal. One that would probably still kill him. He would be coming back to an even more lop-sided fight than if he simply agreed to redo the proving. But maybe he could come back strong enough to do better than GreatJoy had. He was certainly not strong enough now, wounded, exhausted, and heartsick.

The protocol officer regained her composure, straightened her back and cleared her throat. Eyes narrowed, she spoke to RaiseHim like a stern mother. "Lest you forget, *child*, our goal is to keep Bowmark from the throne. Your sick obsession with him is not the concern of the protocol or its keeper. The protocol is about maintaining order, not fulfilling personal vendettas." Shifting her cold gaze to Bowmark, she said, "Your terms are accepted. I so vow upon the protocol and Holy Books."

"Wait," RaiseHim said, desperation tinging his voice. "Nobody is going to believe this sea slug has the courage to commit treason by sailing away."

Father said, "Neither will anybody believe we voluntarily killed ourselves in the treasure room."

The conspirators' eyes widened. Perhaps now they realized the weakness in their plot, surrounded by thousands of commoners who loved the king and Bowmark. Had they truly not thought beyond their desire to make Bowmark prove again?

The protocol officer sucked air through her teeth. "This was not supposed to end in a civil war."

RaiseHim said, "We could suddenly discover the designate has brain rot."

ClimbsHigh laughed. "We can say the protocol officer saw a sore on Bowmark's lip."

Bowmark grit his teeth. One achieved brain rot by having sex with somebody who had brain rot but didn't know it yet. The sores that grew on the face and private parts were hideous. Whoever was discovered to have brain rot was exiled to a special village on Fire Island where their growing insanity and violence affected no one but others who had the same disease or the family members that came to care for them.

"Truth," RaiseHim said. "Even I could believe he *would* voluntarily sail by himself to Fire Island to avoid the shame of his sores being seen by others."

"I prefer rabies," Bowmark said.

RaiseHim pressed the knife a little harder. "I don't care what you prefer."

The protocol officer nodded. "We can claim to have seen a sore on his mouth and that he fled in shame. If he disappears on the way to the island, we all know storms and tearjaws take a few people every year. If the designate becomes disqualified by coming down with a terminal disease, nobody will question the need for another proving. My King?"

The muscles in Father's jaw twitched. "I accept."

ClimbsHigh and KnifeSlash put their knives away. RaiseHim withdrew his knife much later with a grunt of disgust. The officer stepped up to Bowmark. "And when you leave, take this!" She shoved the Atlas into Bowmark's stomach.

"And your ugly monkey!" RaiseHim spat.

Bowmark kept his gaze on Father and Spearmark. He would not waste Sunrise's death. He would take care of both his families, accept the shame that would be heaped on his name, and explore the world. He would do this for Sunrise and all the Sea Predators.

And even if he ended up executed for treason and burned, he would return and kill RaiseHim.

Bowmark held out his arms to make his vows to the protocol officer.

SAFE
HARBOR

HIGH
HARBOR

STONESHELL
ISLAND

NEVER TELL A NOBLE THE TRUTH
LEST THEY USE IT TO BIND YOU.
~SEA PREDATOR COMMONER SAYING

Bowmark jogged along the dark path toward High Harbor. Bitefinger liver poison kept him from feeling his torn-up feet and gashed leg as he followed the route his feet had worn into a groove over the years. A black, flattened conical reed hat covered his head, and a black cape the rest of him. People still danced by the light of oil lamps. They ignored the silent figure as he passed. One of the half-moons shone in the clearing sky. Bowmark slipped now and then on mounds of flower petals. People sat on their verandas and sang about love, fishing, flying mice, babies, and nagging wives with lazy husbands.

Bowmark stopped to catch his breath. A couple holding hands walked by him, humming. Tomorrow, they would learn how the designate had taken ill with a nasty disease, abdicated, and then sailed into quarantine to ensure no one else sickened with his illness. Time pressed on him, for he had vowed to leave before dawn. After shifting his sack of provisions to the other shoulder, he resumed his jog, all of it uphill. SnatchFast clung to the pack bouncing on his back.

When he reached the quiet lanes of High Harbor, his steps slowed. In a nearby pen, a sow snorted. Elsewhere, a baby cried for a moment. Bowmark trudged past the dark houses. An occasional seadog raised its head, but none bugled, for they all knew the young man who often patted them and brought them treats.

On the veranda, faintly limned by moonlight, a figure sat with bowed shoulders. This house alone had light seeping through paper screens. Shadows moved, and inside were voices, sometimes speaking, sometimes wailing. Sunrise's youngest sister sobbed. A cousin joined her.

Bowmark stopped. His abdication meant that RaiseHim would be able to kill a commoner on the Bronze Disc. Would it be another of his friends from this village?

The figure raised its head. MoonGleam. Sorrow's hand gripped his heart and squeezed. Moonlight made silver the tear tracks on her face. She laid her head on her arms again.

He climbed the steps and knelt beside her, laying a hand on her shoulder.

"Go away," she mumbled.

"MoonGleam."

"You!" She leaped to her feet and stumbled into a post. She whipped around, pressed her back against the post, and glared at him. "Have you come to deliver the royal roasted pig to thank us for our *contribution* to the proving?"

"No. A servant brings that tomorrow. I—"

"Shall I announce your arrival so our family and guests can bow and congratulate you?"

"No. No one must know I was here. And. I—I'm too ashamed to see Mom and Dad."

"I just realized—you had my brother chosen because you knew his every move. You knew how he fought. Well said that friendship with nobles is like friendship with tearjaws."

"No. No." He pulled out a heavy bag that hung inside his skirt and then reached for her. She flinched, but he caught one of her hands and pressed the bag into it.

She pulled out of his grasp. "What is this? His ashes?"

"Money. I want you and your family to move to FarSide. The farther away from the palace you are, the safer you should be."

"Oh—you care about our safety—like you cared about

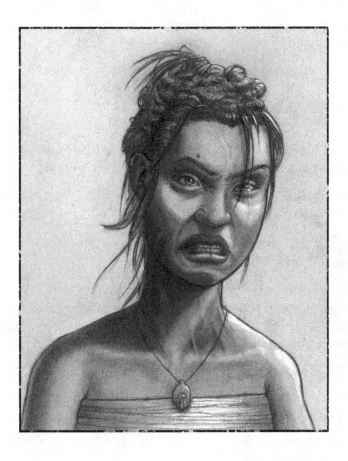

Sunrise's."

"It's not—"

"He called you brother!" she wailed.

"I—He—please, MoonGleam, you—"

"Lava take you!" She slammed the bag of heavy coins on his chest and ran away into the darkness.

The King's Vow coins bounced and scattered on the veranda. "Hell did take me," Bowmark whispered.

The door banged open.

Bowmark vaulted off the veranda.

"MoonGleam?" Dad called.

Bowmark ducked behind the house and fled. After tripping over a pile of retting fibers, he returned to the main path and continued to the cliff stairs. He had vowed to leave by dawn. He had not said where he would leave from.

He worried about Sunrise's family and prayed they would take the money and move, prayed MoonGleam would not fall off a cliff, prayed he would reach High Harbor Bay in time.

The Protocol Officer had not left to chance the destruction of Sunrise. Why would she leave to chance Bowmark's fate? She had vowed that she would never try again to harm the king and his sons, but Bowmark had no doubt she would be willing to send someone else to make sure Bowmark never returned with the Atlas or any unsettling ideas.

His feet seeping blood, he sped through the moonlight down the steps he had memorized. He passed the four huts that clung to the rocky steeps of the tiny High Harbor bay. Bowmark could not feel his feet, and the numbness seemed to be spreading to his knees. By the time he reached the rocky shore, his legs trembled and cold sweat chilled him in the light breeze.

A lamp shone, a tiny spot of yellow, on the short jetty of tumbled basalt boulders. Four fishermen stood around the light doing last minute inspections of net repairs. The outriggers clonked dully as they butted into the rocks and each other. Low tide, and the waves were mild.

The scrunch of his wooden sandals on basalt chips and ground-up coral turned their faces toward him, startled at first. Then suspicions narrowed their shadowed eyes.

The oldest of the men stepped away from the light so that he could better see Bowmark. "Stranger, what are you seeking?"

Bowmark set down his bag and took off his hat. In the eastern sky the black shaded to gray, and the stars retreated like poked sea anemones. He reminded himself that these men had done nothing wrong. He had no right to visit his grief upon them and he prayed that his plan would not harm them. Could he act jovial? He gripped the Giver's Hand medallion hanging from a chain around his neck. "Why does ClamDigger call me a stranger?"

The fishermen looked at each other with mouths agape.

ClamDigger caught up the lamp and brought it close to Bowmark's face. "May a tearjaw eat my liver, is it you, Bowmark? I mean, Royal. I mean, Designate."

SpeaksOut stepped closer in. "We thought you'd be trying out all the pretty maidens to find your queen right now."

Underwater snickered.

"Where's your servants?" DeepWater asked.

Royals had their bigoted opinions about commoners, and commoners had the same about royals. The last king to try out pretty maidens had been TearFlesh, which was how StoneGrove gained a commoner king. CatchaFish had challenged TearFlesh after the king had violated his sister. Grandfather, Father, and Bowmark had never tried out pretty maidens. On the other hand, that unwarranted opinion might help with the story the conspirators required to leave him alive.

Bowmark held up his hands. "Who has the best outrigger?"

The fishermen with plain faces, scarred hands, and splayed toes glanced at each other warily.

Too late Bowmark remembered the saying: Never tell a noble the truth. "Let me see," he said, and splashed out to the outriggers. More black sky slid into gray as he inspected sails for rot and wood for cracks and shipworm, tackle for completeness, including a water distiller, and ropes for soundness. He slung his sack and hat into the largest canoe.

ClamDigger grimaced. Then he bowed and said mournfully, "What was mine is yours."

"Of course it is, after I pay for it."

ClamDigger stared as Bowmark placed six King's Vow coins into his dirty, gnarled hands. Father's carved profile glinted in the lamplight. Oh, that Father could be here for advice. And strength. ClamDigger's jaw moved, but he did not speak.

"And you three." Bowmark beckoned and they stepped up for four coins each. "I just paid you to sail that way, that way, and that way for, ah, ten ropes." He gave them each another coin. "Then set the sails so the outriggers will keep going, while you take your boards and swim back. Tomorrow, you can look for them if you want. If you find them, lucky you, your old canoe back and the price of a new one in your hands."

They frowned and looked sidelong at each other and shifted from foot to foot.

Bowmark handed his last four coins to ClamDigger. "I'm keeping yours and sailing by myself. I'm paying you to leave now, don't stop to talk to anybody, especially ChatterBird. Go visit some cousin of yours in WetSide."

ClamDigger nodded, then said slowly, "May we ask what this is about?"

"You may ask. I will not answer. It is a royal matter. This requires silence."

He knew them well enough that he could guess the thoughts churning in their eyes: Ah, the nobles were capricious at best, with scant accounting for their actions, so there you were. They needed to treat him as designate.

The entire sky shone gray with a pink glow in the east outlining the ancient volcanic cliffs behind them.

Now they could see him more clearly. "Designate." SpeaksOut dropped to his knees, "Storm and wind, I can't believe you need another ordeal. You don't look well and your feet are bleeding something awful."

"I don't feel well." He waded to the chosen outrigger with the name *Sails Far* painted on the prow and pulled himself in. He untied the line, unfurled the sail, and tacked in the light breeze to head northwest between WetSide and King's Island.

Hopefully, the fishermen he had paid in Safe Harbor on the other side of StoneShell Island were already past the reef. Giver of all, how he needed Sunrise, who was smarter than him and surely would have come up with a better scheme.

He passed the northern tip of WetSide with the sun warming his back. The breeze strengthened, steadied, and blew all the familiar smells of the island over him. He took one look back. A smudge of smoke still belched from the evil lake of lava on King's Island.

Bowmark set the sail in a position that let the outrigger skim over the swells in a straight line without supervision. SnatchFast peered over the edge of the boat towards the islands and whined.

Bowmark stretched himself face-down in the canoe, and for the first time since his mother's death, he wept aloud.

WE ARE ALL SEA PREDATORS. ROYALS LIKE TEARJAWS.
COMMONERS LIKE PORPOISES.

~SEA PREDATOR HOLY BOOKS

A long time later Bowmark rose, eyes and nose swollen and with a headache bludgeoning his forehead. He slowly sat on the middle thwart, emptied of emotion and drive. He was on a voyage he had never wanted to take, a voyage Sunrise had longed to go on. Bowmark picked up the Atlas that had doomed them and turned the pages. Sunrise had planned to sail to Ironia first. One place to start. He reset the sail, and still feeling empty, lay down on nets that smelled of rotting fish and gave himself to sleep.

Bowmark awoke when a wave sloshed onto his face. The wind had changed. The canoe juddered against cross-purpose swells. He spat out the water, nearly leaped to reef the sail, then remembered where he was and why. Slowly he raised his head until he could peek over the side. His canoe had sailed itself to within a rope of another outrigger. abandoned for a few days by a fisherman he had paid. And there, far to the east, a spot of color, not water, not sky.

He slowly reset the sail and from the prow lowered a net laden with a rock anchor and his personal supplies in a waterproof bag made from a tearjaw air bladder. There must be a better way to hide the fact he was in this canoe, but his tired brain could not come up with one. This was a common method to keep a canoe almost stationary. Hopefully, the people coming would not think to investigate the weight below the canoe.

Then he hid in the prow to watch the spot of color grow into an orange triangle canvas and outrigger canoe. Sparkles from reflected sunlight gyrated on the sail.

When the canoe drew near enough for him to discern two figures paddling and one handling the sail, he snapped his fingers at SnatchFast, commanding the tiny monkey to keep still and silent, and draped a pile of net over him. Then he slipped into the water and watched the sailors with one eye beyond the prow edge.

Closer, he recognized three distant cousins, PullHard, sixteen, WarCry, sixteen, and Arrowhead, fifteen. Their wavy black hair, more akin to commoners' than the tightly coiled red hair of most of the nobles, was pulled back into bundles by rust-red ribbons. They seemed to be ashamed of their great grandfather's decision to live with a commoner, for they spent much time trying to outnoble the nobles. And they hated Bowmark for no reason he was ever able to comprehend.

Bowmark ducked behind the prow. When the outriggers clonked together, he pulled himself under the canoe and flattened himself like a limpet on its bottom on the side opposite the approaching canoe. Above him, a shadow passed from their outrigger to his. The line twitched from the weight and rebound of a person boarding *Sails Far.*

Bowmark watched. After years of contests with Sunrise, he could hold his breath for over 600 heartbeats. The boy stayed on *Sails Far* much longer than it takes to search a dugout log. What could the dimwit be doing? The line twitched again as the shadow passed back to the other canoe.

The cousins did not move. Bowmark hung on. Ripples refracted light into a dazzle. Still the cousins did not move. Bowmark waited as his lungs protested. Drowning was not how he wished to escape, so he gradually scooted up the side of the canoe. He lifted only his nose above the water and swung his legs under the hidden side of the canoe. The gray seafolks dead on the beach so many years ago had their nostrils on their foreheads. That would have been helpful for him now.

"I saw something! Under the canoe."

A porpoise swished by him to bob near the cousins. It clicked, and then squealed at them.

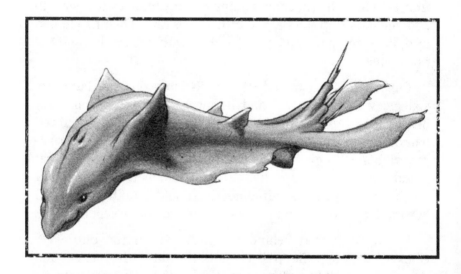

"Just a porpoise. I think it's the one that's been following us. Got any food on you?"

"Only my supper."

"Hand it over. Here, big guy. Do us a favor sometime."

"Why do we do that? I've never seen a porpoise help anybody."

"There's another outrigger over there."

"I saw it. It's bound to be as empty as all the rest."

"He can't have persuaded every fisherman on the island to throw away his outrigger."

"He must have been planning this for months."

Bowmark had only had ten long breaths to plan while the protocol officer said her vows in the treasure room. He breathed carefully.

"I think he's hiding in the Royal Forest, laughing his belly off. He'll take off in some well-provisioned canoe with ten, twenty followers, head straight to the enemy. You'll see."

"That doesn't make sense. The enemy would skin him as soon as they saw him. Let's go home."

"Not until we check that other vessel. If we aren't thorough, we'll be in the hot lava crisping next to that commoner Sunsomething."

Bowmark grimaced as the three mulled over their decision.

"So do we retrieve these two canoes?"

"We're not supposed to split up until after we've checked them all."

"So then, we check that one, sail south to finish the west islands, and then back home."

"Unless we see another sail further west."

Groans. The outriggers separated.

Once, during the candle he waited before reboarding, the porpoise nosed along his side, surfaced, and exhaled right into Bowmark's face. Bowmark caressed the creature's green, rubbery jaw. "Thank you. I owe you my life."

The porpoise chortled, waggled its head, and sped away.

The following week had little to distinguish one day from the next as he journeyed northwest and studied the drawn currents and lands in the Atlas. Rain fell a few times the first week. According to the marks he scratched into the gunwale every sunrise, the second week, fifth day, he came to a thick kelp forest, rich in fish and snails—and perilous with sea snakes. There must be a seamount close to the surface here. After harvesting a lot of kelp and fish to supplement his rice balls and dried fruit, he marked what he figured was the correct spot in the Unknown Area of the Atlas with a waterproof ink of tree resin and charcoal.

The third week, second day, the wind died. Bowmark paddled, rested, paddled, rested, paddled while the monkey paced from one end of the canoe to the other. Bowmark mentally paced with him.

In the light of a westering sun he dragged the paddle into the canoe. His back and arms cramped and stung. His fingers would not release their grip so he held the paddle blade between his knees and jerked his arms apart until his fingers were pulled off the shaft. His hands remained rigid in the paddle pose.

Bowmark scoffed at himself and stiffly moved to the prow and the glass water distiller cradled in a hole in the front thwart. He pulled off the cap and salt-water container. The base filled with sweet water was too wide for him to hook his rigid fingers around. Using his wrists, he lifted the base to his lips, and then dropped the glass bowl. It shattered on the thwart, spraying broken glass and water across his legs. *No!*

He could keep himself alive on the water in fish vertebrae and eyes. As long as there were fish nearby. He could rig the sail to catch rainwater, should it rain. No rain had fallen this week. The Atlas marked some deserts in the ocean that were bereft of fish or other life. He was still sailing in the part marked unknown, so he wouldn't know how good or bad the fishing was until he fished. How had he not thought about how this journey could kill him?

Stop. Think.

He had a gourd that held his dried fruit. Dumping the fruit into the empty sack that had held rice squares gave him a distiller base. The extra sail bunched around the bottom held the gourd stable. The top part of the distiller fit somewhat when he stuffed some seaweed between the glass and gourd. He could breathe now.

Scraping up the broken glass and tossing it overboard, Bowmark wondered what the deep dwellers thought of things like glass shards drifting onto their heads. How great would it be if a shlak swallowed one and choked?

Three days later, during a set of hand-stand pushups, a white pearlescence castle like the one drawn in the Atlas floated into view. The Atlas claimed that varons made these structures shaped like round islands and covered with thin towers that looked like melted candles. He flipped to his feet and stared.

If only he could go there. Varons were the nonhuman people who had made the unbreakable knife. The Atlas said their castles were made of the same pearlescence and showed a picture of a varon who looked like a cross between a seal and a seahorse. According to the human measure on the page, the creature was twice as long as a human.

The Atlas also said that sometimes the varons welcomed fishermen. Sometimes they stole everything a fisherman had and killed him. Since one could not tell what they would do until after the encounter, the Atlas advised sailors to wait until the varons swam to them and invited them to trade and visit. Bowmark watched and waited as the shining castle dwindled from sight, but no varon came to give him an invitation.

Sunrise would have paddled there anyway, gambling that his unexpected visit would be welcome. Bowmark sighed. He had a mission. He could not gamble. He needed a way to become stronger, become more skilled, become the man who could defeat RaiseHim.

The fourth week, first day, Bowmark looked up from his fish gutting to check his lines of drying fish, seaweed, and jellyfish. The outrigger really could not hold much more, so he might as well stop fishing.

A porpoise startled him by squealing near the prow "Do me a favor some day!" he called as he threw the offal to the porpoise. The creature leaped, deftly caught the guts, and dived just in time to avoid a collision with his canoe.

"Showoff." Bowmark strung up the last fish. He tore off a small chunk and handed the piece to SnatchFast who gobbled it down.

He sat and ran his hand over his dreadlocks. They were matting together. He uncorked his small oil gourd and upended the vessel over his palm. Not even one drop issued from the bottle. Bowmark thought about his hair contracting into a helmet instead of separating into individual dreadlocks. "Burn it." He pulled out his obsidian blade and shaved his head.

His curious companion played with the cut hair for a while, then jumped on Bowmark's shoulder to rub his little paws on his bald scalp. "No no no no!"

"It's bad enough the canoe smells like monkey poo. Get off my head."

The monkey clutched his neck and hooted.

"On my return trip I'm going to bring an entire cask of oil and stock more distillers for water. And I'm leaving you on the next habitable land."

The monkey hooted in his ear.

The day after he shaved off his hair, he observed his eighteenth birthday by staring all day at the horizon, holding his steel Giver's Hand medallion, and thinking of how the day would have been celebrated. Servants and royals alike would have feasted on roast pig and pana fruit. Coconut and prickle fruit. Pickled rice balls. Boiled eggs. Crushed roots. Sugar rods.

There would have been costumed dramatic dancing and dances that everyone would have joined in. Giver's Hand, he loved dancing. But there, or here, Sunrise was still dead.

The next day, he paddled to add that little bit of speed as a slow breeze lazily moved his canoe along. A break to exercise his hands and juggle his knives would be welcome. Something tugged on his paddle.

He looked down and jumped up screaming. A tearjaw's mouth closed over the blade of his paddle. Bowmark shoved down to disengage the blade from the rows of backward-slanting teeth, turned the blade, and pulled.

As the paddle slid past the lips of the giant fish, the tearjaw surged forward and clamped on the blade again. Bowmark shoved down, twisted, and the fish twisted with him. The monster shook its head, and nearly pulled Bowmark over the gunwale.

He pulled back with one hand, and with the other pulled out one of his throwing knives. He flung it into the tearjaw's nose.

The giant fish let go. Bowmark fell backward. His back hit the other side of the canoe. The paddle clattered on a thwart. While pulling out another knife, Bowmark listened. Would the tearjaw try to bump over the canoe? He needed a spear. All the canoe held was a gaffer hook.

SnatchFast bounded up the mast, screaming too loud for Bowmark to hear anything else. Excrement slid down the sail and mast. Post-fight shakes made his hands tremble.

Thump! The stern rose and crashed back. Bowmark grabbed the gunwale. He waited.

The tearjaw had probably rammed the knife farther into its nose. Bowmark eased out yet another knife from his large collection that were hidden in pockets and seams of his skirt. His heart beat against his ribs. Holding his knives ready to throw, he scanned the waves, and saw nothing. He continued to wait.

When the sun had moved a hand span across the sky, Bowmark cautiously rose and reefed the sail. He untied the canvas from the boom and mast and swished it one-handed in the sea while clutching a knife in the other hand. Surely the smell of monkey excrement would not attract a tearjaw. Once the sail was clean, Bowmark examined the feces-stained fish he needed to throw away. He glared at SnatchFast who was poking at the fishnets. "I honestly can't say if having you as a companion is making me crazy faster or slower than being alone."

Bowmark tossed the polluted fish, hoping it would satisfy or drive away the tearjaw. This had been a small one. Had he seen a large tearjaw, he might have fought the monkey for the highest place on the mast. Fishermen who had caught the attention of a large tearjaw usually threw their whole catch overboard, and then paddled or sailed away as fast as possible while the tearjaws jostled each other for the dead fish.

He watched until the light grew too dim to see.

In the fifth week, third day, he sailed past a giant, stupid sunfish that one ate only if the alternative was starvation.

After five weeks of mostly fish and seaweed, he felt that he could swim through a lagoon of tearjaws to get some fresh pork and fruit. He had one rice ball left, no more dried fruit, a handful of sugar crystals, and a month's worth of fish and seaweed. So he might die of boredom, but not of starvation. He glanced around: distiller clean and drops condensing on the inside walls of the blown glass, sail in good shape, three gourds filled with sweet water, nothing on the horizon, nothing more to do.

He hated this time of day. With nothing left to occupy him, he would brood into despair as he had every day before. He reached for the tooth-marked paddle, laid it across his lap, and sighed. One man paddling an outrigger of this size could not go far or fast, but paddling aided the work of the sail somewhat, and exhaustion helped him sleep at night, at least briefly before he woke—heart pounding and sweat trickling—from nightmares of killing Sunrise.

Just for ten minutes, he pleaded with his soul, just let him go ten minutes without thinking about Sunrise or MoonGleam. As he dug the paddle into the sea, he thought about his escape—it should have been Sunrise leaving with his blessing! And the plotting protocol officer falling into the lava.

He clenched his teeth. He had wanted to be wrong about the woman and to have spent his gold uselessly on the fishermen. When he came back, vow or no vow, he would need—a thought made him pause.

Why was he blaming the protocol officer? Because she was the obvious leader in the treasure room. Truth. But the woman had truly wanted to find a way to save her precious protocol without further assassination, or else their throats would have been slit and done with. Those lesser cousins were young. The officer had no friends that weren't crippled with age. But RaiseHim . . . . The protocol officer had no imagination. RaiseHim had plenty.

Bowmark pulled the paddle onto his lap and used a fish rib bone to pick his teeth. As he scraped, he thought about his cousin RaiseHim's cruelty to servants and himself.

RaiseHim liked to poke the penned boars with sharp sticks until they lashed their scaly spike-tipped tails against the rails and screamed with frustration. Once he secretly cut a fisherman's net in such a way that at the first cast, the net parted from its towlines and was completely lost. It was the fisherman who had to buy a new one.

He tilted his head back. The officer may have been the leader, but strings ran from her to RaiseHim's fingers. Why hadn't he seen this before? He closed his eyes. Because Sunrise wasn't there to point out the obvious to him.

He opened stinging eyes. And then he dropped the fishbone. The clouds directly west bore a slight green tinge on their bottoms, meaning a reef atoll under them, possibly an island. Almost invisible specks wheeled under the clouds. SnatchFast darted to the bow, then up the mast, and back, hooting. "Gimme mine!" Bowmark jumped up, grabbed the lines, and tacked west.

The sun had touched the rim of the world when he sailed through a gap in the reef into a shallow lagoon filled with colorful sponges and corals, bright striped fish, undulating sea slugs and prickly sea cucumbers. White, tan, and ashy-blue crabs scuttled around crevices in fan and brain coral. Mussels raked the clear, blue-green water next to purple wiggletoes and yellow starfish.

Thousands of seaskimmers and bluefeet rose screaming from the two stride-high island, about a hundred strides long and half as many at its widest. He strapped on wooden-soled sandals to protect himself as he waded through poisonfin, sharp coral, crooked thin edges of barnacles, and venomous snails. He picked his way around a group of shield urchin, their sight tightening his stomach with the pain of remembering the Disc.

The stench of piles of guano, regurgitated fish, rotting kelp and dead birds made war upon his nostrils. While nothing could protect him from the reek, his hat and tough seagrass cape preserved him from most bird attacks and indignities as he moved through their nesting grounds. With relief, he thought through tomorrow's chores. Boil eggs. Collect and dry sea cucumbers. Search for octopuses.

He examined some bits of man-made flotsam caught on the sharp rocks. A bit of rope made of some unknown fiber. A splintered plank of greenish wood with an iron nail rusting out of one end. His examination cut short when a green and brown hump moved in the shallow water. A sea turtle. If he couldn't make something glorious of that plastron and shell, his artisan tutor would be ashamed of him. Dried turtle meat, and look, on that end of the islet, a groaning, barking herd of striped seals.

He set to work. The sun rolled across the sky.

This was not the islet to dump the monkey, so small and short that storm waves would wash over the entire island. Only three seawalker trees rose above its scabby surface. As he was pondering how tired he was of cleaning monkey poo out of the canoe, and dragging the sea turtle toward his outrigger, an unnatural straight-edged shape on the shore caught his eye.

In the fading light, he bounded over the rocks to pick up a thin wooden box that was scraping against the shore. It was half a stride long, ornately carved, inlaid with gold and some type of stone with shifting colors. The box weighed more heavily than its size indicated. The golden lock was shaped like a twisty six-legged snake and so realistic he had to squint to make sure it was ornament. The metal snake did not move.

He tapped the golden shape and the *clink* of metal convinced him it was sculpted, not taxidermy. He grimaced. The venomous six-legged snakes were nasty, much meaner than the larger eight-legged ones.

SnatchFast jumped on the box and sniffed it.

The phosphorescent sea outlined his dark outrigger as he carried the box toward the canoe. Although the glowing algae and shrimp helped him find his vessel, the dim shine did not help him find his footing. At rock's edge, he set down the box, pulled the outrigger onto the coral sand, and searched with his hands for the tiny lamp within one of the storage gourds. A flint ignited a small flame.

The eyes of nesting birds shone like stars drawn near as he studied the box. How to open it without a key? He pulled out the bronze knife from his belt and inserted its tip in the key hole set in the middle of the snake legs.

The golden snake lock writhed. Its tiny claws scratched the knife.

SnatchFast screeched and ran behind a rock.

Bowmark dropped the knife and backed up, his skin prickling. The priests, the protocol officer, the artisans, the historian—none of them had told him about anything like this. The metal snake might creep anywhere at night. How could he sleep now?

He pulled out his obsidian blade, and, as slowly as moss growing, he placed the tip against the stilled keyhole. The snake stayed flat and still. But the stone blade was far too fat to fit into the hole and was no good for levering.

A quick search through the outrigger brought him back with a long, thin knife of bone.

SnatchFast hopped back towards the box and pawed at the jewel. "Gimme mine!" Bowmark shoved him away, but the animal capered back. The monkey clung to the top of the box and sniffed the edge over the lock. Bowmark pushed his little face away.

Again, slowly, slowly, Bowmark extended the sharpened bone fragment toward the hole, and into the hole. He leaned away before he twisted the knife in case the metal snake moved again.

The box burst into flame with a rushing crackle. Bowmark fled into the sea, tripped on a stone, and fell as white flame whooshed over where he had been. The sea birds shrieked. Hundreds of beating wings roiled the air. SnatchFast's scream cut short as the fire engulfed him.

Bowmark pushed himself back up. Flames licked up his sail. He snatched off his hat and used it to scoop up and splash water on the sail. Scoop and toss, scoop and toss, water and flame splashed and fell hissing into the sea.

The fire on the sail winked out. Seals groaned and wailed. A cacophony of shrieks filled his ears as burnt birds plopped into the water all about him like rain. The stench of burnt feathers vied with the reek of guano.

Bowmark cried out, "SnatchFast!" *No.* "SnatchFast!" He searched but found no trace of his pet. With an aching throat, Bowmark trudged to his boat and sagged against the side. He peered at the blackened sand where the box had been sitting.

The white flames surrounding the box shrank to an orange, crackling ball, and then to a red glow.

Bowmark leaned against his outrigger and watched the red fade to black. He then pulled the canoe away from the shore until he stepped off an underwater precipice, bobbed back, climbed into the canoe, set the anchor, and slept fitfully.

Gray dawn found him trying to decide what to do. The sea bubbled with fish and small tearjaws feasting on charred birds. Sunrise would not have dithered. He would have gone back instantly to see what was left of the box. Bowmark stared gloomily at the tiny island. That was magic. What else could it have been? He found the paddle and pushed back towards the shore.

Dead birds, and crabs tearing at them littered the scorched rock.. With his foot, he nudged aside carcasses, revealing his glass lamp melted to a puddle, the beautiful stones on the box cracked to sand, and the wood and bone burned to white ash. The inlaid gold snake had transformed into a glinting ring. Could the ring transform back to snake? His skin prickled again.

SNAKE RING

In the midst of all this ruin lay a strange cylinder, silver with shifting blue and green colors, the diameter of his wrist, and a length as long as his forearm. Each end of the cylinder was capped with a metallic round fist of four clawed snake toes. Like the golden snake on the box, the craftsmanship on the claws radiated the sense of the preternatural.

Holding his breath, he nudged the cylinder. The metal did not snap at his sandal. He dipped his hat into the ocean and poured sea water over the object. The cylinder neither moved nor steamed. Rocks did not rouse the thing, nor did a brief touch with knife or finger. He picked up the cylinder. Sunlight shone on intricate inscriptions in another alphabet, one based on circles, radii, and parts thereof. He had never seen the like. StoneShell seemed a tiny dot in a wide, wide world.

He touched an inset circle.

Zip! A blur near his face made him jerk his head back and blink.

His hand stung from a sudden reverberation. Bowmark held his breath and moved only his eyes to see where the suddenly long, thin pole—extended from the hilt he held—pressed onto the now chipped stone next to his left foot. The metal cylinder was almost as tall as him.

He inhaled. He exhaled. He gently pulled the pole off the stone, leaving a shallow hole and an almost invisible shaving from his sandal. Gently, he bent his knees and lowered the pole. He needed to turn his wrist to lay down the weapon and accidentally touched again the indented circle.

Zip!

The pole collapsed back into its original length.

Bowmark swallowed and took another breath. Angling it well away from his body, he slowly touched the circle again. *Zip!* And back. *Zip!* The pressure he applied to the circle determined the speed at which the staff changed. He examined the claw fist that had chipped the rock and noted no scratches or dents. A wondrous weapon, this: a long, thin staff that could punch into stone. Much better than his bronze knife.

If he learned how to use this telescoping staff, it could be what kept him alive during his mission. Such a weapon could persuade the protocol officer that new weapons could protect the people better against the enemy. Truth. This was great fortune, despite the loss of SnatchFast.

But what good would it do? Since RaiseHim had surely proved to designate, the rules of their fight were the same as the challenge to a ruling king. Bowmark would step barefoot on the Disc *without* a weapon.

As he mulled this over his eyes returned to the transformed ring resting in the middle of the blasted terrain. He used a shard of shell to pick up the gold ring and studied it. Incredibly, it had the detail of a snake -every scale and claw reproduced in miniature- but wrapped into a circle. The thing did not protest being handled now, but Bowmark did not trust it. He put the ring and his new weapon into an empty sack at the farthest end of the canoe.

Bowmark spent the next two days collecting eggs and then baking them, drying seal and turtle meat, and mending the sail with seal gut. The giant turtle shell made a vessel to hold all his new provisions, and more seal gut and sap made water bags. He drew the uninhabited island onto the Atlas, naming his discovery FlamingBird Island.

With the clean salt air blowing the stench of the island away, he tacked northwest.

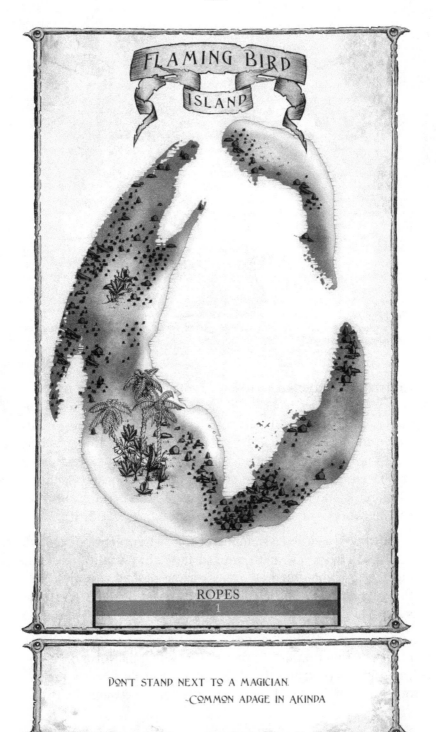

FLAMING BIRD ISLAND

ROPES
1

DON'T STAND NEXT TO A MAGICIAN.
-COMMON ADAGE IN AKINDA

An island or cape—he did not know which yet—rose from the sea. After three more weeks of sailing through barren ocean and increasingly cool nights, Bowmark welcomed the sight of cliff, slope, and forest as thick as seal fur. This could be Ironia. Maybe. If he understood the maps aright and had sailed correctly. The crash and boom of surf on stone soothed his heart. Clouds of white birds and gray skaters circled and searched the cliffs and roaring waves.

Bowmark paddled, scanning for the swirl or froth that would indicate a rock close to the surface that could wreck his outrigger. No landing here unless being dashed to splinters on the gray cliffs could be called landing. On a whim, he turned south.

Later, he rounded the rocky arm of a broad bay where brown blades of kelp tumbled in the wash. A small platform of pegged wood perched on the tip of the rocky arm that nearly met the other arm of the bay, leaving a narrow pass between the two.

Huge tree trunks and branches stripped bare and silvered by sun and salt crowded the eastern side of the bay. Driftwood he understood, but there amid the floating logs stood a number of dead trees, their single trunks straight and tall, their bare branches stretched out like whale ribs. Some of them slanted and some had nearly surrendered to the ocean, leaning over so far only their branches emerged above the water.

He only knew of a few kinds of trees that grew in shallow ocean near the shore. These looked nothing like them. His attention then latched onto something stranger than all the unused wood.

In the middle of the floating logs were a number of straight stone shapes, two domes, and a broken tower with crooked lines of cracks in the walls. Water lapped gently against their sides. The cliff behind the lines, domes, and tower had a hollow spot, as though a giant hand had scooped away part of the land. His eyes could not resolve what he was seeing into anything he could recognize. Perhaps they were weirs of a sort, like the fish traps that five families on Scab Island maintained. With their weirs, they were able to keep the families on Rice Island supplied with fish. He thought of the eight inhabited islands that made up StoneGrove. It should have been Sunrise trying to figure out what he was seeing.

On the west side of the bay were two wharves: one collapsed, one with some tiny buildings standing on rocky ground nearby and much larger buildings on the side in the water. Had the sea risen here to surround trees and buildings?

His sail sagged, becalmed. The reek of rotted seaweed left behind by low tide mingled with the pungent fragrance of unfamiliar trees. Why did none of the seabirds circling above sport in the waters of the bay?

As he paddled toward the wharf a bell tolled five times.

When he reached the half-decayed wharf, a man with crutches thumped over the wooden walk to the dilapidated ladder to which Bowmark moored his outrigger. Bowmark looked up. The man looked down, and they studied each other.

The man had earthworm-colored skin seamed from obvious years of outside work. The top of his head had few hairs, but he had curly brown hair all over his lower face. Thick, black hairs bristled on the backs of his hands. Did all people here have hair on their faces and hands? Were the women hairy? Instead of a tunic, the man wore something shorter that hugged his body and had fasteners along the slit that ran from neck to waist. Instead of a skirt, he wore sleeves on his legs with fasteners at his crotch. The right sleeve was folded and pinned closed at the knee, for his lower leg was missing. His sandal was a solid, dark casing that covered the entire foot and ankle. A glint alerted Bowmark to the knife he held in one hand.

The man studied Bowmark from head to foot, and the outrigger from prow to stern. Bowmark stayed seated and held up both empty hands with fingers spread wide.

After several moments, the man spoke in Common with an accent that shifted the vowels and softened the consonants. He said, "Where in the world did you come from?"

The one question he must never answer. "I am from a place some hundred days from here. You will not have heard of us."

The man pursed his lips before replying, "I just implied that, don't you know?" His gaze went to the bay entrance, then back to Bowmark. "Where's your ship?"

Bowmark looked down. Had his vessel become invisible? He could see it. "This is my ship, *Sails Far.* I paid for it."

"Where is your big ship?"

"This was the biggest I could find."

The man rubbed the back of his neck. "We're using the same word, but I don't think we mean the same thing. It is not possible for you to have sailed thousands of kilometers on two logs connected with rope and sticks. Where is your ship like that?" He pointed to a gigantic two-masted box on the other side of the wharf.

Bowmark looked under the wharf. "Giver of Life, that thing floats. I thought it was a fixed building. It's built like a huge box.

Families could live on that." He looked back at the man who appeared puzzled.

"I think you've never seen a ship like that."

"I haven't seen much. This is the first land I've come to in months. Is this Ironia?"

"Ironia? What business do you have with Ironia?"

"It is a place where many trade routes cross. I thought a land such as that would not immediately kill a stranger."

The man shook his head and seemed to relax. "Come on up so I can sit while we talk. These crutches are uncomfortable."

In half a second, Bowmark stood beside the hairy man who stood a double hand span shorter than he.

The man squinted one eye while looking up at Bowmark. "They don't wear much where you're from, do they?"

Bowmark glanced at his bare feet, legs, and chest. Perhaps the man thought he should be wrapped in sleeves.

The man looked down at the outrigger again. "Where do you sleep? Where do you eat? What do you do when it rains?"

Bowmark pointed to a jumble in the middle of the canoe. "I have a cape and hat."

The man shook his head again. "I've got a new story to tell the wife." He turned and thumped back to a bench where wharf and shore met. The bottoms of the crutches were heavy balls crusted with rust.

Bowmark approved. Even a crippled man should help protect his people. Being hit by one of those would really slow an enemy down. What if the smith added one of these to the butt end of a spear? No, that would ruin the weapon's flight arc.

The man maneuvered himself onto one end of the bench and indicated that Bowmark should sit at the other end. "Name's Staylik. Yours?"

Bowmark sat, feeling the weight of the obsidian knife hidden in his waistband and the throwing knives in the seams. Now that he was separated from his canoe, perhaps the men that had surely been summoned by the bell would attack. "In Common, my name is Bowmark. My parents hoped that I would have the strength and suppleness of a great bow that is wielded in intelligence to speed the arrow to its purpose, the bowmark."

"Hmm." Staylik reached down and picked up a box made of oiled wood with a purple and yellow grain. He used his knife to continue a chip carving on the lid. "I got named after my uncle. Don't know why. Nobody liked him. So, young man, ever hear of the ungols?"

"I don't know that word." Maybe the Atlas had mentioned ungols, but he could not recall any such mention.

Staylik watched Bowmark out of the corner of his eye as he carved. "You're looking for a place that doesn't kill strangers. Why would that be?"

Bowmark almost answered, "Because I need to stay alive," but that wasn't what the man was asking. The man had a right to know that Bowmark was not a spy or someone who would kill the people here as they slept. On the other hand, his mission stated baldly wouldn't sound like something they would want to encourage either. So, how to say this so Staylik would continue to carve the box, and not him?

"I have some things to trade. Or I could work for what I need."

"Someone who lives on a log doesn't need much."

"Ah, I need . . . . My people have sent me on a mission. I cannot return until I have collected the most precious things from ten lands." *Idiot!* Why had he said that? "I have not come to steal. I will give you value for what your people consider precious."

Laughing, the man shook his head. "Your people don't like you much, do they?"

Thinking of MoonGleam, Bowmark turned to look at the sun and pretended that that was why he needed to wipe his eyes. "Some don't. Some—we need to learn about the bigger world that we have forgotten."

"They say it's a wide world and full of wonders. Me though, a good woman is wonder and treasure enough. If your people don't know the ungols, go back and tell your people to stay where they are. Hmm. You aren't one of three sons sent out and whoever collects the most loot gets to marry the princess?"

"No." Bowmark slumped. This was absurd. RaiseHim had won and there was nothing he could do about the coup. If he had stayed and redone the proving, maybe he could have injured RaiseHim into ineligibility before his cousin killed him. Instead, he had run like a coward.

Staylik blew a chip of wood off the box. "I'm sorry to tell you that you came to the last place you should have gone if you wanted treasure. We don't have a fleck of gold, a chip of ruby, or a single silver spoon. Everything we have is wood or iron."

Bowmark's breath failed. Iron was the second most precious commodity on StoneGrove. Not as rare as pearlescence, but more valuable than gold. Could he carry a load of iron in his canoe? No, iron weighed too much.

Maybe they had something lighter, like an iron or steel medallion. "You would have me believe that there is never salvage."

"Smart one, you. Still, it's true. Got time for a story?"

Bowmark studied the man's face.

"Don't you know, at one time this was a busy harbor, with iron and lumber going out, coal and prisoners from Ironia to work the mines coming in. Those dark, cold mines." Staylik shuddered.

"What are mines?"

"Huh? Mines are holes in the ground that doomed men crawl into to dig out ore. The ore is smelted and you get metal. On *this* island, you get iron."

"Why don't you trade with the shlaks, the ocean people who look like crabs?"

Staylik's eyes widened. "I've heard of them, but not from anybody that's seen them." He waved a hand. "Back to that later. Let me finish the story. Two, three dozen cargo and pleasure ships a month came through here. Some Ironian lesser nobility lived in yonder castle to oversee and tax and meddle and so forth."

Bowmark looked over his shoulder.

"Oh, you don't see a castle? Coming to that. Several thousand people lived here then. The prisoners, the men with whips, the men who built tracks for the ore cars. The fishermen, guards, bankers, bakers, weavers. Some farmers inland, servants for the nobility, so on and so forth. But Rolocton had a problem. Oh, this island is Rolocton. Ironia is three, four days that way." He pointed north.

Bowmark closed his eyes and visualized the maps and commentary in the Atlas he had studied. Rolocton, Haller's Crown, some tiny islands, all of which belonged to Ironia, and then Ironia itself. Rolocton was a good place to sell fine fabrics and hunting supplies. He opened his eyes and looked at the decayed wharf.

Staylik chipped off another sliver of wood. "Ungols are the problem. They have human captive slaves and stolen fast ships that fairly twirl around the heavy cargo ships, and they have hearts harder than any iron. I suppose that as long as there are people, there will be those who find taking wealth easier than making wealth. More fun, too, if your idea of fun is shooting men and women with poison arrows. So, every four, five years or so the ungols and the bears they ride came and divested Rolocton of whatever they could find. Oh, hey, Broon, meet my new friend Bowmark."

STAYLIK AND BROON

A man slightly taller than Staylik, with light brown hair on top of his head, crawling out his ears, and covering his chin, walked up with a stool which he plunked down in front of the bench and then placed himself on, nodding to Bowmark.

Bowmark nodded back, hoping that was a friendly greeting. The Atlas hadn't mentioned ungols. What were ungols riding bears? What were bears?

"Ah," Staylik continued, "the nobility got tired of that, and they couldn't afford to keep an entire garrison here for years on end, waiting for the one day they would be needed. So what do you suppose they did?"

Broon chuckled.

Bowmark watched both men warily. "Did they train the farmers how to fight?"

That made both men laugh. "No. The way of it was this: They hired a magician. If they had bothered to ask farmers or bakers, they would have been told to stay away from magic. But they didn't ask and they did hire. Did they hire him to make sure the mines held up? Of course not. Did they hire him to make the townspeople safe? Of course not. Did they ask for good weather or good crops? No."

"Don't you know it," Broon said in a reedy voice.

"Way it worked out, maybe we're glad they didn't think to include us in their request. They paid that magician Fencock to put a spell on all their treasure, that it would never be stolen again. That magician stayed around town long enough to throw some fancy powder around and spook everybody and then hired a ship to take him somewhere else to cause trouble. So, the nobility had reason for a party, and a party they had. Fancy food, a thousand candles, casks of wine, and everybody dressed up in their best clothes and as much jewelry as they could wear without falling down. They would never be robbed again. Hooray! They danced away the hours until midnight.

"Midnight. Midnight, when the lord held up his golden cup to make a toast and the musicians finally got to catch their breaths, and the servants sat and the nobility stood. Midnight, in that blazing hall with light shouting out of its glass windows. Everyone grabbed a cup and waited. That's when our disaster happened. Rolocton stretched and rolled over in its sleep. Earthquake, some people call it, when the ground shivers and twitches and the candles fall out of their holders and people grab onto furniture but the furniture falls faster than the people even. Wine splashed on the marble floors. And then a noise like I hope never to hear again and don't know how to tell you what it sounded like. A crash, a boom, a mountain screaming in agony, whatever it was—it woke the world. And the bluff that castle sat upon slid into the bay like butter off a hot plate. Not a soul survived."

Bowmark marveled at how many words Staylik could stuff into one breath.

Staylik pointed with the knife. "There you can see the walls of the hall. If you dive inside, you can see the skeletons of those people still wearing all their gold and all their gems."

"I don't understand," Bowmark said. "I thought you said there was no treasure here."

"Well, keep on listening. Remember, there's a spell on that treasure. What guards it now is what ruined all the fishing and crabbing you once could do in the bay. What guards it now pulls down all the seabirds that try to rest on the water. And what might that guard be, you want to know. It's this: fish with fangs, fast fish, about the length of my forearm, that go about in great packs. Fish that can strip the flesh off a man in seconds."

Bowmark raised his eyebrows.

"There was a man like you once, strong, at least he was after recovering from a mine accident. Never was any man happier than that man when all the mines collapsed in that earthquake, this time with no one inside them. Don't you know, after the earthquake, all the nobility and whip holders were dead. Mines gone. Ships sunk. Message hive gone. Everything in chaos. The miners took over every ship that could float and sailed away as fast as they could. But that injured miner missed the great evacuation. No prison mines, no ore, no coal, no reason to come here except for the hunting, and with no castle to stay at, the hunters went elsewhere. The bankers and traders left. Half the town had been serving at the party, so everybody left in town mourned their wives and husbands, including the beautiful Jaditha, who was taking care of that injured miner.

"That miner recovered. He figured he had better things to do than stay on this broken island. He got a friend to throw some game into the bay over here on the westernmost side which drew off those packfish. He rowed over to the ruins, dove and grabbed a load of treasure before the fish returned, and figured he could row back to the mainland of Ironia. It would be tough, but he was strong. He would pick up enough treasure to buy him a house and servants when he reached Ironia. Don't you know, he only got as far as the opening to the bay. The ground quivered and a wave like the fist of the ocean overturned his little boat and crunched it on the rocks. He was just pulling himself out of the water when the packfish arrived. Took his leg off clean to the knee."

Bowmark looked at where Staylik's missing leg would be if he still had it.

Staylik blew off another chip. "When he recovered from *that*, he realized that Jaditha was as great a treasure as any man could have, and her house as fine a castle."

Bowmark thought a moment. "And because no ships come here anymore, there is no salvage."

"That's the way of it. Of course, some townspeople had rings, earrings, and gold hidden behind bricks. But the ungols came back, and if we didn't give them anything, they said they would kill us all. Did you see that offering platform over there? They agreed that they wouldn't burn down our town if we left enough wealth for them on it. We gathered the rings and such and laid them there. The ungols took all we left them. Everything was fine. Instead of using money, we do favors for each other. That works all right when you have a couple hundred people. More than that, we would have to work out something for money. Oh, back to the point. I'm sorry; you came to the wrong place."

Broon stretched. "In a week or so, it's going to be the wrong place for all of us. Or maybe not."

Bowmark looked at him, and Broon stared back. "If you just happen to meet an ungol, you can tell him we really don't have anything to give them, and this time we're prepared, with weapons."

"Ah, Broon, he's not a spy, and he's not a lick-spittle messenger."

"No?"

"No. In fact, I think Jaditha and I will invite him over for an evening meal. If he's staying that long."

Both hairy men looked at Bowmark. He looked over at the sunken castle. "If I understand aright, you are expecting an ungol raid soon. You have nothing to give them. You expect to be slaughtered."

"You see why we're twitchy."

Bowmark stood, still looking at the castle. "I have an idea. But first, I have something I want to show you. Maybe you can tell me what my find is."

He ran to his outrigger and returned with the sea turtle box he had carved.

Staylik whistled. "That shames my box. What is that beauty made of?"

"Plastron. I had a lot of time to carve while I was sailing." Bowmark lifted the lid and took out the cylinder he had found on Flaming Bird Island.

Broon leaped off his stool and ran into the town. Staylik tossed aside his crutches and threw himself face down before Bowmark. "Forgive me!" he cried.

Bowmark looked from the metal cylinder to Staylik and back. Had he somehow revealed he was a royal as well as a foreigner?

"I didn't know you were one of the craft! I am sorry for my words. Everyone here says I speak like a fool. Please don't hurt the good people here for my ill words."

Bowmark knelt beside Staylik. "I don't know what you're talking about. I found this in a box on an island. The box burnt up when I tried to open it. I don't know what this rod is. I don't know why you think you offended me."

Staylik turned his face to look at Bowmark's. "Salvage? You simply found it?"

"Truth. On a small island filled with birds and their debris."

"May I see it?"

Bowmark gently laid the rod near Staylik's hand. "Be careful. It—"

"I know. This is a staffshifter. Only magicians have them." The man pushed and rolled until he was sitting on the wharf. "They have the secret of memory metal. Hmm. And somehow the memory can be modified not only with these markings, here and here, but also with the thoughts of the magician. Anybody can make it zip in and out; it takes a magician to . . . see these claws? . . . to make them open and grab."

Gingerly Staylik picked up the staffshifter, keeping his fingers away from all symbols, and examined the embossed designs. A grin transformed his face as he showed Bowmark an incised circle with one horizontal diameter and five evenly spaced rays in the bottom half. "That's Fencock's mark." He handed it to Bowmark and laughed, slapping his stump. "Oh, this is delightful. Wonderful! That pile of dung outspelled himself! That earthquake must have created a tsunami that swamped his ship. Ha ha ha! Wait 'til I tell Jaditha!" Then he sobered. "Tough luck for the sailors, though. They do say, 'Don't stand next to a magician.'"

Bowmark shifted his plastron box to show Staylik the gold ring. "What does this do?"

The blood drained from Staylik's face. "Did you put it on?"

"No."

"Good. Don't! You have no idea what might happen."

Bowmark grinned. "That's what I just implied."

"No, no. I don't know either what might happen. You might swell up and burst. You might have visions. You might go insane. You don't know, and you don't want to find out."

Bowmark stood and glanced at the sun. "The day still toddles. I have my need, you have yours. Perhaps they can meet and kiss."

"Huh?"

Bowmark lightly lifted the staffshifter and ran to his outrigger. Within a heartbeats he had unmoored and paddled part of the way to the sunken castle.

ROLOCTON HARBOR

WE THANK THE GIVER WHO WATCHES OVER THE LIVESTOCK
AND CROPS. THE ROYALS AND COMMONERS.
THE FOOLS AND CHILDREN.

-HOLY BOOKS OF THE SEA PREDATORS

Behind Bowmark, Staylik stared, shaking his head as he felt for his crutches on the bleached wood of the wharf.

Broon walked up with a platter piled with cheese, hard sausages, and fruits hard and soft. Under each arm nestled a bottle of wine. He laid the food and drink on the bench. "Where—? What's he doing? I thought I'd appease the magician, but I guess we'll eat this instead of him. Does he think he can counteract the spell?"

Far beyond Broon a few people watched, peeking out from behind a dilapidated warehouse.

Staylik fingered his beard. "He's no magician. My guess is he's thinking I'm a liar."

"Don't you know, who would believe an ugly mug like yours?"

"Not as ugly as some I know."

They sat with the platter between them. Broon picked up some cheese. "Want some?"

Staylik shook his head. "What a waste."

"I know it. A momma somewhere is going to be crying."

"Broon, you're not that long come back from a hunting trip. Think you could make a contribution here?"

"Ha, it worked so well the first time we tried it. Besides, I came back empty-handed."

Staylik studied him.

Broon spread out his hands. "You don't even know the man, or boy, or whatever sleek-skinned shimmery thing he is."

"I know what it means to be cocksure. I know what it means to want something. I know what it means to take a risk to win it all."

"What you know is what it means to lose."

Staylik kept gazing at him. Finally, Broon slumped. "I have a rooster. Stupid thing wakes me up every morning, and, don't you know, I don't need it when I have a wife with sharp elbows. I'll be back."

A time later, he returned with the rooster under his arm. He went half way down the wharf, grabbed the bird by its wattled head, and swung it around twice. He easily pulled off its head and threw it far into the bay. The leathery wings fluttered and the taloned feet kicked as Broon tied a string around one green foot. He swung the rooster again, spattering blood, gaining momentum, and released it to splash in the water. He pulled on the string with small jerks.

Staylik rubbed a hand over his scalp. "He's reached the logs."

"I hate to see him become fish food. But you told him." The water near the wharf boiled and flashed. The string zipped out of Broon's hands.

"Oh, wow!" A small boy who looked like Staylik with more hair ran to the end of the wharf. Other people from the village hesitantly gathered around to watch.

With a small net tucked into his waistband, Bowmark crouched in the prow of the outrigger to contemplate his course. He inhaled and exhaled in a slow rhythm, extending the staffshifter to help his balance as well as to keep from impaling himself on it. He ignored the faint shouts of those on the other side of the bay and steeled himself with memories of Sunrise and the conditions he needed to fulfill. Some of the logs were firmly fixed by boulders or silt, others rocked freely in the tide. He had some good memories of time spent walking on logs and narrow ledges. The shattered tree trunks, some the size of the royal hall in the Bamboo Palace, amazed him. Such a wealth of good canoe and fire wood here.

Hoisting the magic staffshifter, he leapt onto the first log and began the race of keeping the goal in sight while always judging the fitness of the next log, the next log, running and jumping, the next log, wobbling at the sudden sink and roll of some of them, pounding the end of the staff into a stable log while pushing off a rolling tree trunk, staggering, and running. This took less stamina than running on sand, but a great deal more judging and planning and balancing. A profound stillness was interrupted only by his breathing and the clap of his bare feet on the silver-tan, splintered logs.

The first wall of speckled granite rose before him, slimed with bird droppings and algae. *Zip!* He tucked the shortened staffshifter under his belt behind his back, leaped up, caught the crumbled upper rim, and pulled himself to a straddle atop the wall.

The water was not as clear as that around StoneGrove. Instead of blue shades it was murky green. But he could still make out seaweeds and sponges that obscured beautiful friezes and carvings. The walls stood only a hand span taller than Bowmark. Perhaps the hairy Broon was the tallest of his people.

Ah, and there the secret to why much of the stone castle had remained more than rubble when it slid into the sea: ornate, rusty iron straps, a hand in width, held together the walls and attached walls to floors and roofs. The demonstration of wealth was staggering. If Bowmark were to collect all the iron from all the islands of StoneGrove he could probably hold it in his arms. Here they used it as support beams! But apparently these people didn't care about the precious metal. So he continued to scan for other treasure. But of jewelry or gold, there were none. Perhaps this was where Staylik had already raided. Perhaps Staylik had been having fun with him. After all, no fish were to be seen.

Bowmark followed the wall as it tilted into deeper, darker water. The roofs had fallen into most of the rooms, covering whatever had been in them. But some of the roofs had buckled in their descent, leaving gaps showing the floors of alternating black and white tile. There, a faint gleam from a crushed cup, and another glint enmeshed in small bones, perhaps a ring, showed in spaces between feathery algae. He pulled out the staffshifter, and dove.

Silt swirled around his probing fingers. The cup required that he brace his feet against a sponge-encrusted beam and pull. The ring necessitated the dismantling of hand bones, which then also yielded a heavy bracelet coated with muck.

He came up for a breath, then dove again. He swam through an ornate doorway with seaworms hiding in the crevices into a room that still held up a cracked, domed roof. Light spilled in through a missing section of dome between two arching iron ribs, but only directly illuminated a small portion of the room. Roof slates, rusted beams, scattered bones and whole skeletons looked insubstantial and green underwater. And there, a slumped skeleton on a throne presided over the doomed party.

Bowls, cups, tongs, tiny tridents, spoons large and small and
minute, knives sharp and dull, jars, vases, saucers, trays, and
mangled unknowns, all of them made of gold, corroded copper,
and onyx with gems and engravings—obscured by worm casts,
holdfasts, broken shells, and barnacles lying in random piles—
filled the room. Bowmark opened his net.

A silver flicker in the doorway caught his attention. A whiptail fish zigzagged in and propelled itself into the air bubble trapped in the domed ceiling. The fish splashed back and jumped again.

At the wharf, Staylik grimaced, pulled his son into a loose embrace, and said to his friend, "Broon, how do you feel about a swim?"

"Don't think so. I took a bath last month."

Staylik squeezed his son. "Boy, someday it's going to be the hardest thing you'll ever do, but please, when you're a little older and know more than me, please keep believing me."

The boy frowned in confusion.

Bowmark brought the staff around and faced the doorway. *Zip!* He shortened the staff and pointed the weapon. Something was scaring that whiptail into panic. Holding the staffshifter in his right hand, he retrieved his bronze knife with the left. Just in case.

A jaw full of teeth with a fish around it surged through the doorway. *Zip! Zip!* The fish's shattered jaw leaked blood and tumbled in the eddy left by the retreating staffshifter claws.

Another packfish tore past the carcass of the first. *Zip! Zip!* Three more packfish shot into the submerged room. Bowmark zipped the staff three more times, catching the last one less than a hand span from his arm. He needed to breathe. Another one. *Zip!* Miss. *Zip! Zip!* More blood added to the haze.

Bowmark pushed up into the air bubble under the dome. He looked down in time to fend off two more packfish. A cloud of fish clotted the doorway.

Bowmark grabbed a stone carving that capped a pillar. He kicked and pulled and wedged his hands and feet into the lintel, rising into the air, and pressed his back against the rounded ceiling. He panted and his heart thudded. Mere thumb-widths from his feet, packfish swirled, clicking their jaws. On the floor, they darted about the net and bowls.

Fumes and ashes! He might kill a few before they sliced him to shreds. Maybe. The hairy man had not been joking. He licked his lips while he searched his small space for a way to survive. No exit except the two doorways opposite each other and both underwater. No weapons other than what he already had. No shield.

The packfish circled below, checking corners, swimming around leaning lampstands, in and out of the shaft of light. The hole in the roof was completely out of reach.

But Bowmark looked again. A corner of a ceiling tile not far from the corroding, iron rib he clung to was marred by a tiny chip. He shifted to brace foot and knee so he could use his left hand to insert the bronze blade into the chipped hole. His muscles vibrated with cramp and fatigue as he pushed the blade in and pried.

Slowly, a crack widened along the mortar. He pushed in deeper and pried again. The tile broke loose, carrying his hand into the water. He pulled back and grabbed the rotting wooden lath that had backed the tile.

The packfish converged on the falling tile and followed it to the floor. After milling about, they swarmed out by the doorway Bowmark had entered. None came through the door opposite it. He breathed in relief.

On the wharf, Staylik closed his eyes and hugged his son tightly. Broon muttered, "What a waste."

Bowmark sucked in air. He pushed off the ceiling, splashed down into the cold water, grabbed some nested bowls, shoved them in the net sack, and then kicked toward the opposite doorway. He swam into a large columned room with a partially collapsed dome that let in more light and air. He pulled himself up one of the tilted, crumbling columns, burst into the air, grabbed a ledge, pulled up, and sat precariously with his back against a dome rib and his feet just above the snapping fish that had followed him.

A long crack, an eighth of the ledge supporting the dome away from him, was not large enough for him to squeeze through. Serene sky shone blue past the crumbled stone and rusted iron. Water roiled beneath his feet.

After he caught his breath and the black stars had left his vision, he pointed his staffshifter toward the packfish and jabbed again and again randomly. It didn't matter where he aimed. He always hit at least one fish. The water turned darker and darker as blood and the bodies of fish filled the gaps between thrashing, live fish.

This is untenable. The sea thickened and thickened, and now the fish wriggled through the bodies of the living and dying and dead to find an elevated platform from which to flip themselves higher and closer to him. The ocean seemed all triangular teeth and gore and tearing and gnashing; a frenzied, boiling soup of bloodied scales and snapping jaws surging closer as his feet slipped on the scummy column. His staffshifter served only to stir the bloody mess.

Tile dome, stone ledge, iron ribs, crack. The crack. He fingered the staffshifter and considered how easily it could punch into rock. Could he punch through the stone ceiling without being dislodged into the maelstrom beneath him?

He aimed at a spot in the dome a stride above his shoulder. *Zip!* The recoil jarred his arm. He teetered on the edge. His heart wrenched inside his chest as he wedged himself back, his foot nearly slipping into the writhing mess. He deliberately slowed his frantic breathing as he shortened the staffshifter and considered his next move. Panic blinds you. How many times had Father said that?

He looked up. The metal claw-fist had punched through the tile layer of the dome. He inserted his fingers and probed behind the granite tile. Then he pulled, breaking it loose, revealing lath and outer slate shingles. He reached in the hole and found an iron strut he could get his fingers around. Good, a firm hold. For one hand at least. There was no way to break through at this awkward angle. Resolutely he forced his feet off the ledge and hung dangling over the pool of death and his net of treasure pulling down on his waistband. He had to pull his legs up as high as possible to keep his feet out of the water, and still, a flopping fish found purchase on the back of his skirt. The dangling packfish thrashed as though on a fishing hook. With a yell Bowmark thrust the staffshifter up towards the fractured ceiling, pressing the button hard to extend it as fast as it would go. Zip! Crash! The metal snake fist burst through the layers, bringing down stone, rotting wood, and ceramic tile shards all around him.

When he could open his eyes and blink away the dust, he was still hanging by one arm, gripping the outside iron rib. The crack had become a hole large enough to escape through. He retracted the staffshifter and hooked his elbow around the cold metal strut.

With a roar, the inner ceiling caved in. Bowmark nearly followed. Years of agility and obstacle training caused his body to react before he could think. He flipped to the outer rim of the dome and was forced to let go of the staffshifter. *NO!* It slid down the roof and splashed in an adjacent room. Slowly, the dome crumpled, splashing, screeching, the stones cracking against each other, the iron twisting slowly. Bowmark slid down till he could clutch a stone gutter, gasping.

On the wharf, Staylik's son shouted, "Look, Da! The dome fell down!"

Staylik opened his eyes and shrugged. "That's almost the last roof to go. Come on, son. The show's over. Let's go home."

"No. I think I saw him!"

At the castle, Bowmark peered into the formerly domed room. Fish, scraped bloody by the falling tiles, tried to leap out of the water at him. He checked himself: still had the net, still had his knife, still had all his body parts, but blood ran in rivulets from a gash on his hand, and seeped from many scrapes across his chest and shoulders. He examined the gash. Somewhere in that last scramble, a packfish had gotten to him. The wound did not hurt yet, and thanks to Giver who watches fools and children, the gash was not deep. What he thought was a muscle spasm in his thigh turned out to be a particularly tenacious fish, still affixed to the back of his skirt. The fish— taking more work to remove than Bowmark would ever admit— finally succumbed to an awkward knife thrust between his legs. The fish took a chunk of his skirt with it into the depths.

Below, in the next room over, the staffshifter gleamed atop tumbled shingles and sponge-encrusted beams, and, oh ho, several knives, large and small, curved and straight, with gem-studded hilts showing through rotted leather sheaths. No fish except the dead skirt-biter. Only one doorway in the far wall. He dove, snatched the staffshifter, two of the ornate knives, and kicked back to the dome wall. He looked back as he cleared the water. A cloud of fish streamed into the room.

Bowls, knives, he had enough. He had more than enough. If that magician did not drown in the accident that put the staffshifter on Flaming Bird Island, Bowmark hoped he would find him and slit his throat. What kind of man killed and crippled hundreds of people who had done nothing to him or his nation just for money?

A few deep breaths, and he was off, racing along wall-tops as silver flashes in the water kept pace, leaping along logs that tilted and rolled and dipped with nearly every step until his eyes and knees burned with fatigue and sweat replaced all the sea water on him. He flung himself into his canoe.

The fish pummeled the sides as he panted. The thumping was soon replaced by chewing and tearing wood fibers. How long would it take for them to chew through his canoe? A new surge of fight burned through his veins as he seized the paddle and started shoving fish and sea. Too, too slowly he pushed away from the logjam. Too, too slowly he strained toward the bay arm, batting away the leaping fish, paddling with a paddle grown heavy with fish hanging on. The edge grew ragged with bite marks and half-moons of wood torn off.

When he reached the rocks of a bay arm, the paddle was hardly more than handle and wriggling fish. The prow crunched between two boulders. Bowmark vaulted out of the canoe. Fish flung themselves against the rocks.

As he scrambled over the black boulders, the ground vibrated. Rocks shifted as the vibration intensified. The offering platform swayed. Bowmark swung the net bag of treasures onto the wood planks. One leg of the platform collapsed but the treasure stayed in place. Bowmark stumbled back over the shuddering stones and fell into the canoe.

The land groaned and settled. Now that the treasure was no longer moving away from the castle, the fish left his vessel and the spare paddle alone as he headed for the wharf.

Broon cracked a nut. "You sure he's not a magician?"

Staylik's boy Jofar jumped and danced.

Staylik's brows drew together. "You saw him. Did he look withered to you? Did he look like he'd had his life sucked out, chewed up, and spit back in?"

Broon looked at the empty tray. "Don't you know, I ought to get more food."

"Take Jofar with you. Might be best if everybody went somewhere safe while I talk to this whatever-he-is."

"Be careful."

"I always am."

Broon scoffed and herded everyone off the wharf.

A MAGICIAN AND THEIR TOOLS ARE NOT EASILY PARTED.
                                    -IRONIAN SAYING

By the time he reached the wharf, Bowmark was shivering and clumsy, and hollowed out with fatigue that promised to stay for years. The ladder looked harder to climb than a cliff, but Staylik looked down at him; and one must never show weakness before a potential enemy. He climbed the rungs awkwardly with a numb right hand.

Staylik stared. "You should have died," he whispered.

"I nearly did."

His face changed. "You fool! You idiot! You, you, you foolish idiot!"

One corner of Bowmark's lips twitched up, and though he wanted to lift his hands in warding, they refused to move. "You sound much like my father." *And CrunchIt.*

Staylik shouted, "And he was right if he told you that no one should be as stupid as you just were. You think the spell won't notice when you try to take that stuff off the offering platform?"

"Please, Uncle, why would I try to take it? Who needs treasure with a curse like that on it?"

Staylik's gaze shifted from Bowmark's face to the offering platform to the sunken castle and back to Bowmark several times. He scratched his chin. "Bowmark, right? I am listening as hard as I know how to listen. What did you do? Why did you do it?"

Bowmark wanted to lie down. He wanted to lie down while somebody stuffed fruit into his mouth. Hunger pinched his stomach. His right arm ached as though he had pinched a nerve. "I took some of the treasure and put it on the offering platform for the ungols to pick up. Whoever the spell does not kill, your people should be able to destroy."

Staylik's eyes widened and his mouth elongated. He let go of the crutches and wrapped his arms around Bowmark's chest. "My boy!"

Bowmark held still. "Uncle, what are you doing?"

Staylik looked up with a face filled with joy. "I'm hugging you. Your people don't hug?"

"During a wrestling match." The tops of his ears heated. "A man and his wife. Young children and their parents. This hugging is a mark of approval here?"

"Approval? Approval? You just saved the wind knows how many lives. Come, please, let us feed you." He waved at the people bunched near the warehouse. "We need to celebrate!"

Bowmark ambled through a mass of cheering, smiling people. With a relief he did not understand, he noted the women had smooth faces. Someone handed Staylik his crutches and he thumped beside Bowmark onto the main street. The rough-hewn stone road wound up a slope and flattened into a space crowded with two-story houses. The houses had stone roofs and red walls of a substance Bowmark could not identify. He had never seen such tall buildings. Shrieking children danced and darted through the crowd.

They neared a home no grander than the rest, where a black seadog rose from its spot against a wall and growled. The quills along its back rose and its yellow eyes narrowed.

"Down, Guardian!" Staylik said. "Don't you know, this is a friend." He opened the front door, which swung on hinges, like a box lid, and gestured for Bowmark to enter.

Bowmark grabbed the lintel so he would not fall down. "Uncle, I do not wish to dirty your home. Let me wash first."

Staylik squinted. "Uncle? You keep calling me that." Then he called to his son, "Hey, Jofar. Get our guest some water." The boy grabbed two of the wooden buckets by the door as Staylik turned to the growing crowd. "The rest of you, come again for a celebration after our brave guest has eaten and rested. And you, body-patcher, go and get some ointments."

Most of the people moved away as Bowmark bent to pick up the third bucket by the door and then nearly dropped it. Was it made of gold to weigh so much? No, it was made of wood and lined with sap. His throbbing right hand was still weak and tingling. "I'll go with him. I may need a lot of water." Used to multitudes staring at him, he walked without self-consciousness beside Jofar to the community well carved into the cliff face that sheltered the town from northern winds.

Bowmark took note of the stone-paved paths, the tiny windows with . . . fabric? scraped animal skin? . . . stretched over them, lack of verandas on the houses, flower designs of white, yellow, and red around the doors, and...the exceedingly clean smell of the town. What did the people do with their wastes and that of their animals? He could think of no polite way to ask.

Jofar bounced beside him, banging the buckets, asking question after question. "Why do you dress like a girl?"

The women here wore skirts that fell to midcalf and something like a short tunic with narrow sleeves. "Why do your women dress like warriors? Are they stronger than the men?

"Did you see any packfish? Were you scared? You got scars on your arms and leg. Did you get them fighting? Did you ever kill anybody?"

"Truth." Before sudden misery could join his fatigue and shove him into the street where he stood, Bowmark extended his hands and said, "See these scars? I got them when I fell on some coral. Coral is poisonous, and all the cuts grew red and hot. I had to rinse them several times a day with saltier water from the distiller and—"

"What's a distiller?"

How like Sunrise. Bowmark loved the boy.

At his host's house, Staylik and Jaditha, a tall woman with a face strong enough to quell kings, stood and watched their son and Bowmark walk to the well.

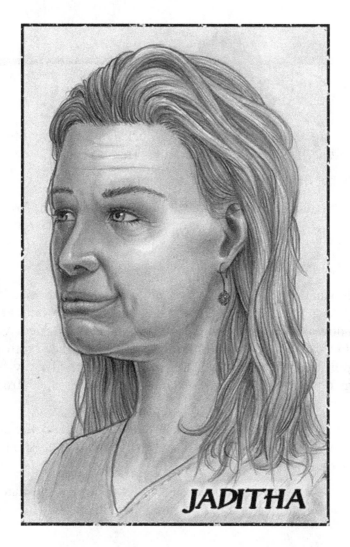

JADITHA

"Don't you know," Jaditha said, "a lot of women are making some unfavorable comparisons with their boyfriends and husbands."

"But not you!" Staylik said. "That boy hasn't a chin hair on him. His pits are bare. I could beat him in ten minutes flat. I could skin him like a pig."

"I know it." Jaditha kissed him on the cheek. "If the weapon of choice were the tongue."

At the well, Bowmark upended a bucket of water over himself. "Woh-ho!" he shouted involuntarily. "That was cold!"

"What did you think the water would be?"

"Not cold." Bowmark rubbed the frizz on his scalp. "We live on volcanoes. Our rocks and the water we store in the rocks are warm."

Jofar squeaked, "You live on a volcano?"

Bowmark rubbed and splashed cold water on skin that wanted a warm blanket. Questions poured over him like a typhoon rain. A movement caught his eye, and he turned. A tiny person dressed all in black and a twin-peaked hat—with odd proportions and a strange swaying gait—scuttled away from them down a dark alley. Someone's toddler escaped from a kitchen? "Who's that?"

Jofar looked at the alley. A few more steps and the short person ducked around the corner of a house. "I don't see anybody."

Bowmark looked askance at the boy. Perhaps he had the close-sight. Or perhaps that was an odd animal.

Staylik supervised the laying of the table as neighbors brought contributions and Jaditha scurried between kitchen and door. Broon quietly stacked wood by the fireplace before nudging Staylik on the way out and saying, "You owe me a clucker dinner."

Jofar bounced in before Bowmark. "Da! Da! His people are so rich they make their *floors* out of glass! And their well water is hot! And he says our girls dress like warriors! And those drawings on his shoulder and forehead don't wash off!"

As Bowmark dried off with a heated, rough towel, he studied the furniture. There were no sitting mats. Platters of food covered a high platform held up by four sticks. Smaller, shorter platforms on three sticks ringed the high platform. If you sat on the bare wooden floor, the small platforms would come up to your chest. Staylik was sitting on one of the short platforms. "Oh!" Bowmark said. "Small thrones. Your people sit on small thrones to show that you rule yourselves?"

Staylik laughed. "You're a lot of fun."

Bowmark untied his skirt and let it drop.

Staylik's eyes widened and his gaze swung to the pantry door where Jaditha was looking for herbs.

Bowmark knotted the towel around himself. He faced east, placed his palms on his chest, and said, "Thank you, Giver of sky and land, for this food and for these friends." He sat, and a fierce hunger drove him to gulping foods with odd textures and tastes. The only thing he rejected after one bite was a bowl of nasty white cubes. Jofar watched in awe as Bowmark ate an entire bowlful of fruit.

Staylik twisted a curl of hair on his chin. "Jofar, go see if the widow Berla can give us more of that. Bowmark, do your people always eat like they're dying of starvation?"

Bowmark paused with a brown, spongy square of something halfway to his mouth. "If I'm rude, I'm sorry. I don't understand how I feel so hungry that the world can't fill me, and so tired when there is much afternoon before the sun sets." He pushed the square into his mouth and picked up a roasted root.

Staylik considered as Jaditha sat beside him. "Did you use that staffshifter?"

"Truth. It saved my life."

"Ah. Where do you think the power of the staff came from?"

"Magic?"

"It came from you."

"I have magic?"

"No. Uh, I don't know. You don't look like it. It's more like the magic used your strength."

Bowmark blinked. Warmth and strength was returning to his right hand. Testing it, he picked up and drained a mug of...something. Then he tried some chunks of gray meat in red gravy using the small ladle they provided. It was edible. It wasn't fish. He helped himself to more, using tiny tridents like the ones his hosts used to spear the meat. The tridents seemed a worthy invention to bring home.

Jofar returned, slamming the door behind him.

Staylik chewed and then cleared his throat. "Are you going to keep that staffshifter even though it sucks your strength?"

"Truth, I am. It's a marvelous weapon. Using any weapon takes strength." He poked at a pile of fried insects. Those could wait for later.

Staylik and his wife glanced at each other. "That's not what I would choose. But since you don't seem to be bothered by magical things, perhaps you would do us the favor of taking ours."

Bowmark rolled a ridged, oblong nut along his fingertips, considering whether or not he wanted any more magical things.

"Da hates it," Jofar said.

Staylik sighed. "You should know Jaditha repaired some of that cursed magician's clothing and ran some errands for him. Instead of *paying* her, he gave her one of his cursed toys, a small ball that glows with a heatless light when you say, "Light, come." Then it sucks the heat out of you while it glows."

Jaditha made a motion like throwing something away. Outside, some musicians began playing a variety of pipes and drums.

Staylik continued, "I threw it into the bay. Next day, there it was on the shore, washed up tangled in seaweed. I went out on the jetty and threw it further out. Next day, I bought a fish from Nelk the fisherman, cut it open to clean for supper, and there was the ball in the stomach of the fish. I think what I heard in Ironia is true: magic things don't mind being sold or gifted, but they cannot abide being lost."

"Coincidence," muttered Jaditha. "Sheer coincidence."

Bowmark thought of howling, dark nights at sea when a lamp could not remain lit. "I could use something like that."

"I thought you'd think so. You're a brave fool."

"Staylik!" Jaditha protested.

Staylik rose and hobbled to a large upright wooden box with hinged doors that swung outward and retrieved a wad of blue cloth. "It's important that I say this proper."

Handing the crumpled package to Bowmark, he spoke solemnly. "I give this gift to you."

Bowmark slowly unwrapped a milky white ball that was uncomfortably close in size to a man's eyeball. He held it gingerly. Staylik plopped onto his small throne and prompted him. "Now you say you accept it."

"I accept it. Thank you." Bowmark examined the sphere. "So I just say, light come?" Everyone at the table recoiled slightly as the ball illuminated the room with a pure white light like starlight. A slow coldness creeped down Bowmark's fingers. "And, ah. How . . . how does one make it stop?"

Staylik reddened. "Ha, dropping it works for me."

Bowmark gently placed it on the table and the light winked out. He wrapped it in the cloth reverently, then flexed warmth back into his fingers. "Wonderful. But I worry at taking more from a people so destitute and endangered. Do you think the ungols that are destroyed by the magic curse will have allies who will seek revenge? Have I thrown trash in the receding tide only to have it come back tomorrow?"

Staylik pondered. "Well, from what we can tell, the ungol are a fractious people. They divide into small tribes and war amongst themselves constantly. My guess is that the tribe that's been threatening us will not be missed. Worst case is another tribe finds us. But then we'd be no worse off than before. No sir. You have done us a great good. And taking that tricky trinket is yet another favor."

Jaditha leaned forward. "Enough of such talk. Bowmark. If I don't find out, the women of this town will never forgive me. Do you have a wife or betrothed?"

"No." He shoved another spongy square into his mouth and tried hopelessly not to think of MoonGleam. He had enjoyed their easy camaraderie. Her frankness sometimes left him speechless. In the palace, tens of noble and royal girls had paid lavish attention to him. No, not to him, to his *position*. What any of them really thought of him was not something he was allowed to hear.

That led to another unfortunate thought. How could a man not think of women, constantly, in great and fantastic detail? His mind paced, trapped in a cramped four-compartment cage. He could think about Sunrise and relive another thousand times the moment the spear entered his chest. He could think about his father and brother with knives pressing their necks and his own vein indenting on a sharp blade with each pulse. He could think about MoonGleam and her accusations. He could think helplessly about women, any woman, parts of women. His brain was weary and desperately needed another subject.

"I'm sorry," Jaditha said. "I did not mean to make you so sad."

"Oh. No. I'm tired. That's all. Uncle Staylik, would it be rude to ask what your crime was?"

Staylik laughed and slapped the table. "Ha! You caught that, did you? Ha! After what you have done for us, you can ask me anything. It would not go well for you to broach that subject with other people here, but I'm happy to tell you. My crime was sheer, knuckle-headed stupidity."

Bowmark licked some gravy from his thumb. "I had not known that was a crime. The Ironians are a stern people."

Staylik chuckled. "I thought I would better my life, marry a high-placed woman, get rich, the usual ambitions. I had a small shop that sold fabrics. I planned to add a tailor shop so I could make clothes for the nobility. So I backed a certain nobleman in his attempt to replace the king with himself. I was counting on his gratitude. He might have been a grateful man, don't you know, but he lost his head and I lost my shop and freedom."

Jofar interrupted, "Why do you keep calling my da 'Uncle'?"

"It is what our people call a wise man whose advice we should heed."

Jaditha covered her mouth and laughed.

Staylik cocked one eyebrow. "When did you heed me?"

"From this moment on. I have heard much valuable advice from you. For example, I must stay away from magicians. And I must not do anything you have done."

Staylik and Jaditha laughed until their eyes leaked tears.

Feeling relieved that he had judged this family correctly and could tease them, he continued to eat. Suddenly, his eyes closed. Only great effort could open them.

Jaditha took his arm and led him to a small, stuffy bedroom with a thick mat on an elevated platform. He had time only to fuzzily wonder why all the furniture stood on sticks before he fell asleep.

When he awoke, afternoon sunlight slanted in through the small windows. He had slept the afternoon, night, and morning away. Hunger and renewed energy let him spend the evening eating and watching the people of Rolocton dance. The dances involved a lot of hopping around each other in intricate patterns. He worked hard to avoid laughing at their choppy motions.

"May I see your flute?" he asked one of the musicians, a man with curly, black hair all over his lower face and neck. When the man handed it over, Bowmark studied the silver instrument. He had not seen silver since the day all the silver had been given to the shlak. The holes were spaced a little differently from his bamboo flute. A tentative blow proved the sounds to be a little different as well.

A thought made him stop. The Southils owned thousands of flutes made from the bones of Sea Predators. His ultimate purpose in life was to protect his people from the enemy who wanted more of their bones. And now he needed to protect them from RaiseHim as well. And the shlaks. How could one man, especially that one man being him, do this?

Jaditha interrupted his thinking with the request, "Play something for us."

Ah, he had learned to play the flute only because Mother had wanted him to. Sadly, he'd never gotten good at it. Still, if he played something they didn't know, perhaps they would not notice the missed notes. Bowmark played the happiest song he could think of.

When he had finished and lowered the flute, Jofar asked, "Was that music?"

At least one of them noticed.

Jaditha said, "That sounded like bird twittering."

Ah. *Beauty of the Morning* was based on the song of the blue-eyed longtail but was a great deal more than that. Bowmark thought. These people needed—he needed—simpler music, like what the musicians had been playing for the dances. He raised the flute and played the children's song *Come Walk with Me*. The drummers joined in and soon people were dancing again, more to the beat of the drums than to his sour notes.

The musician looked relieved when the song ended and Bowmark handed the flute back to him.

Another night of sleeping on a moss-filled mat, was followed by a breakfast of more spongy slices topped with amber syrup while a variety of girls came in offering more food. In late morning, Bowmark walked onto the wharf with Staylik and Jofar, watched by a crowd staying back a respectful distance.

"Don't you know," Staylik said, "I'm sorry I can't talk you into staying longer."

"I have an obligation."

Jofar grabbed Bowmark's hand and skipped beside him.

"I wish there was more we could do for you," Staylik said as he maneuvered around a rotten board.

"Uncle, there are two things you can do for me."

"Anything."

His father would have called that a fool's response. "The first thing I want is a treaty of peace between my people and Rolocton."

Staylik stopped and squinted at the bright sun. A brisk breeze played with his beard and diluted the stench of rotting fish floating in the harbor. "I don't know what you are to your people, but me, I'm just a maimed man whose job is to watch the harbor. We don't have a governor or mayor or anybody like that to make such a treaty. I can tell you that any of your people are welcome here." He repositioned the crutches. "If, say, your people attacked Ironia, we would be on Ironia's side. They haven't come by to tax us for a number of years, and we haven't reminded them we're here. But we still belong to Ironia."

"We have no desire to attack you or Ironia. We simply want to know that there are people in the world who don't want to slaughter us."

"Rough neighborhood, eh? I can safely tell you this: if you don't bother Ironia, Ironia won't bother you. What's the second thing?"

"I need a treasure to take home as proof that I was here."

Staylik grimaced. "If we had any, it would be yours."

"You do. Would you give me the carved box in your bag?"

Staylik drew out the small box. "This? It's nothing. And there's nothing inside it."

Bowmark took the box and ran his finger over the design of a radiant sun on the lid. "You err. This carries your friendship. What is more precious?"

Staylik hugged Bowmark and patted him on the back while Jofar rescued the crutches Staylik let fall. "If ever you can visit us again, please, please do. I want to see what you look like when you've finished growing."

"Peace for you and your land." Bowmark laid his hand of blessing upon Staylik's bald head. He climbed down into the canoe, stowed the box and a bag of strange dried fruit and bread, and took up the new paddle—carved with unfamiliar flowers and vines—that the people had given him. If all the humans on this side of the world were as friendly as these people, perhaps he would survive this journey. With a lighter heart, he pushed away from the wharf.

The euphoria lasted until the horizon had risen to cover the island. Bowmark turned the box in his hands. He would bring this back to StoneGrove and present the wooden container to the protocol officer who might or might not agree that this counted as a treasure. Could he count on the protocol officer to keep RaiseHim from murdering him before he could get him on the Disc? No matter how many times he ran the scenario in his mind he came back to the same conclusion. As drastic and unlikely as it may be, the best chance to save his family and people was to fulfill the terms he had agreed upon.

What would RaiseHim do to destroy Bowmark? He might wait for the proving, but he might simplify events by accusing

Bowmark of treason. That might or might not work to get Bowmark bound in a cage and thrown on flowing lava. Probably the protocol officer would fight that because if Bowmark were guilty, then so was the officer.

Somehow Bowmark would need to reach the palace without being stopped and then present the treasures while at the same time challenging RaiseHim before the pig's anus had a chance to plot.

Bowmark's fingers traced over the chip pattern. Truth, if he moved quickly enough, he could likely avoid the cage, but he would likely still end up in the lava. He needed to get stronger, learn how to fight a man with weapons while he had none.

How?

The wind shifted direction and Bowmark adjusted the sail. Mom often told him to not borrow trouble from tomorrow. Truth, he needed to think about today's task: obtain treasures and seek news of the Southils. He dismissed the urge to worry and the desire for a warm monkey snuggling on his neck as he put the box in a strong sack.

One thing at a time. Right now the thing was sailing.

DISCORIA

MEMORIES ARE FOUND MOST QUICKLY THROUGH THE NOSE.
-SEA PREDATOR ADAGE

Bowmark sat in his canoe, miserably bailing as a cold rain poured over him and roughened the sea. Ahead, a plethora of lights above a dark shore indicated windows, hundreds of them in mounded patterns, shining obscurely in the black night. The Atlas had not told him that Ironia's seas and rain were so cold. The chill seeped through his cape, hat, and sodden skirt. Closer lights, swinging in blurred arcs, indicated but could not illuminate narrow docks and a flotilla of massive, curved ships.

He had been foolish to reject the Roloctoners' offers of coats and shirts. Then, he had thought only of how little the canoe could carry. Now, the utility of such clothes became apparent. Frigid rain dripped off his hat and plopped onto his lap and bare forearms. Why would anybody live in such a cold place?

The Atlas said that the Ironians were used to seeing all kind of humans and other peoples, so even if he did show up in the dark, his offer of a pearl for a hot meal and a night's rest should not startle anyone. He reviewed the comments in the Atlas about the Ironians: "*They are a proud people, quick to perceive insult, and unwilling to hear if another nation has grandeur. It is always safe to admire any facet of Ironia. Among the things that cause offense: pointing to any person, touching one's nose while talking to someone, sniffing behind someone, appearing stingy. The docks of Discoria, the capital, are uncommonly safe and theft-free. This is not true once one has left the docks."*

The wind changed direction every few seconds, so he had to paddle in. That served to warm him a tiny amount. He collided with an unlighted ship, but his speed was so slow that it did no harm. His canoe dragged so badly that he might need to find another. If only he had thought to check and repair his canoe before leaving Rolocton.

With all these ships, including the one he just hit, there must be a pier somewhere. He slid along the hull and found a kelp-and-barnacle-coated piling. Bowmark moored, and then groped for a ladder. Roaring rain hammered the pier and filled his eyes, so he could discern nothing in the darkness. He reached up higher on the pier, and there was the edge of the dock well over his head. He gripped the edge and leaped onto the wood, landing on his side.

Wiping his eyes, he sat up. If he followed the lights slowly, he might not fall into the sea or trip over someone's goods.

Before he could stand, a point pressed into his back. Under the rain and wind and sea slapping the ships, an old man's voice quavered, "What might your plans be, what?"

"I have come to trade." Rain pelted Bowmark's legs as he waited. The point did not leave its place between his shoulder blades as rain trickled down his hat and cloak. Wind tugged at reefed sails and ropes. Somewhere, a chain clanked erratically. Bowmark still could not see anything on the dock. He made sure to make no threatening moves as he drew his legs under himself slowly so he could spring away if need be. Why didn't the guard say something?

Then he did. "Zzz. Sunfolks have never before come here to trade directly. Why have you bypassed the seafolks, why?"

What people did the guard think he belonged to? He wiped rain from his eyes. "I have seen everything on my island. I wanted to see more of the world."

The point withdrew. "Zzz, zzz, zzz. We may have much in common. I, too, wish to travel. Zzz. With your tiny vessel, the only cargo worth carrying must be gems."

Bowmark rose, but the guard's voice did not. Bowmark's cape flapped about his knees. "Master," he shouted into the spray, figuring that it was better to overestimate a man's rank than to underestimate and give offense. "Am I allowed to enter Discoria?"

The voice quavered from below. "Yes, quite yes. Would you care for advice about the inns, would you?"

Bowmark shivered. Would it give offense and make an enemy if he left for warmth right now? "Please, pardon me, Master. I don't know what the word 'inn' means."

"Zzt! It is the Common word for public businesses you go to for food or for a bed to sleep in."

Bowmark sneezed. *Please, Giver, let that not be an insult!* There were businesses that provided for strangers? He had planned to knock on doors until he found a family willing to take him in. Then he thought of the multiple tens of ships' lights he had seen; trading ships, not local fishing boats. Inns made sense. The Atlas had not mentioned them, or the ungols. Ah, the Atlas would not remark on what everybody knew. His ignorance could kill him. "I will be grateful for anything you can tell me."

"The cleanest and best priced inn is the Orange Crab. Go up the nearest street to the Sailor's Plaza. At the plaza, you turn right and go to the seventh building on the left.

"Thank you! May the sun rise on your happiness." Bowmark peered through the rain and dark. Street was another word for lane or path, if he remembered correctly. He took one step toward a tiny, blurry light, did not fall off the dock, took another step, and still did not fall off. With a bit more confidence, he kept heading for the tiny light.

Even moving slowly, he stubbed his toes on boxes and barrels and piles of odorous rope. When he reached the end of the dock and the pole holding up a swaying lantern, Bowmark turned to see what manner of guard he had been conversing with. But everything was obscured by the sheeting night.

Stupid. There was a joke about looking for a lost knife under a lamp far from where it had been lost, because the light was better there. His teeth clicked together as his shivering increased.

He found the road going uphill and shortly stepped into a flat space bounded by tall buildings, some with light streaming through tiny glass windows. Every bit of ground was covered with building or streets of patterned stone. Not a single house rose on stilts to offer shelter to a traveler.

A statue of a ruthless whale with arms reaching for a boat occupied the middle of the space. Perhaps this was a plaza? He turned, and there on the right was a street with enough light to keep him from running into something. Water raced by in stone gutters and rain rattled against the windows.

The seventh building on the left held a large front door, hinged, bright green with an orange crab painted in the middle. This amused Bowmark. Ironians gave names to buildings as if they, too, were people or canoes.

A sudden gust caught his cape and tried to strangle him. "Safety to you!" he shouted at the door. "I am Bowmark, and seeking shelter!"

The door stayed closed. Muffled voices inside continued conversation.

He pulled the cape into place. "I am Bowmark. Please let me in!"

As sheets of water gurgled by his feet and rain tapped his hat and shoulders, Bowmark waited, his body cold but his face heating up. As a king's son, he had never needed to beg. He resisted the urge to use his staffshifter to break down the door.

A man wrapped in dark red garments brushed past him to open the door and enter without a single word of greeting.

Bowmark followed him into a dim, low-ceilinged room thick with the smells of sweat, ferment, and wet clothing. People, mostly men, clustered at round tables, many wearing something red. A skin of mud coated the wooden floor, and a layer of smoke hovered under the beam-and-board ceiling. A dried mud and stone fireplace dominated one wall. There, a young man turned a boar haunch over a fire.

As he studied the room and its people, every man glanced at him before returning to business. The women, though, their gazes lingered on him, tracing him from head to foot. Their calculating looks puzzled him. Since they could not know he was a royal, what did they have to calculate?

A passing boy, carrying a tray of filled mugs, pointed with his chin and said, "Sir, yonder is a chair for you."

"Thank you." Bowmark slid his hat to his back. He sidled carefully through the crowd to a table ringed with men wearing ragged clothing with a purple patch on each shoulder. They ignored him as they continued to play with small blocks of wood on a checked red and black cloth. Their yellow hair looped about their heads in complicated braids.

The young man poked at the roasting boar with a large fork and knife. A slice slithered off and fell into the fire.

A man in a blue shirt shouted, "It's done! Let's eat!"

Black smoke billowed up the chimney and then billowed back in.

"Hey!" a man at his table shouted. "I would have stayed on the ship if I wanted to breathe smoke!"

"Don't you know, this fitful wind keeps pushing it back," the young man said.

Several men hooted. One shouted, "Barkeep! Why don't you hire someone who knows what he's doing, instead of country rubes like him?"

The young man tore off his apron, wadded it, and dashed it to the floor.

The smoke of the burning boar reached Bowmark. The stench and taste of Sunrise burning on the lava coated his nostrils and mouth.

Bowmark surged out of his chair, knocked over sailors as he scrambled around the table, and ran, swerving around people and accidentally upending a tray of soup. People shouted angrily. He crashed through the door.

He staggered in the dark against a wall, shivering, the rain sluicing off his back before he realized he had fled the inn. That smell. Sunrise falling into the lava! His throat spasmed as he slid to his knees. *Sunrise, my brother!* Hot misery pricked his eyes.

He pulled the heavy, wet cape around him as he stared up into the black night. It wasn't right he was here instead of Sunrise. What was he doing here? Bowmark didn't know how to enter an inn or ask for supper or pay for anything. His throat hurt.

Bowmark pushed himself back up and crossed the street to a yellow door with two black mugs painted on it. He opened the door as he had seen the stranger dressed in red do, and entered a room crowded with tables holding empty bowls, and several men wearing green patches on their shoulders climbing stairs at the back of the room. A few people with red beads clipped to their hair sat and talked quietly. At the fireplace, fragrant steam escaped from a black cauldron.

An elderly woman with white hair frizzing out from under a red cap limped up to Bowmark. "Sir, may I hang your wet cloak by the fire?" When he untied and handed the cape to her, she said, "Oh, my," and hurried to the fire, where she hung the cloak from a peg on the beam in front of the fire by black cloaks and red coats.

Bowmark sat at an empty table near the fire and shivered. Everyone took a careful glance at him, and some more than a glance. At an adjoining table, a rumsha, wearing a patchwork tunic and a purple tri-peaked hat, hummed. His thick neck and head projected forward from muscular shoulders instead of above. Bells hung from his long whiskers and upright ears. The animal—no, *person*—with bells, eyed him with apparent amusement before saying, "Your race must be a sturdy one." He tugged on his green and orange jacket with three clawed fingers.

Bowmark studied the non-human person. The Atlas had described rumshae as a jovial people who traded fairly. The only complaint listed was that they would not make promises for future trade or even make dates for delivery. The seafolks would set dates to meet, show up, and wait to see if rumshae showed up or not. If the rumshae did not, there was havoc played on the seafolks' tight schedules.

Beady eyes in a snouted face crinkled. "Here at the docks, you can run around naked, but in town you might want to wear more." He laughed, a bubbly sound like water over rocks. "Or not. Depends." He laughed again causing his whiskers to vibrate and the bells on his drooping moustache to chime. "You certainly catch the ladies' eyes."

RUMSHA
MERCHANT

Bowmark opened his mouth to say, "I'm not naked," but
thought better of it. His father had a phrase that brushed off
people politely, so Bowmark said instead, "I will consider it." He
continued to study the first rumsha he had ever seen. The Atlas
had also described them as a peaceful people. They could afford
to be, for who would attack anybody who had clawed hands like
that? One swipe could disembowel a human.

The old woman hobbled over. "Does Sir want a meal?"

"Yes, if it is hot. And I would like a place to sleep."

"And what will Sir use for payment?"

Bowmark squeezed out an oval silver pearl from his belt pouch and laid the small gem on the table. With a wrinkled smile, she picked it up and shortly brought a large bowl of soup and a small loaf of bread.

"My good Madam, you forgot to bring his change," the rumsha boomed. He rubbed under his chin and grinned, revealing teeth and lips much like a rabbit's except for their black color and four short fangs. His long mouth whisker bells made subdued tinkling sounds.

The woman glared at the rumsha. "We don't know how long he's staying, do we?"

"We do not." He continued grinning until the frowning woman placed several octagonal coins on the table. After she left, he leaned over and said, "You have paid enough for one night and two meals."

The rumsha winked at him before striding upstairs. When he walked, he lowered his chest and head, making his eyes level with his massive hips. His thick hands nearly brushed the floor, and a blunt tail projected straight behind him. In that position, he stood half Bowmark's height. He needed to stretch upright to be as tall as Bowmark's nose.

Bowmark ate in silence while he watched three more rumshae whispering together while motioning with their fingers. They looked exactly like the drawing in the Atlas. Sunrise would have given everything to see them. He *had* given everything. And achieved nothing he wanted. Bowmark's eyes grew hot again.

Cold still pained his bones when the lady came back apologetically explaining that since he had come so late, there were no beds left, would Sir mind a mat in front of the fire? Nothing more attractive existed at that moment.

Sometime that night, he awoke and listened intently, not knowing what had awakened him. Cold, damp darkness pressed against his eyes. A faint sound, the gentlest of footsteps, passed across the common room. He peered into the dark until he could see by ember glow the vague shapes of a few tiny people scuttling with an odd, bobbing gait from a tiny portal near the door toward the kitchens. Thieves? They were not furtive, merely difficult to see as they hastened under a table that was taller than them and around the chairs without a misstep. Once they were gone, he closed his eyes and noticed nothing until a boy needed him to move so a new fire could be laid.

After a breakfast of eggs and bread, he jogged through a thick fog to his canoe. A guard with a knife and hooked staff watched him trot onto the deck and jump off the end.

The canoe bobbed under his weight. He sorted through his belongings. Everything was still there. He stopped in mid-step. A wrinkled, black bundle large enough to hold a toddler lay in the back of the canoe. Snags and bumps covered the surface.

Around him, sails were hoisted, and men shouted greetings and orders to each other. Gangplanks thudded onto the dock, and men carried boxes to a wagon pulled by a twelve-legged, low-slung creature with stiff horns radiating from the back of its skull. A driver held reins tied to two of the horns, and three passengers sat on saddles behind him.

Bowmark watched the mysterious bundle in his canoe as fog condensed on his eyelashes. Who had put that black bag there, and why? He crept closer. A faint buzzing and the smell of ginger rose from the bag. Bowmark reached forward and touched the bundle.

A petulant old man's voice wavered from the bag. "Tonight. Wait until night to talk." The bundle shifted a bit. The voice sounded like the guard from last night. Did each ship get its own personal guard? Tiny personal guard? Was this the variant of human called a littlefolk? Was Bowmark supposed to pay him? He looked out at gray water and ghostly ships obscured by fog. Every clank of a chain, every scrape of a rope, every word of the men on the docks sounded as clear as though he stood next to them.

He touched the bundle again. "Master, I need more advice. How do I buy pants and shirts and," he sifted through the new words he had learned in Rolocton, "boots?"

"Zzz. The Sailor's Cobbler. The Quick Needle. Go away."

Bowmark blinked. The bundle resumed the buzz. With a sigh, he sat back and mulled over plans of action as he fingered the edge of his skirt, feeling the pearls and diamonds sewed into the hem. His thoughts were punctuated by the deep tolling of a huge bell on a buoy out in the bay. Shivering, he pulled himself up onto the dock and watched crates being unloaded from one ship, and chests being loaded into another. Each ship's sailors wore distinctive patches of color on their shoulders.

What was the polite thing to do here? What was the thing that would get him into trouble? Ah, he'd forgotten that his canoe needed repairing. He called down. "Master, I'm sorry, but you will need to leave my canoe for a few candles. I'm going to dismantle the outrigger and mast, and then drag the canoe ashore."

The bundle stopped buzzing but did not move.

"The canoe drags. I must repair it."

The bundle moved slowly. "If you must."

"I must."

The bundle unrolled to reveal not a bag or blanket but a wrinkled, spiky creature with huge two-part ears that unfurled into a butterfly shape. Circles of metal pierced with tiny holes covered its eyes. Though upright, its clawed fingers touched the thwart it stood on.

Giver! Bowmark stepped back as his breath jerked. A kratchnak!

NO MAN WHO WANTS POWER DESERVES IT.
-SEA PREDATOR COMMONER SAYING

Bowmark had stopped believing in kratchnaks by the age of nine. Before then, he had spent many night candles shivering in his hammock awaiting the coming of the giant bug that ate bad boys.

He took another step back. No. This short monster had not eaten or harmed him yet. His breath still juddered. "I—" The Atlas had not mentioned kratchnaks. Bowmark could not tear his gaze away. Slits in a double row ran up the face instead of a protruding nose. A belly that overhung legs so short that only the clawed toes could be seen. The monster yawned, exposing teeth as sharp as sharks'.

AN UNINVITED GUEST

Bowmark clenched his fist over his heart as reason berated him for his little-boy terror. He was easily two and a half times taller than this creature. This naked monster had no weapons save his teeth and claws. Bowmark had knives aplenty. And— And—

He blinked. Why would a monster that ate bad boys at night be guarding his canoe? What—? Thought stalled as he stared at the grotesque creature that had featured in many of his nightmares.

The creature said in his mosquito-whine voice, "You should have told me that first. Two docks over is a boat ramp with a boatyard on the west. Take me there before you dismantle your canoe." It started to curl up, stopped, and straightened up. "Do not tell anyone we have spoken." Then it folded and stretched its skin into the black bundle shape.

Take that thing to a boat ramp. Get in the canoe and paddle while sitting an arm-length away from it. Follow the directions of a... ... a what? Bowmark pivoted and walked back to the lantern post and the guard leaning against it and idly sliding her sword in and out of its sheath.

She looked up at him and raised her eyebrows. "Can I help you?"

"What do you call that kind of person?" Bowmark pointed with his chin at his canoe at the far end of the dock.

She craned her neck. "I don't see anybody."

Static electricity crawled up his back. Was he the only one that could see that? The night creatures at the inn. The little person Jofar could not see. Were these things invisible to everybody but him? If so, what did that mean?

The guard said, "You and those sailors were the only people who passed me this morning. What do you call that skinny boat of yours? And what are the sticks on the side for?"

The floaty feeling of unreality dissipated a bit as Bowmark replied. "That skinny boat is properly called a canoe. The sticks make an outrigger. That is my outrigger canoe." *With an invisible monster in it.*

"Could you say that again? Your accent is difficult to understand."

He repeated his explanation.

"Canoe. Canoe." She altered his pronunciation of canoe and then her face brightened. "I've heard of them. Canoes are what sunfolks use." She ran her gaze up his body. "That's the first canoe and you're the first sunfolk I've seen personally. Are all sunfolks as tall as you?"

"Ah... ... no. Ah... ... I need to repair my canoe. Where may I do that?"

She gave him the same directions the kratchnak had.

He returned to the end of the dock and climbed down the ladder he could now see in the daylight. He settled on the thwart like he was sitting on thistles. He picked up his paddle and studied the silent figure on the prow thwart. *I'm going to say something stupid. Something mountain-sized stupid.* He cleared his throat. "Are you... ... planning to eat me?"

The kratchnak made a slight motion. "Eat you? Raw? How disgusting. Stop talking."

"Please, only one more question."

The kratchnak wheezed.

Bowmark took that for assent. "What are your people called?"

"We are The People. Other species call us tezledek. Now go away and tell no one we spoke."

He couldn't go away until his canoe was repaired. Who would believe that he talked to invisible monsters? Bowmark pressed his paddle against the piling to begin his short trip to the boat ramp on the west side of Dock 3.

A man came out, crossed his muscular arms, resting them on the top of a piling, and watched Bowmark tug his canoe partly out of water and dismantle the outrigger. He paid no attention to the tezledek climbing out of the canoe and waddling to a hole in the bank under Dock 3, nor did he watch the throngs of people, animals, and wagons passing on the promenade behind him. He did wordlessly bring out a huge basket for Bowmark to put his belongings in and plopped it down next to barrels of large iron pins, strips of copper, and a covered metal container sitting over a flame.

Bowmark flipped over his canoe. The man whistled, walked over, and ran his hands over the divots the packfish had gouged out of the canoe wood. "How did this happen? How did you survive if your canoe was dancing on the rocks?"

"Some magic fish wanted to eat me."

"Tah! Don't tell me then. I don't care." He scratched the stubble on his chin as he poked into the gouges. "The wood is thick enough that I can plane down the rough edges. And I can fill in the holes with tar."

"What is tar?"

The man lifted the lid on the metal container and lifted a ladle filled with a black substance that oozed slowly. Its evil odor overwhelmed all the smells of sea, algae, and cargoes of spice. Bowmark pinched his nose. Volcanoes smelled bad but this was worse. "What good is putting something drippy in the holes?"

"The tar solidifies when it gets cold."

So did lava. So then, perhaps that would work. They talked price and then Bowmark left to find the stores that the kratchnak, the tezledek, had told him about.

After visiting the shops, he needed to wait for his boots and clothes to be made.

Bowmark drifted into an inn through a black door with three red squares painted on the door's center. The large fire in the dining room was for heat only, so there would be no smoke of burning boar to chase him out. He ordered bread, honey, fruit, and ramchew-leaf tea, and then placed coins one by one on the table until the server reached for the money.

Few sailors and many merchants sat about the wooden tables. Why had he not yet seen one of the gray-skinned seafolks? A sailor with an orange patch stepped by his table to say, "If you be looking for work, the Wind Rise could use a husky lad as yourself."

"I'll consider that," Bowmark said. A safe, all-purpose reply.

Five men with blond hair entered. They wore brocaded vests over silk shirts, fur cloaks, and intricately folded caps with tassels, trim, and dangling gold-chain loops. Instead of the common pair of red beads clipped to the hair, they each wore a long blue bead.

The only table left with open seats was Bowmark's. They sauntered over and motioned with their eyes that he should leave.

He had only begun his meal and declined to move.

One reddened slightly, but, tightlipped, they sat and turned away from Bowmark. One sniffed.

They had to be minor nobles with no retinue and plenty of arrogance. As he ate, he watched them while they rolled twelve-sided dice and laughed about what somebody had said at some party. Every so often, someone would enter the inn and sidle up to one of the men, slip him some money, and the man would give the someone a small packet that was instantly hidden away.

Ah, this larger land of Ironia was surely separate enough a nation from Rolocton that he could obtain his second treasure here. "Masters, give me pardon."

Four of them rolled their eyes. One said, "Jeeto, give me permission to roust this barbarian."

Jeeto turned and studied Bowmark. He had a squeezed nose, a thin mustache with ends that hung below his jaw, and rings on every finger. When the others saw he was paying attention to the large islander, they turned their heads and studied him also. Jeeto smirked. "Are you asking pardon for appearing in public naked?"

Bowmark chose not to say one more time, "I *am* dressed," but did say, "Master, I am newly come to this country and hope that you might enlighten me. Sir, what is considered most valuable in Ironia, and where may one obtain such treasure?"

The men sat back and sniffed. Jeeto shifted his chair around, tugged at his mustache, and narrowed his eyes in calculation. "All here agree that the most valuable things are the Ground Jewels of Old Terla. Why do you want them?"

JEETO

"A life mission is laid upon me. I doubt that I would need all of them. How are they purchased?"

The men glanced at each other, amusement dancing in their eyes.

Jeeto placed one fingertip on the table and thought with pursed lips. He did not move, even when the server set a mug of something spoiled beside him. His followers sipped cautiously as their gazes flicked between him and Bowmark. Finally, he leaned forward. "What ship are you working for?"

"I came in my own ship, the *Sails Far.*"

"How many men have you?"

"I came by myself."

The man leaned back and thought some more.

Bowmark finished his lump of spongy substance the Roloctoners called bread, and most of the tea.

After one more glance at his companions, Jeeto leaned forward again. "How are you with a knife?"

Bowmark pulled out his obsidian knife, stood, picked up the table knife and juggled them. He added the spoon, caught a knife behind his back, changed the pattern, and then the bronze knife that he had surreptitiously palmed plunged into the table exactly at the tip of the leader's fingers.

Jeeto pulled back with an oath. The followers sprang up reaching for their daggers, but the leader waved them down and Bowmark continued to juggle.

Jeeto frowned and cleared his throat. "Maybe you're good enough."

Bowmark caught the utensils and sat. "I would hope that three to six candles of dexterity and weapons' practice a day had some usefulness." He spoke calmly, hoping that formal, polite speech would garner him favor.

"Candle?"

How did these people measure time? "The length of time it takes for a particular kind of candle to burn from tip to end."

"Would you be interested in doing a task for me?"

Bowmark considered. "Only if it will help me purchase a Ground Jewel. I do not plan to stay here long."

Jeeto's voice dropped. "They cannot be purchased. Once, they belonged to my family. Then that evil," he made a motion of throwing something away, "Pounter stole them from us. If you could retrieve them, I would let you choose the best jewel for yourself."

Bowmark studied his side bowl of sweet-smelling, round, fuzzy fruit. How did people eat these? "Where does Pounter have them?"

"Somewhere in his mess of Castle Pile. It has been added to for hundreds of years. Lots of things are lost or hidden in unused rooms. But I have found out where the Jewels are hidden. I haven't been able to use the information before."

Bowmark listened some more and agreed to meet again at the inn the next day with an answer.

At the Quick Needle, he picked up two shirts: a dark red shirt with armhole vents, sleeves that ended mid-forearm, and bone buttons down the front; and a felt-lined dark blue pullover cloak with longer sleeves and a hood. The black pants baffled him at first. You pulled on the legs and were left with a gap in front and two dangling wings of fabric with pockets that had straps at their tips. The soft-spoken tailor demonstrated how the wings crossed in front and the straps wrapped around the waist through loops to meet and button in the front as a belt. He would need to transfer all the jewels and knives from their hidden sheaths on his skirt. But he kept his old boarskin belt with its built-in sacks and loops. Wrapping it over his new pants worked. The cloth pants and shirts were scratchy, but warm.

At the Sailor's Cobbler, he picked up flexible boots with multiple holes in the sides ("To let out the sea you will get in your shoes, don't you know,") and solid, thicker boots with hidden sheaths for knives. He hobbled his first couple of steps as his feet became accustomed to the stiff wrapping. As cocooned as any pupa, he strode about the shop.

The artisan who fitted his boots noticed the staffshifter sticking out of Bowmark's jacket pocket and quickly averted his eyes.

Bowmark's weapon brought him far too much attention. He asked the artisan if he could create a sheath for the weapon and the man quickly nodded, saying he could produce the accessory before the afternoon was over.

With his skirt tucked under an arm, Bowmark spent the rest of the day wandering about Discoria, the capital of Ironia, looking into small shops that sold candles and soap, vegetable markets with produce he could not recognize, and a number of temples dedicated to odd gods. At each one, he asked the priests to let him see their Protocol. This puzzled all of them. The books they brought him said nothing about how a king was chosen in Ironia.

Most of the buildings were of clay brick or stone and two or three stories tall. Wouldn't all the people be crushed when an earthquake hit? Why did they build like this?

In the narrow alleys and streets, the people bumped into each other without remark. Most looked twice at him when their eyes slid past, but no one bothered him. Most of the wealthier-looking people wore two red beads in their hair. Would it be rude or dangerous to ask about the beads? Should he wear some? Of course not. He often forgot his royal dreadlocks were gone. His hair was growing back shamefully slow.

Everywhere he wandered, he marveled at how clean the city smelled. Had the city no cesspools, pits, latrines, or middens? Privies they had, and even those smelled clean. Whatever they did, he wanted to know. The shlaks might appreciate such knowledge.

Discordia's people were no neater than his. In fact, many of them were slovenly, openly dumping food scraps into the street gutters. Wandering pigs with blunted spikes and seadogs with shaved quills took care of the scraps, but who took care of what the animals left behind?

And then something that looked much like a seadog but covered with curly hair dashed by barking like a seal. What was that? No one else but he paid attention to the creature.

A crowd of gray-skinned seafolks crossed an intersection. Bowmark stared at them and their colorful skirts and tunics. Father claimed the seafolks were a human variant. How could that be true? They had webbed hands and feet, and nose slits on their foreheads.

Eventually he made his way back to the Sailor's Cobbler and was pleased the artisan had produced an exquisitely fashioned sheath from fine leather, tooled with intricate patterns. Bowmark's brow creased. How much was the man going to charge him? However, the artisan would not take payment.

"Please remember my service in the future," the shopkeeper said in a hushed voice as he stared at his feet and held the sheath out.

Bowmark's tongue jammed on the explanation that he was not a magician. He pulled his hand back from bestowing the king's blessing. "Thank you." He hurried out of the shop.

On the way back to the dock he came into a square crowded with people and a raised platform. A line of ragged and hopeless-looking people stood roped together with bindings on their wrists. Across the square from the platform, several families huddled together and wept. A finely-dressed man on the platform shouted numbers while people in the crowd waved colored bits of cloth.

No one objected as he wriggled in closer to the front of the platform and studied the eyes of the people roped together. He had seen those looks of helplessness or stifled rage before on the faces of the servants RaiseHim had abused. A large, muscled man untied the smaller man at the front of the line and led him away.

Bowmark turned and worked his way to the back of the crowd where he found a young man watching with interest but not waving any cloths. "Give me pardon. May I ask what is occurring here?"

The blond man with a wispy, braided beard raised his eyebrows. "This is the monthly sale of debt slaves."

Bowmark stepped back, startled. "People are sold? Like food? Like clothing?" The man focused more attention on Bowmark. Enunciating slowly, as though Bowmark was stupid, he said, "Slaves are people who have been purchased. Whoever bought them owns them for the rest of their lives and makes them work for him for no wages other than food and bed. Most slaves are freed when they become sick or feeble."

"That—that is evil." When Father said the Sea Predators don't allow slavery, was this what he was talking about?

The man elaborately shrugged. "The creditors think it is evil not to pay one's debts."

Bowmark backed away. This was worse than how the nobles treated the servants. Servants were paid well in Father's household. The hopeless eyes of the slaves filled his thoughts as he wandered more streets.

He watched a juggler and a street singer, and batted at a huge gold bug that buzzed by his head. Non-humans moved easily through the city. Humans who merely looked different from either the black-haired or red-haired Sea Predators would not have been able to move safely in StoneGrove. Thousands of people thronged the streets, filled the shops, and worked at their crafts. His entire kingdom of thirty-five thousand was not as populous as this one city in Ironia.

Once he was caught up in a parade of people singing and stamping their feet. Their elbows and ankles had bells strapped to them. It took two cross-streets of walking before he could work his way out of the throng and lean against a building to watch them stamp by. A fellow onlooker said disdainfully, "Jinglers."

What would Sunrise have thought of these people?

When the watchmen lighted the street lamps, Bowmark returned to the docks, arriving shortly before sunset. His head was swimming with all the new sights and ideas he'd encountered. Wearily, he reconstructed his outrigger as the tezledek crawled back in. Was he really the only one who could see the tezledek? He pushed off the ramp and paddled back to the first dock.

The sun set behind the hills of Discoria.

"It's night," he announced.

The dark bundle on the prow thwart stirred.

"I don't know your customs. What do I pay you for guarding my outrigger?" He held up a magic ball to better see the monster as it unrolled.

The creature blinked humongous bright copper eyes with deep, black pupils. His shiny black face had two vertical rows of miniscule slits instead of a nose. His long, thin forearms bore six bristled fingers, three on each side of a divided palm. His loose skin wrapped around him like a cloak. The tezledek still appeared as it had that morning.

Bowmark still recognized that shape as one existing only in scare tales. "I'll be staying in my canoe tonight so you don't need to guard it anymore."

"Zzz zzz zzz. You're a sunfolk. I wished to speak with you."

"While I must not tell anyone you did."

"Correct. I have heard that there are still islands where my people do not yet live. Do you know of such islands? Do my people live with yours?"

"No. Never." Unless the monsters on his island were invisible.

"Zzzzzz." He smiled, revealing a single row of serrated teeth like a tearjaw's. "Are you returning to your people, are you?"

Those teeth! What if it *was* a kratchnak? "Once I have accomplished my mission, yes."

The creature smiled wider, and his ears fluttered. "And I, Scolla, shall accompany you."

Bowmark gaped, then took a deep breath. If he brought back a stranger, especially this thing that looked like a kratchnak, he might as well march up to the volcanic caldera and throw himself in. Revealing where StoneGrove hid was treason. The penalty for treason was to be thrown onto molten lava. Should no molten lava be handy, the criminal was bound in a small cage and thrown onto a bonfire. "Is there a reason you did not ask me if I wanted you to accompany me?"

"Obviously you need someone who can tell you of local human customs. Also you need someone who can correct your atrocious accent. Zzz. You need someone to tell you where the dangerous places are."

Bowmark deliberately unclenched his fists and rubbed his short hair. "What you say is true. What you have not told me is why you should be that person." Father would have been proud at how calmly he said this. Speaking politely to this…… this thing of horror…… was wearing.

The creature answered, "It is custom here not to remark when we join a traveler. We join, we leave when we wish. I seek a new land and a new beginning. I have found no woman who wants to be more than a friend. Surely there is somewhere in the world a woman who will find me attractive."

I don't see how. Bowmark tried to puzzle out the implications of these things riding with travelers. He asked cautiously, "Are you claiming that you will be my guide? Are you expecting to be paid? What about your guard duties?" *And why didn't the Atlas mention anything about people like that?*

A red tube tongue whipped out of the creature's mouth and wiped one of his eyes. "I ask for no pay. I am not a guard."

"Then what…… were you doing last night?"

"The guard did not see you or your vessel. I did. I wanted to speak with you."

"I see." How was he going to get rid of this creature without having his hand bitten off?

The creature scuttled over Bowmark's belongings until he reached one of the dock's pilings, which he climbed with surprising speed. On the dock, he turned, and his copper eyes glowed like moons in the light of the ball. "I go to pick up my travel needs. We shall speak again at dawn."

As long as he was talking to this tiny monster: "Wait. If you would be of use to me today, please answer me this: are the Ground Jewels of Old Terla the most precious things in Ironia?"

"Yes. Quite yes."

"Is it true that they have been stolen from nobles that wear blue beads in their hair?"

"Yes, yes, yes." He scurried away into the darkness.

"Light, leave," Bowmark said. He tamped the magic ball into a pocket. His hand had become cold and stiff so he tucked it under his arm until his fingers had warmed. The sea lapped against his canoe and shushed the evening while cloud fragments slid past the moons. What was he going to do? That thing made his skin crawl.

On the other hand, the creature had not hurt him yet. Indeed, it had helped him. Add to that everything it had told Bowmark so far had been true. He could handle vicious boars; what made him think he couldn't handle this tiny thing?

The inside of the canoe had dried, and the night promised to stay clear, so Bowmark rolled up in his cape and lay down to sleep. But his mind was full of strange animals, people, food, clothing, buildings, boats. How could he ever hope to navigate this world full of things and people and rules he didn't understand? Thankfully, exhaustion saved him from his thoughts, plunging him into a deep sleep.

THE MAGICIAN'S GIFT MOVED AS IF ALIVE.
FOOLISHLY ACCEPTED. THE RECIPIENT DIED.
~MORALITY PLAYS OF KORINSIN THE BARD

He woke up feeling less lost than he had the day before and warmer in his new clothes. A light fog was already clearing. He knew where most of the odors originated and could walk the faster tempo these people used. Although he had not yet found a place to bathe, he knew which guard to ask. And it looked as though he might soon have his second treasure.

He stretched languidly, sat up from his bed made of cape and nets, and then stopped abruptly. Webbed black bundles lurked on the trampoline, the rope net strung between the spars of his outrigger. "Scolla! What have you done to my canoe?"

The largest black bundle rolled a fraction of an inch. "Supplies. Go away."

"You can't tell me to leave my own canoe. What have you stuck on the trampoline?"

"Eggs. Messenger bugs. Books. Jewelry for my kind. If you are quiet, you may stay. Zzz."

"If I'm—if I'm—" Bowmark surged to his feet and leaped up to the dock. After he obtained the treasure, he was going to cut Scolla's food off the canoe and throw it into the sea. He might throw Scolla, too. His new heavy boots made ridiculous loud stomping sounds on the dock as he left the annoyance behind.

At the appointed time, Bowmark strode into the Red Squares Inn freshly bathed, fully dressed, and short hair combed. New steel and bone knives hid in his boots, pockets, and belt. Unlike his obsidian and bone blades, hiding these knives held no risk of snapping them in two.

The nobles sat in a dim back corner. Before he joined them, he scanned the room. Among the diners, two men plainly dressed seemed especially tense and interested in him and the corner where Jeeto sat.

He approached and sat before the leader. "I believe I would like to help your family regain the wealth that was stolen from them."

The leader placed the back of his fingers against his mouth to indicate that Bowmark should be quieter. The server set a platter of small, sweet breads and a pitcher of fermented juice on the table. Bowmark declined the spoiled drink and watched as the other men drank deeply of the nasty smelling stuff. One could learn to tolerate anything if one needed to. May Giver grant he would never need to tolerate that.

Jeeto laid a parchment on the table. The paper was fantastically smooth, unlike the banana fiber pages of StoneGrove or the waxy velum of the Atlas. "Tonight, we'll lead you to the Pile. We have someone inside who will let down a rope over the wall on the eastern side. Can you climb a rope?"

Bowmark had been scaling cliffs from the age of five. Sunrise and he had loved gathering the black eggs of the cliff-dwelling fishpiercers. Gaining numerous scars on their shoulders from the birds' teeth seemed to make the eggs taste even better. "I can."

"Once you are atop the outer wall, you will conceal the rope and take these stairs down as far as they will go. You turn right. The first door on your left will be locked. Can you pick a lock?"

"Can I what?"

The leader laid a row of thin, angled tools on the table, followed by a large iron lock. "Frech, you're the best lockpick of us. Show him how."

Bowmark watched intently. His acute hearing appeared to amaze the men; he could easily hear the tumblers shifting inside the lock.

A few breaths later, the leader resumed tracing Bowmark's route on the crudely drawn map. "You will have choices here. Go forward and down the stairs here, then right. Two corridors later, turn left."

"What is in all the rooms I am passing?"

"That doesn't concern you."

"I want to know."

Jeeto's lips thinned. "Stores mostly, old furniture, broken weapons. It leaks so badly in this section of the Pile that no one lives there. You won't have to worry about tripping over any scullery maids." He paused.

Apparently a response was required here. "I shall consider that." Bowmark winced inside at sounding inane.

"Uh, good." The leader pointed. "Here, and around this corner here, are guards. After you dispose of them, you will go down these stairs to this door. It looks like the wall, so you need to look carefully for the lock."

Bowmark was mentally translating the Common word 'dispose'. To throw away. "Wait. Dispose. Dispose of the guards." He paused. "Do you mean that you want me to kill these guards?"

The followers glanced at each other and snickered. The leader looked disgusted. "How did you think you were going to reach the Ground Jewels? Can you turn yourself invisible and dance past these guards?"

"There must be some way around them."

The leader began to roll up the parchment. "There may be. We've never found it." He motioned with his chin to his followers. Their chairs scraped back.

"Wait." Bowmark's chance to gain the second treasure was evaporating. "Wait. Give me a few candlemarks to think."

Jeeto slipped the parchment into a pouch. He tugged on his mustache. "We will stay here for twenty minutes more." He uncapped a leather cup and rolled out dice. They clicked across the table.

Bowmark's stomach grew queasy. He needed that treasure. He needed to destroy RaiseHim. He stood. They ignored him. He wavered, made aborted motions to sit, to walk away, to explain, to—*Do not show weakness.* The tense men watched him with narrowed eyes, their feet and bodies shifting, their hands resting on what could be hidden weapons.

"I shall return," Bowmark said. He strode deliberately from the room, blinked in the momentarily-painful sunlight, and ran, his boots crunching on the cobbles, to the docks. He slowed just before reaching the new guard at his dock, nodded at him, and then ran again to the canoe. The dock thundered under his feet.

"Scolla!" He dropped into the canoe.

The tiny stowaway peeked at him from under a fold of blanket.

Bowmark sat and hugged his knees. "I don't know what to do." What was he doing? He knew nothing about Scolla or his people or his purposes. Where was wisdom in blabbing his needs and intentions to every halfway-friendly person he met? As the news spread, who knew the variety of ways his mission would be interpreted? Here he was, asking advice from a kratchnak, the giant bug that eats bad boys. Without Father, without his teachers, without Dad and Mom and, Giver preserve him, without Sunrise, whom could he seek for counsel? He placed his elbows on his knees and clasped his hands behind his head. *Think—*

Scolla's croaking voice could barely be heard over the lapping water on the hull of the canoe. "Will I know what to do, will I?"

Bowmark closed his eyes and shook his head. Lost and stupid. "I need. There is something I need to obtain. To get it, I need to pass some guards. I am expected to kill them."

"Zzz. Many human thieves like to kill guards."

Flame torched his neck as he glared at Scolla. "I am no thief! I don't want to kill the guards. They haven't hurt me or my people. They work to support their families. They have mothers. They have sisters. They may have wives. They may have children. Who am I to devastate those people by killing men who are only doing their jobs? Who am I to shed—" He covered his face with one hand. Giver, how had he shed Sunrise's blood?

The creature stood, holding the blanket over his head like a tent and peering through one of the holes in the blanket now draping his face. "A compassionate human. Zzz. How rare."

Bowmark grasped his knees. "What? There are many compassionate humans. The people on Rolocton. The tailor here."

"These guards are not of your people."

Bowmark frowned. What did that matter? Then he remembered the gray seafolks killed in StoneGrove. Shame cooled his indignation. "I need—this object. I need to kill men to do so. I will *not* kill them."

The creature watched him through squeezed eyes. "You cannot resume your journey without this object, can you?"

"That is so."

"Zzz *click!*" Scolla stood hunched. "I am able to procure a solution for you."

Sunlight sparkled on the fretted surface of the sea and danced, reflected, on the underside of the dock. The wind bore the smells of salt, tar-seamed ships, and barrels of spices being unloaded and bargained over.

"You have a way for me to get past guards without killing them?"

"Yes."

"Can you get it by tonight?"

"Yes." Scolla scurried up the mooring pier and with his bobbing, floating gait scuttled toward the land. Porters and sailor swerved around him as they did their work, but none looked at him.

Bowmark caught up to Scolla. "What is this solution?"

"Go away." Scolla accelerated, his tiny feet a blur.

"I need to understand—"

"Go away." Scolla bobbled faster.

Aggrieved, Bowmark stopped and slapped his thigh. Sailors looked at him, some taken aback, and some disgusted. Bowmark breathed carefully to abate his anger and observe his surroundings. Scolla ducked into an opening in the rocks protecting the shore. Bowmark had violated a social rule, but he didn't know what that rule was. Was it slapping his thighs? Or talking to a monster no one else could see?

Time. The twenty minutes had nearly passed. Bowmark sped up the hill and through the grid of streets to the Red Squares Inn.

The nobles still rolled their dice.

"What happens after I get past the guards?"

With a close-lipped smile that had nothing to do with friendliness, Jeeto unrolled the parchment. "You use their keys to enter the snake quarter. Pounter has released snakes into this area of passages." His finger traced a large square.

"Are they six or eight-legged snakes?"

The leader frowned. "There are no such things as eight-legged snakes."

Bowmark, who had speared a number of eight-legged snakes during Royal Forest inspections, remembered another commoner adage: Never contradict a noble. He kept his facial expression calm, but inwardly, he winced. The venomous eight-legged snakes avoided people, but the even more venomous six-legged kind bit whatever they could reach.

"The Ground Jewels are moved randomly from room to room in this central area, usually one of these four rooms. They could be hidden in a box of nails or a bucket of rags."

Bowmark balked. "Why would they move them? Who moves them if the rooms are full of snakes? Why..."

Jeeto slammed his palm on the table. "These are things you do not need to know. *This* is what you need to know. You need to find all six of the jewels. They are rubies, the size of a thumb, set in six gold torcs. They were worn by the ruling Sextet Sentries over a millennium ago."

"Six kings at one time?" What were torcs?

"Almost. One of them was an ancestor of mine. After you find them, retrace your steps, climb down the rope, and meet us back here. Do you understand?"

Bowmark nodded while repressing the urge to ask more questions. They arranged a time to meet that night.

The next few candles, Bowmark roamed another section of the city. Once, he wandered into a private home and was angrily chased out. After the nearby guard understood that Bowmark had meant no harm, he laughed and showed him the difference between business and home doors.

Bowmark bought a roasted root from a street vendor, watched a school of girls practicing dance steps, purchased some fragrant oil for his scalp, listened to some flower vendors sing about their bouquets while a guard flirted with them, caught a boy's runaway ball and returned it. In the midst of all this humanity and activity. he felt far lonelier than he had at sea.

What would Father be feeling while he trained RaiseHim as designate?

In the late afternoon suffused with a golden haze and quiet air, Bowmark returned to his outrigger and found Scolla huddled near a black bag. It was difficult to tell the two apart. Scolla must be the one with spines like snagged threads all over his skin.

Scolla unfolded. "Your solution." He reached into the bag and pulled out a coiled thin gray rope. "A magician's cord."

Stay away from all things magic. The weight of the staffshifter pressed against his thigh. He smiled as he looked down at Scolla. "Show me how it works."

"Cord, stick!" Scolla threw the cord at Bowmark.

He reached to catch it, but faster than he could see, the cord sped around his arm, his chest, his legs. The cord tightened, pulling in his arms and lashing his legs together. Bowmark toppled against the side of the canoe, and unable to right himself, rolled into the sea. He kicked, and the cord raced to truss his lower legs. The back of his head bumped into a log as he bobbed up back-first. He tried to twist to put his face into the air, but every twist tightened the cord, squeezing his chest. Air bubbled from his nose.

He pulled his head up and still could not reach air. Then he pulled up his knees to prepare for a thrust, but the cord writhed over them and tied them fast to his torso. More air leaked from his lungs. He floated face down, totally helpless. The cold sea made him shiver. The outrigger! His fingers arched and slipped on the algae coated wood. Another try pushed him away from the log.

Lava overtake Scolla! Why had the kratchnak killed him? He hadn't harmed the bug! The last of his air huffed out. *I tried, Sunrise. I'm so sorry.* The sea water seeping into his lungs burned.

Suddenly the cord released him. He flailed, smashing his hand on the outrigger log. He breached the water, grabbed breath, and choked. He reached the canoe and pulled himself up with his head hanging over the side so he could cough out the water. Chest heaving, he sat up. Scolla clutched the outrigger and held the cord.

Bowmark coughed some more, spit, and shouted, "You! You kratchnak! You traitor! You drowned me!" He wheezed. "Why shouldn't I kill you?"

"I did not know you would fall. I needed to touch the cord to recall it—"

"You waited long enough!" Bowmark leaned over the canoe to cough out more sea.

"I cannot swim. None of my people can. If we fall in water, we try to walk to shore. Few of us make it." He held out the cord. "You asked me to show you how to use it." He huddled against the log when the shadows of several people fell over him.

A cluster of sailors looked at him. "You all right, mate?" called one.

Bowmark gasped. "I will survive."

The sailors left.

Bowmark pulled off his wet shirt and pulled on the blue hooded jacket he had planned to wear that evening. His pants he laid over the trampoline. His boots he grimly emptied out while watching Scolla stay put. Finally, he said, "I won't kill you. The cord is a great weapon. How do you recall it?"

Scolla carefully crept across a spar to the back of the canoe. "You touch it and say, 'Cord back.' It is simple. But, you ask yourself, how do I keep the guards from shouting, how?"

Bowmark cleared his throat. "Instead of showing me, could you simply tell me?"

Scolla smiled, exposing those horrendous teeth, and pulled out of the black bag a stoppered clay vial. "Don't open it now," he said as he passed the vial to Bowmark.

Scolla's hands had three taloned fingers opposed by three more taloned thumbs around a circular palm. That had to give him tremendous dexterity. Bowmark touched the human-shaped Giver's Hand lying on his chest and wondered for the first time in his life what actual Giver's hands looked like.

Scolla interrupted his thought. "Once the guard is down, fling a few specks of the powder from that vial into his nose, and he will go to sleep in a few heartbeats."

Bowmark frowned. "Is this poison? Do you mean that he'll sleep forever?"

"No. Quite no. He will sleep for six to seven hours and waken well-rested after many vivid dreams."

Bowmark tried to remember if the Common word 'hours' had been in the Atlas. "Forgive me. What is an hour?"

Scolla's ears perked. "Do you not have clocks on your island, do you?"

"Another word I'm unfamiliar with." Was this creature toying with him?

"Zzz. I suppose it would be inevitable that some branches would revert more than others."

More nonsense. "Please. I am forced to try to accomplish a deed in a land I know nothing about using objects I'm unfamiliar with, and now you wash strange words over me. Can you just tell me how long the guard will sleep once the powder is used?"

"Sssss . . . half a waking day. You will not need to rush."

Bowmark rolled the vial in his fingers. "Oh. So just like the pollen of the jabbock flower on the west islands. When you poke them, they spray and you sleep." Scolla's face scrunched in a way that Bowmark could not translate. Curiosity? Interest? Surprise? "So then, thank you for helping me to right a wrong."

Scolla took the cord that had snaked into a neat coil in his other hand and offered it to Bowmark. "It is important that I offer you this cord, and that you accept it," Scolla buzzed. "Otherwise you will need much time for the cord to learn you. Most magic objects are obedient to only one person at a time."

Bowmark reverently took the cord. The magic weapon darted to thread itself through a loop on his belt next to the staffshifter sheath.

Bowmark pulled up his cape. "I intend to nap until nightspread. This time, you go away."

With no apparent upset, Scolla clambered over Bowmark's belongings to the farthest end of the canoe and rolled into a blob.

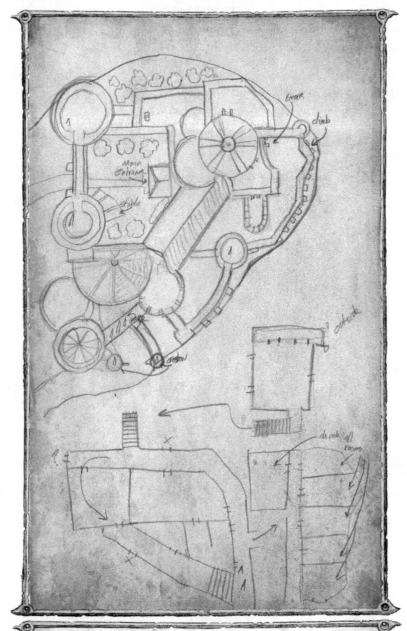

THE PILE AT DISCORIA IS A COLLECTION OF KEEPS AND CASTLE
THAT GREW OVER EACH OTHER DURING THE WARRING HOUSES
PERIOD THAT STARTED IN 1867 AND LASTS TILL THIS DAY. EACH
TURNOVER OF POWER SEES NEW CONSTRUCTION OVER THE OLD.
-SEAFOLK ATLAS

The minor noble Frech blew out the lantern he was carrying, and the clouded night covered him and Bowmark. They stood near a tiny ledge dividing sea-inlet cliff from massive Castle Pile wall. He whispered directly into Bowmark's ear. "Do not wander from the wall, or you will find the crabs below. The rope is about fifty steps that way. We're depending on you."

At the bottom of the five-story-tall, north wall of the Pile, Bowmark slid his hands along the stone blocks and his feet along the narrow ledge in deep darkness. He found the rope and jerked on it several times to check its fastness. As he climbed, he thought about the cliffs and birds of home—and about his friends. He tried not to think about RaiseHim sitting beside Father every day. Father was a man of duty, and he would instruct. RaiseHim would ignore him.

After Bowmark reached the top, he began to coil the rope, but reconsidered. It was too dark for anyone to see the rope, and since he was likely to leave precipitously, perhaps it would be better if he left it in place. Leaving the rope tied to a hook of unknown purpose, he dropped the coil back down the outside of the wall.

Following the memorized directions, Bowmark soon crouched at a small door with a lock. Probing the ancient metal with the delicate picks, he listened intently. He didn't want to use the light ball in case it drew attention, so he worked in suffocating darkness until the lock clicked. He slid the picks into a pocket and slipped into the castle.

He pulled out his magic sphere which lit a dark stone corridor. Still air stank of mildew and dust. He located the door that should lead farther into the disused areas of the castle. With a gentle push, the door snicked open a thumbwidth. Beyond, a chair scraped across flagstone.

He grasped the magician's cord, set his shoulder to the heavy plank door, shoved through and rolled on the floor of a room lit by a single candle in a niche. The roll turned into a leap. His eyes had barely registered the man fumbling with his sword before his hand flung the magic rope. "Cord, stick!"

"Jorno!" the man shouted as the cord whipped around his arms. "Jorno!" He stumbled and slammed against the wall.

Bowmark held the back of his fingers against his mouth, but the man continued to shout even as he thudded onto the stone floor.

He stopped when Bowmark pulled out a knife. The anger in the guard's eyes shifted to fear as Bowmark crouched at his head. "Don't," the man stuttered. "I can't move. You don't need to—" His eyes followed the vial. "Don't. Please."

"Give me pardon," Bowmark murmured as he removed a pinch of powder and then flicked it under the man's nose.

Despair clouded the man's eyes. "Should I thank you that I won't feel pain as you slit my throat?" He wriggled against the cord. "I don't know where they are. No one knows. You are killing me for no good reason." He sighed deeply and slumped.

Giver should throw him away for this. Bowmark reached for the cord. Hearing steps behind him, he changed his motion to a push off and roll to stand.

A sword smashed the floor and a chip of flagstone zinged off.

Bowmark sidestepped a jab and wild swing.

"You pile of dung!" screamed the man who must have been Jorno. "He was my brother!"

Bowmark took another step closer to the door and farther from the cord.

"Demons spit and roast you!"

Bowmark ducked a high slash. He flipped backward and kicked Jorno's wrist. The sword arched up and clattered off a wall.

Jorno screamed in pain and rage as he retreated and fumbled for his knife with the other hand. "Demons eat your kidneys!"

"Cord back." Bowmark dove for the magic cord, rolled as it slithered into his outstretched hand, then in one smooth motion, threw it toward the other guard "Cord stick!"

Jorno shouted incoherently as he slashed at the writhing cord. It snaked around the knife, the hand, and jerked his arm against his body. He kicked at Bowmark. The cord entangled his feet. His knees cracked against flagstone, and from there his struggles toppled him.

When Bowmark knelt beside Jorno, his face turned grim. Jorno's voice trembled and blood dribbled from his nose. "I will haunt you. I will spit upon your every meal." Tears escaped his eyes as he struggled to breathe against the constricting cord. "You killed my brother. I'll kill yours."

"Give me—" Sharp pain closed Bowmark's throat. He tossed the powder into Jorno's face.

The man bared his teeth and struggled against the rope. "Demons strangle you when you lie down and demons bite your back when you rise up. De—de—" He sagged.

Bowmark tugged at the cord and it slithered back into place on his belt.

My brother. Bowmark stared at the low ceiling and tried to swallow past the knife within his throat. Nausea rode his stomach. Spearmark would be compelled to see murderous men each day in court and live with the sickening knowledge that neither he nor Father could do anything about those men. If only he were home showing Spearmark the tiny creatures in tide pools, tossing him into the surf, and drawing goofy pictures in the sand for him to gleefully stomp out. Instead, he was months away in a cold, dark place, leaving Spearmark next to a liar and thief.

He examined Jorno. Bowmark had humiliated these men and shamed them with fear. He had not meant to hurt them, but he had. They were sure to be dismissed. How could he undo this harm?

Despite his heart beating, "Hurry, hurry, hurry."' at him, he pulled out two pearls from a hidden pocket and tucked one into each brother's boot. He stood, then knelt again, and pulled out two stones, a ruby and a sapphire, and placed them beside the pearls.

He found the semi-hidden door behind a ragged moldering tapestry that may have once depicted these people's massive boxy ships sailing into a harbor. The door unlocked easily. "Light, come," he whispered to the ball held in one hand. With the other hand he held the staffshifter. He nudged the door open, slipped in, and shut it securely behind him. The people who lived and worked in the Pile, let alone the brothers, did not need vicious six-legged snakes among them. How much time did he have? Surely somebody was going to investigate all the noise the brothers had made.

He spun, trying to see everywhere at once in the irregular hall while the dancing shadows of his fingers obscured most of the walls. Holding the ball in his palm distributed the tingling cold better, but in order to maximize the light, he had to pinch it between thumb and two other fingers. This concentrated the sensation to three small points, making his fingertips feel like they were vibrating.

Nothing but dust, insect debris, and a faint odor of mildew. Somewhere, water trickled. The first room he checked had tables with warped tops or broken legs. The second room held chairs with faded, torn, or stained upholstery. The third room held boxes of ripped and discolored linens. When he shifted one box, a gray and blue striped rat shot out from behind it. The rat scurried into another gap between boxes.

When he turned to open another box, he nearly laid his hand on a snake. The handspan-length snake struck where his hand had been at the same time that Bowmark slammed into the door. His first thrust with the staffshifter shattered the box and flung the snake unharmed behind a rickety stack of boxes. Shadows jumped as the light ball fell out of Bowmark's hand. The ball dimmed before he snatched it up again.

A golden reflection shone between rags in the broken box. He inched forward, and then inserted the lengthened staff into the box. If only those claws could open so that he could snag whatever that gold was. The staff startled him by twitching one claw. But the metal claws did not move again. Bowmark must have misinterpreted a shadow. He gently raked inside the box.

Rags and a golden torc spilled out. So did a longer snake which had half engulfed a rat. That snake, he whacked with the staff.

The first snake surged out from behind the boxes and bit his boot. Bowmark stomped it with no hurt to himself. That's what boots were good for. He had wondered.

Two snakes down. One torc. He used the staff to pull the torc closer to himself before picking up the rigid necklace and shoving it into the net hung on his belt. Then he used the staff to smash the box to pieces. There were no more torcs in the jumble.

The stench of dead snakes, rat urine, and moldy linen swirled around him as he smashed box after box. A corner box of snarled tassels yielded a second torc. Dust clogged his throat. A growing weariness in his arms reminded him that the staffshifter took its strength from him.

Cautiously, he opened the door into the hallway a crack, then slammed it on the head of an arm-long snake trying to enter from the hallway. The reptile banged against the door until he crushed its head with his staff. Fumes and ashes! He leaned against the door momentarily to catch his breath, and then dashed through the hall to the next room to encounter an arm-and-a-half-long snake that had been nosing into a rusted chest plate. Bowmark dispatched the monster as it turned. Armor clattered against the wall. Surely the whole Pile could hear him.

Torc number three rested under a pile of bent daggers. A tiny snake nearly snagged his wrist as he reached for the torc. He leaped back, tripped over a lance, and landed on a heap of armor padding that shot up clouds of dust. He scrambled up in time to stomp on the snake.

Back in the hallway, his staffshifter hit two more snakes. His fingers grew so cold that he had to transfer the light ball to the other hand. Thank Giver he had trained to be ambidextrous. He opened another door.

The next room held no snakes, two torcs, and sacks of withered dirt-encrusted, root vegetables.

A snake leaped at him from the door lintel as he passed under on his way out. A wild swing knocked it aside. The venomous creature hissed and leaped again. *Zip!* He broke its back.

He thumped the door lintel on the next door to make sure no snake waited for him. The room held two snakes trying to swallow the same rat. Those were easy to kill, but a third snake he had not noticed nearly got him in the thigh.

Bowmark jumped onto a chest. Its lid collapsed. The third snake leaped again, and he hit its neck with the shortened staff. It bunched for another leap.

Zip! The staff's metal snake fist crashed into its head. The snake writhed uselessly, its six short legs dragging its smashed head along the floor. When he stepped out of the chest and shook off the rotted wood splinters, he found the sixth torc wrapped around his ankle. He touched his Giver's Hand medallion. Giver should have skipped the gift of snakes.

Creeping back through the halls gave him no more surprises, but he did not breathe freely until he had closed the door to the snake-filled halls. He stepped over the brothers. *I am sorry for what I did to you.*

He hesitated at the base of the stairs, listening intently. He slid his boots off, knotted their straps together, and slung them over his neck so he could run more quietly along the stairs and wall. Nothing but his own rapid heartbeat, the tiny pops and creaks of ancient buildings slowly surrendering to gravity, and the susurration of the sea interrupted the silence. The heavy torcs in the net pulled at his waist.

A final deep breath, and then he sped lightly, near silently, up the flights of stairs, crouched along the wall, and to the rope. He put the magic ball away and waited for his fingers to regain their strength. Then he swung easily over the edge and descended. *Be careful.* Giddiness and relief of tension swept over him. Done! He wanted to laugh.

Someone above him did laugh.

ONLY A FOOL KEEPS ALL THEIR TREASURE IN ONE PLACE.
-DISCORIAN ADAGE

Bowmark halted. His hands clutched the rope and his toes gripped the wall. What? He crouched. Who?

The voice above him, triumphant, said, "Thief! I hold an ax. The man beside me holds a bow. At both ends of the path are guards waiting to dismember you. If you do not immediately hand over whatever it is you have stolen, I shall cut this rope. It's a long fall to rocks already covered with crushed skeletons."

Bowmark glanced over his shoulder. A wavering point of light, a torch, flashed around the corner of The Pile.

"Do you surrender?"

Think: Hanging by a rope. Ax above, soldiers on the path, cliff below, and below that, piles of sharp rocks edging the sea. Knives, staffshifter, light ball, magician's cord. Would they kill him if he surrendered? Air refused to enter his lungs. Bowmark grabbed one end of the magician's cord and pressed it against the wall. "Cord, stick." The end threaded into a crack in the mortar between stones.

"Repeat that," the man holding the ax in the darkness above him called.

Bowmark pulled on the magic cord.

Someone above him shouted, "Happy flying!"

Steel struck brick and the rope fell loose.

Bowmark fell, then jerked to a stop as the cord circled over his shoulder tightened. He let go of the severed rope and clung to the magic cord.

"Thief down!" shouted the voice above him. Shouts and jeers answered.

Bowmark fumbled in the dark, his cold-cramped fingers and toes probing for holes as he rappelled down.

There was no room to kneel on the narrow ledge at the base of the wall, so he used his toes to stick the end of the cord against the rock below him.

"He's up!" shouted a guard.

Bowmark hopped backwards and swung down over the edge. The rough cliff gave his feet a place to push against as he rappelled. Then an undercut left him swinging. He looked up at the torch light glinting off an ax. Could magicians' cords be cut?

"There!" shouted someone.

Bowmark twisted to increase the swing. Something zoomed past his head. He touched rock with no handholds. A swing the other way showed a rippling torch reflection far below. The sea. He lowered himself some more until no more cord dangled below his feet. Why wouldn't the magic cord stretch like his magic staffshifter?

A torch roared toward him and glanced off his shoulder. The brief light showed a natural ledge to his left.

The sound of metal striking rock echoed.

He swung toward the ledge, yelled, "Cord come," slammed into the cliff, dropped to the ledge and slapped the cord against wet rock, "Cord stick!", and toppled off. The cord held on the cliff face, and he pulled himself back to the ledge.

When he looked up, only blackness met his gaze, so he must be under the overhang. The shouting was muted and jumbled from rock echoes. A wet, salty wind whirled around him. His arms and legs trembled.

Several breaths pressed some strength into his limbs, and he resumed his dark descent. Once, he laid his hand on—truth—an arrow that had just struck the rock beside him, a miniature one. Its sharp point persuaded him the arrow was no toy. *Too close.* He kept to the shadows.

He sagged with relief when he finally reached the sharp, wet boulders and then the sea. The water sucked out all his warmth as he probed his way through cracked boulders and shattered wood and, *Oh, Giver,* a skull jammed in a cleft, and finally into deep enough sea that he could swim away. Lights and more lights gathered on the Pile, and slowly lights crept down the cliff. Fractured reflections rippled on the sea. By the time boats with lights along the gunwales approached the base of the cliff, Bowmark had found a treed place across the inlet to climb out and hide in while he shivered some heat back into his body and watched the search.

Bowmark stumbled through the dark, past bugling and growling seadogs, through the foggy streets of dockside Discoria and to the Red Squares Inn. All was dark and quiet inside, but the banked fire gave off enough heat that Bowmark found comfort in sitting against the fireplace wall. Where were Frech and Jeeto? Perhaps he could ask the innkeeper at sunup. He fell asleep while waiting.

He awoke, awkward, sore, and with salt-stiffened, damp clothes. Bowmark yawned. The ribs that had slammed into the cliff radiated pain with every movement.

The innkeeper hovered around the edges, serving the few early risers and keeping a constant watch on Bowmark. Unbidden, he gave Bowmark a hot cup of broth redolent of pungent bulbs and eels.

Warmed and strengthened by the savory broth, Bowmark dozed off and on as he continued to wait. He decided a dozen times to go to the bathhouse, and a dozen times decided that he must not go until he had delivered the Ground Jewels to the rightful owner.

The front door opened, admitting a pale gray light, Jeeto, the three followers, and six unfamiliar large men. Two of them stationed themselves by the door like guards, two disappeared into whatever was in the back of the inn, and two approached the early eaters who abruptly decided that they could finish breakfast another day. Overhead, doors slammed.

Bowmark stood.

Jeeto sat at a table, and with an open hand indicated the chair across from him.

Bowmark strove not to wince as he hobbled over. He carefully lowered himself onto the chair. The two large men who had been intimidating the diners moved to stand behind him.

Holding one end of his long mustache between thumb and forefinger, Jeeto asked with barely-suppressed excitement, "Do you have the Ground Jewels?"

"I do." Bowmark untied the string about his neck and pulled the net containing the torcs out from his shirt.

Jeeto seized the net and counted. Glee suffused his face.

"Your Majesty!" exclaimed Frech.

Bowmark stared. "You're a king?"

"I am now!" The leader clutched the net bag and held it up. "I am now!"

The followers bowed with arms held stiffly behind their backs and hands splayed.

An electric feeling of something gone horribly wrong tingled down Bowmark's spine. Still, he said evenly, "Which torc would you recommend I take as my reward?"

Jeeto glanced at the guards before looking at Bowmark. "You knew when I hired you that I couldn't give you one of these. One needs all six to prove one's claim. Why do you think they were all separated and hidden at random?"

Bowmark sensed the guards shifting behind him. He was only breaths away from a knife in his back.

Jeeto made a motion with his head. Frech stepped up as he pulled out a velvet bag and emptied gold and garnet rings upon the table. "Take whatever you want of these."

Bowmark stirred the small pile of jewelry with his forefinger. "Your Majesty, among my people, these are baubles." The muscles between his shoulder blades bunched in anticipation. "I gift you the torcs." He stood and then stepped resolutely toward the door. The astonished guards only stared.

Outside, he strode with measured tread until he had turned a corner. Then, he ran. He raced downhill, expecting any moment that one of these people's miniature arrows would pierce his back, raced without wasting the time to look back, raced past shop boys opening shutters and through a herd of multi-legged cart pullers and onto the docks swarming with people shouting orders at each other.

Scolla bounced when Bowmark hit the canoe. "Sss!" he hissed as Bowmark jerked the mooring rope free.

Bowmark grabbed a paddle and dug savagely into the water. "Sss yourself! Loosen the rigging!"

CONTROL THAT IS PERCEIVED
IS CONTROL THAT CAN BE RESISTED.
-ZZTAK OF THE PEOPLE

Scolla unrolled and waddled to the mast where he studied the ropes and sail with obvious incomprehension and irritation.

Bowmark paddled faster.

Once they slid away from the confinement of the large ships, Bowmark's hands blurred with speed as he shoved Scolla aside, set the lateen sail to catch the gusty wind, unrolled an oilcloth-covered set of new-forged throwing knives, and returned to paddling, looking back to the docks as often as forward. Not until they had passed the dolorously-tolling buoy did he return to the stern to control the sail.

Sea birds circled the canoe plowing through morning-sun-glittered waves.

Bowmark's damp clothes clung to his skin and threw his warmth to every gust. He shivered.

Scolla angled his ears to cover his squinting eyes and said calmly in his quavering, old man's voice, "You must have succeeded in stealing your treasure."

Bowmark flung away the lines, the sail wobbled, and he pounded the side of the canoe with his fist. "No! I'm not a thief. I'm a fool! A fool."

"You are damaging yourself."

Bowmark continued to pound an emphasis to each phrase. "I risked my life, and for what? To put a lying man on the throne! I'm a fool. I was cheated. I'm so gullible. I'm so stupid!"

"You are human. All humans are stupid."

Bowmark grabbed a flapping line and glared at Scolla. "*You* told me. *You* told me the Ground Jewels were stolen. I thought I was retrieving stolen property!"

"Zzz. So you did. Zzz. Did you give them to a richly dressed young man with a long mustache and a single blue bead in his hair, did you? He conducts business of a sort near the harbor."

"Truth."

"That is Jeeto, son of Nokitch, House of Brakor. The Ground Jewels were stolen from them by House of Lunteen. House of Brakor stole them from House of Kartola. House of Kartola stole them from House of Freesik. Thus it goes from noble house to noble house."

"But, but then every king is a thief!"

Scolla licked an eye. "It is written that all royalty are thieves."

Bowmark's knuckles whitened. "Not my—" He swallowed the word "father" and stared at the horizon until his anger had subsided enough for him to speak with a veneer of calmness. "I wish I had known this."

"I wish I had known what you planned to steal. I could have gotten it for you."

The line slid between Bowmark's fingers and the sail swung wildly until Bowmark noticed and hauled back the line. "What?"

"My people could have gotten copies and used them to replace the Ground Jewels. Should there be a next time, tell me what treasure you need, and I shall obtain it for you. I am eager to reach your island."

"How?— You— . . . Why?" Bowmark held the line and closed his eyes. He hated how his tongue jammed when he got upset. "How.. . . . . could.. . . . . you get.. . . . . past the guards? And the snakes?"

"We go wherever we wish. Also, we have a, zzz, lotion that repels snakes. I could have given you some."

Bowmark did not know who he was angriest at: himself, the new king of Ironia, or Scolla. He wrapped the line around a cleat, flung off his clothes, and dove into the sea.

He disappointed himself by being able to swim alongside the canoe for only a short distance before his burning arms insisted they could not do another stroke. Spent, he dragged himself aboard, and after a minute's rest, sluiced sweet water over himself. Then he rinsed his clothes and laid them on the trampoline to dry. He oiled his hair, chewing a twig until the shredded end could scrape his teeth clean. Then he rubbed a small pumice stone over each fingernail until they were smooth and even. When he looked back toward the port of Discoria, no one pursued them.

Now he could speak to Scolla without knifing him, but the fellow slept on the prow thwart as soundly as a mushroom. Clouds slid over the sun and quietly piled up without dropping their rain. The glittering seas segued into gray and darker gray.

Bowmark ran his thumb over the spear point tattoo on his shoulder and then rubbed the small arrows tattooed along his eyebrow. He muttered, "No one else has these marks so I'll be easy to recognize if I return to Discoria. I'm such a fool. What should I do now?"

He nearly jumped when an old man's voice quavered, "Go north." The bundle that was Scolla had shifted and bright eyes showed between ears parts that were flopped over his face.

"Why should I?"

"In the harbor of Bysea I can obtain replicas of the Ground Jewels for you to take home."

"My people might find it odd that I should have one set and king of thieves Jeeto should have another."

"They need never know."

Bowmark adjusted the sail. "Your people may not have a sense of honor, but my people do."

"Sst!" Scolla curled up tighter. "A *human* thinks he can tell me about honor!"

Bowmark shrugged. Let Scolla be the one insulted this time. How long should he continue sailing away from Discoria, now south of him, before he could lower the sail and take a nap? Maybe a candle. Languor occluded his anger and tension.

Where should he go now? If the winds and current stayed consistent, Bysea was at least two days away across a strait and on the southeastern edge of the huge continent called Akinda. Much of the interior was unmarked in the Atlas.

Scolla interrupted his thoughts. "From Bysea, it is but a short journey inland to The Central Place of the rumshae."

Was that marked in the Atlas? Fatigue clouded his memory of that area of the world. Bowmark unwrapped the round book.

"SSSSS!"

Bowmark looked up.

Scolla stood, his body swollen, sharp spines thrusting out from his now tight covering of hide, his lips pulled back to show every serrated tooth. "Sssss! Only the seafolks have those. You must have murdered a ship full of our allies!"

"No."

Scolla's tube tongue lengthened, stiffened and pointed straight at Bowmark.

"Scolla, what are you doing?"

Splat! A black gob spattered across Bowmark's chest. He dropped the Atlas. A stench, as if he had fallen face first into a privy, burned his nostrils. Tears squirted from his eyes and obscured the sight of Scolla aiming again.

"Stop!" Bowmark vaulted into the sea as another gob streamed through the air where he had been.

The clean sea closed over his head. Bowmark tried to rub the gooey mass off before he surfaced to catch a breath.

Scolla leaned over the gunwale. "Ssss! Killer!"

"No! Sco—" He ducked another missile. He reemerged as the canoe sailed past him. Scolla gripped the stern. Bowmark shouted, "I didn't do it! The man was dead when I found him on a beach!" *Please, Giver, don't let him ask how the man died.*

Scolla paused, and the canoe sailed farther.

Bowmark swam after his outrigger canoe. The nearest land was a faint darkening on the horizon. "Scolla! I did not kill him! You can't sail the canoe without me." The distance between them widened. Scolla intended for him to drown. Bowmark was still naked and without a single knife on him. How could he get close enough to Scolla to kill him? How could he make him change his mind? What could he offer Scolla?

Bowmark shouted, "I want to find a seafolk and return the Atlas. I haven't found one yet."

Scolla deflated somewhat and backed away from the stern.

Bowmark kicked desperately and caught up to the canoe. He pulled himself in and watched Scolla warily while pulling on his skirt with its hidden knives. Scolla, in turn, had completely deflated and retracted his tongue, and now watched him, but did not interfere when Bowmark gathered his throwing knives.

The reek still assailed his nostrils. He fought to not gag. "This assault is more than I will tolerate. When we reach Bysea, you and your supplies are leaving my canoe." He held one of the throwing knives hidden by his thigh.

"Bysea is not your island. I stay until we reach your home."

"My home is hidden for a reason. I will not reveal it to you."

Scolla sat and yawned. "Your people need us. You need me."

Bowmark pointed to the splotch on his chest. "Not this bad, I don't." He grimaced, for his skin was blistering under the gunk. "How do I get this off?"

Scolla yawned again. "Some soap. Much rinsing."

Bowmark pawed through his bag of new belongings and found the bottle of soap. He smeared it on his chest and medallion. "You dirtied the Hand of Giver. I won't forgive you that."

Scolla said nothing.

Bowmark collapsed the sail and dove into the sea again. When he pulled himself back on board, the filth was gone. The reddened patch of skin still stank, though not in an eye-watering way. Bowmark gingerly rubbed fragrant oil on the spot while he watched Scolla lean against a gunwale.

Scolla locked fingers over his wrinkled abdomen. "Prince, what did you do to earn exile, what?"

Bowmark grabbed a knife. "How do you know?"

"Many marks so indicate: your elevated speech, your large vocabulary, your uncommon care for your appearance. You bow to no man. Therefore, men must bow to you."

Bowmark almost threw the knife. "Do you plan to betray me for profit?"

"Zzz, zzz, zzz," Scolla said in a tone Bowmark now recognized as laughter. "Our only profit lies in getting you home. Show me your trade goods."

Anger, bewilderment, and a fear that he would not own collided and jammed Bowmark's tongue. He shook his head.

"Zzz. I have no need to rob you. I do need to see if you have enough to obtain your treasure and return home."

Bowmark glared. Was he supposed to forget that Scolla had tried to kill him? Yet Scolla had freely given him the magician's cord and advice, and he seemed to switch from enemy to friend again based on a few words from Bowmark.

"Are you going to apologize for wrongly attacking me?"

"No. There is no reason."

Bowmark's jaw tightened, but he laid down the knife. As soon as they reached land, he would dump Scolla and his belongings. In the meantime, he should pretend to be cooperative. He pulled three lumpy pearls, two rubies, a tiny sapphire, and four gold earrings out of his waistband. Scolla glanced from the jewels nestled in Bowmark's palm to his face and back again. "Is that all, is it?"

"Truth. I needed to purchase much in Discoria."

Scolla clicked. "You are a pathetic trader, you are."

With trembling hands, Bowmark reinserted the jewels into the waistband of his skirt.

"I will get you more in Bysea."

Bowmark almost dropped a pearl. "Just like that?"

"We have plenty."

"How?"

"Zzz, zzz, zzz. Humans shower us with gifts. Zzz, zzz, zzz. Sometimes a gaggle of human boys will think to harm us simply because we are smaller than you."

Bowmark thought of RaiseHim tormenting any animals or people he could get away with. Then his face heated as he remembered the time Father had discovered *him* on the beach throwing rocks at a sea bird with a broken wing. Father had caught him up, cast him into the surf, and chucked pebbles at Bowmark's head while roaring, "Leave it alone or kill it, but do not *torment* it!"

Scolla whined, "You saw that we have ways to defend ourselves."

Bowmark resentfully laid a hand on his chest. "Truth."

"Every boy so marked runs home eventually. To punish the boy, the tezledeks assigned to his home will withdraw."

"His family will withdraw?" *Wait, how can boys throw rocks at people they can't see?*

"If there is no gift and a promise to leave us alone within a few hours, we withdraw from every human household that is adjacent to the offender's home."

"Your withdrawal from humans is *punishment*?"

"Quite yes. We are important."

Bowmark strove to keep his face impassive. The creature was so important that a small boy could look straight at him and say he sees nobody. *Are these people invisible or not?*

"If the gift and promise have not arrived by the next day, we withdraw from the next circle of houses. Thus we do each following day until the assault is paid for. Never in our history has the process gone more than four days."

That couldn't be right. However, he was cooperating. "What do you do with these gifts?"

"We use the gems to buy the things we do not care to make for ourselves."

"How do you buy from people who can't see you?"

"Zzz zzz zzz. They see us. They don't look at us. We lay down a fair price and take our goods. No one questions us."

Bowmark rubbed the back of his neck. *I don't want to look at his ugly face either.* "But I don't see how your people in Bysea will give you trade goods simply because you demand them. Are you their king?"

"Zzz, zzz, zzz. We have no kings. Those who won't work must live in the wilderness. My people will contribute to my mission."

Bowmark waited. "Your mission."

"Establishing my people on your island."

"I'm not taking you or any of your people."

Scolla patted his fingertips together creating a slight clicking rhythm. "This argument is tedious." He rolled up and pulled his loose skin over his shoulders.

Bowmark's lips thinned as he stared up at the sky. *You don't murder someone because they irritate you.* "You behave as though your people own all the world."

In a muffled voice, Scolla said, "We do."

Bowmark's anger flipped into great, body-shaking laughter that hurt his bruised side after a while, yet still he guffawed. He wiped tears from his eyes and hiccupped. What an absurd creature.

When he finally caught his breath, he said, "Are your people really going to give us enough trade goods to travel to nine nations, obtain what is valued most in each nation, and then enough food and supplies for an ocean voyage of many months?"

Scolla uncoiled like an explosion. "What is this nine nations, what? You said you needed the treasure of Discoria before you could sail home!"

"I do—Or did—I.--It." Bowmark stopped the stutter with a deep breath. "The current flows like this: I need ten treasures from ten different lands, nations, or tribes before I can return. I obtained one in Rolocton. I had hoped for one in Discoria. Then I would have required eight more."

"Ssa! Why did you not tell me this, why?"

"Why didn't you tell me about your snake repellent, why?"

Scolla turned and wobbled to the prow of the canoe, hissing and spitting the entire way. He gave an entire impassioned lecture to the air in a buzzing, sibilant language which he ended sadly with two words in Common, "Snickering Doom." He sat hunched, looking out to sea, gently kicking the wall of the canoe with his tiny front feet.

Snickering doom? Bowmark raised the sail and caught a steady breeze that readily bore him north. A short while later, he remembered he had planned to sleep away the night's exertion and lowered the sail. Scolla still sat with his arms wrapped around the carved prow.

Bowmark laid himself on his cape and placed his hat over his eyes. Sleep came so quickly, he had time for only one yawn.

When he awoke in the late afternoon with a growling stomach, Scolla still sat on the prow. "Scolla? I thought you slept in the day."

"So I do. However, I am considering walking back to Discoria."

Bowmark crept up to the small creature. "Can you walk that far underwater?"

"No." He wheezed. "I had hoped that my traveling days would soon end. I would write a book about your tribe and send copies to Discoria and the Great Library. I would raise beautiful children who prized learning. One of them would grow into love with me. Then I would start my own family." He paused and turned his shiny round head to look at Bowmark with his eyelids open a slit and mostly covered by his ears. "Why were you given such a difficult task, why?"

Bowmark clenched his fists. What kind of bizarre incest was he talking about? The kratchnak thought his island needed him? He mulled over several responses. Finally, he was able to say, "You don't tell me everything. I don't tell you everything." *Like how disgusting you are.* "You claim to rule the world yet there's no mention of you in the Atlas. My people use descriptions of your people to frighten children, and you tell me it is punishment for your people to *leave*. It is clear to me that honesty is not part of this relationship."

Scolla wheezed. "Zzz. Let us begin a lesson on your pronunciation of Common."

He did need lessons in pronunciation. He also needed the truth, but this insane creature would not give him any. He sat back on the thwart and considered. He had survived the getting of the first treasure. Nine more to go. Despite the unreliability, maybe this kratchnak would be useful.

Bowmark set sail for Bysea.

To be continued . . .

We're so glad you read this book. If you enjoyed the experience, it would be kind of you to leave a review, even if the review is only three words long. Reviews on websites help other people to discover this book. So does asking your local library to buy the book.

Note from the authors:

One of the unique things about the book you're reading is that it's in a prolonged beta state. Like software development, we are hoping to engage a fanbase and iterate on the final work based on *your* feedback. The world of Talifar has been in development for over 20 years, and we have many other novels in the queue. We've given ourselves the unique challenge of building Talifar using scientific-plausibility as a filter for our ideas. And since we can't be experts in everything, we are always looking for experts in almost anything to give us feedback about how we can tweak or change our world and stories to be more realistic and fascinating. For this purpose, we've set up a website that has a form that you can fill out with any feedback you have. Please visit https://breathoflifedev.com/contribute/collaborate-contribute-knowledge/

About the authors:

Josh Foreman has worked in the video game industry for decades. As an artist and designer, he's has been building worlds professionally for many games including Descent 3 and GuildWars 2. Tales from Talifar is his dream project which he plans to develop into film, games, and all other media. He is happy to receive comments, corrections, and adulation at www.breathoflifedev.com or his Youtube channel https://www.youtube.com/scrybe

Rose Foreman was born and things progressed from there. After gaining a degree in Clinical Lab Technology, she swam in the South China Sea, the Atlantic Ocean, and the YMCA. She has climbed Mt. Fuji, Mt. St. Helens, and viewed Mt. Denali. She has raised and released five children (including Josh Foreman).

Cyborg (cochlear implant) and avid gardener, she enjoys collaborating with her oldest son on stories set on Talifar. Don't get her started on talking about Rwanda.

If you would like to sign up for a newsletter to learn of new releases and offers, you can sign up at www.breathoflifedev.com

Editing and Story Development Assistance:

Bloocifer	Kim O'Hara
Jeff Gerke	Frank Foreman

Science Advisors:

Domika Clarke	Ian Dwyer

A special thanks to our beta readers:

A.J. Bakke	Kessandra Pendragon
AJ Scudiere	Lucas Michalczyk
Brian Schaab	Melanie Tryk
Damon Rath	Michael McClelland
Isla Rose	Nicole Stufflebeam
Jennifer Hoffman	Sigrid Sol Karll
Juls Finney	Kessie Carroll

And more thanks to our Patrons, as well as all the Guild Wars fans who supported Josh throughout the years!

Now turn the page to read the first chapter of

THE SCARRED KING II

THE SCARRED KING II

JOURNEY

AS TRADE IS THE LIFEBLOOD OF OUR PEOPLE:
SO CRIME. STRIFE AND WAR ARE DISEASES THAT SHALL
BE GIVEN NO MERCY. SWIFT AND SURE SHALL BE THE REMEDY.
—BYSEA CITY CHARTER

Bowmark contemplated his problem. How could he make sure he killed RaiseHim before the lying designate killed him? That RaiseHim intended to kill him was a given. Bowmark would step on the Bronze Disc set over flowing lava with no weapons and no sandals. The usurping designate would have sandals and he would have all the weapons he wanted.

Bowmark leaned against the mast of his outrigger canoe and chewed on a twig. Cold sunlight sprinkled gem sparkles on the sea. A brisk wind blew through his short, coiled, red hair. He had not seen land for a day.

Nine more treasures to obtain before he could return home and step on the Disc to save Father, his little brother, and the rest of the Sea Predators from the murderous rule of RaiseHim.

Bowmark gripped the edge of the thwart, rolled to a handstand, and did vertical pushups. If he was strong enough, could he take a spear to the gut, charge RaiseHim, and shove him onto the lava before he died? The wind tilted him off-balance. He flipped and straddled the canoe with a foot on each gunwale. He ran through stances.

"Stop thumping." Scolla sounded like a wheezing old man but looked like a monster. Bowmark tried to not hold that against the tezledek. He tried to be grateful the stowaway had given him a magician's cord.

"Stop thumping!"

If he had stayed designate for more than two days, Bowmark would have learned royal-court methods to deal with irritating people. "My canoe, my rules. I need to exercise. Or would you rather I stepped off the canoe to exercise?"

"Quite yes. I need to sleep."

"Perhaps you should step off the canoe to take a nap."

Wheezing, Scolla shifted his skin around and wobbled on the prow thwart. "Snickering Doom."

What that meant besides Scolla was unhappy was a mystery to Bowmark. He dropped onto the middle thwart, rummaged through the bags in the prow, deliberately shoving Scolla aside, and found the bottle of fragrant oil he had purchased to use on his hair. Instead he rubbed the oil on his chest over the blistered area Scolla had given him.

Bowmark soaped his Giver's Hand medallion and swished it through the ocean. Again. How his steel and resin medallion could still reek was another mystery to him. However, why should he care whether or not he learned the answer to either mystery? Somehow, someway, he would find a way to fling out this Scolla.

Now for staffshifter practice. Keeping the weapon in its baton shape, he told the metal, clawed fists on the ends, "Open." Warmth drained from his hand. The exotic metal gently vibrated. Two claws straightened—one more than yesterday. The magic weapon was learning to follow his commands.

Two days later they sailed into the port of Bysea, much smaller than Discoria but much, much larger than Safe Harbor back in StoneGrove. Bowmark hid his magic staffshifter and magic light ball under a pile of net that smelled like rotting fish. He furled the lateen sail, and paddled the rest of the way in. A woman riding high upon the head of a house-sized sea turtle slowly plied the bay. To the east he saw another with ropes attached to the shell tugging the stern of one of the massive box boats, rotating the ship. Bowmark had wondered how such large and cumbersome craft could maneuver into their assigned slots along the docks.

A crowd of rumshae and humans watched Bowmark and his conspicuous canoe pull up to a dock. They speculated about the outrigger floats, spars, trampoline strung between the spars, and the triangular sail. A light drizzle did not dampen enthusiasm for calling out questions about loads, speed, distance, and crafting.

Scolla murmured near Bowmark's knee, "I go to purchase honey and make arrangements. Do not look for trouble."

Why look for what chased him? Bowmark watched with surprise as Scolla deftly climbed the mooring ladder like a spider. The creature seemed so unstable when he walked, but in climbing he rivaled a monkey. Bowmark's brow furrowed as he was reminded of his monkey Snatchfast's end in a magical blaze. Scolla waddled invisibly through the crowd.

The day workers who had hoped to unload cargo wandered off, claiming they were looking for more profitable ships. Off-duty sailors detained Bowmark to talk about his outrigger and their adventures in the distant Eastern Islands. Overhead, seabirds squealed. A line of several large, impossibly fast golden insects flew inland from the sea to a warehouse in the center of the docks. One sailor followed his glance and said, "Therein's the hive."

Bowmark nodded as if that meant something to him. As the talk surged and ebbed, he listened for accidental news about the Southils. When he announced his hunger, a large number of the men took him to the Cauldron Inn. There they talked for more candles over a meal of marinated vegetables, hard-shelled fruit, bread, and braised boar loin. Bowmark practiced his improved pronunciation. He also learned some vocabulary he would not repeat to Father if he ever saw him again.

Then he walked the city for a few candles. Unlike his home and Discoria, Bysea was flat, built on a silty delta. Deep gray skies made the sun difficult to pinpoint, and all the houses and buildings looked alike, with barrel-vaulted roofs, arched doors, reddish-brown plastered walls and round windows filled with a green-tinted, bubbly glass.

Where were the docks? He rotated at one intersection, then another, looking for any landmark he could recognize. He followed a crowd that dispersed one by one into individual houses. How did they know which house was theirs?

The last man turned and pointed a knife at Bowmark. "Robbing me will gain you only hurt."

Bowmark backed up. "Neither money nor hurt do I want from you. Which way are the docks?"

The man snorted and waggled his knife the way they had come from.

Bowmark ran that way until he had to turn a corner or run through someone's home. At the next intersection, a substantial number of male rumshae congregated, gesticulating widely, hooting softly, and wearing tunics and caps that rivaled the flowers of StoneShell in brightness. One of these rumshae was much larger than the rest. This one wore no clothing, only several leather satchels on belts. Where the other's stood semi-upright, this giant's body was level with the ground, his heavily muscled tail balancing his large head. A head with a much larger mouth than the tame sea pup mouths the others had. This one had large dull fangs jutting from his muzzle. Bowmark braced himself against a wall as he grieved that Sunrise was not there to see the rumshae, the strange homes, and the strange humans.

To stave off his pain he visited a weapons shop and marveled at the tiny bows and arrows. How could they aim these toys? His bow, back in StoneShell, was as tall as he was, and the arrows as long as his arm. The shopkeeper let him shoot in a narrow, walled back yard at a target on a bag of rags. A half candle of practice, and he had mastered the tiny bow and arrows. He bought a bow, twenty iron-tipped arrows, and a quiver. Why stop being a pathetic trader now? He handed over his pearls. At least the iron-tipped arrows would be worth more than a couple pearls back home.

Scolla had not returned when he hid the bow near the stern in a bark wrap, so Bowmark ate another meal. As a king's son, he had never paid for anything before, and so he found it fascinating and alarming how fast one's wealth evaporated when every necessity needed to be purchased. How could he order cheaper meals?

At the Blue Banner Inn, Bowmark found an open seat at a table where sailors, wearing a variety of ship's patches, and a dockworker, whose armless shirt displayed bulky muscles and a delicate flower tattoo, sat trading traveling yarns.

Setting down his mug of hot tea and wishing the rotted juices and yeasty grains that the others were drinking did not smell so noxious, Bowmark sat among them. Had his ancestors decided that Sea Predators should hate what everybody else seemed to drink with relish? He remembered to smile. "Might a stranger ask an odd question from simple curiosity?"

"We listen," said a sailor with bright green eyes, blue-black skin, and slate-gray hair curling around his shoulders.

"What do people here in Bysea consider the greatest treasure?"

"Good ale," the dockworker said, hoisting his mug.

"Dead pirates," a sailor with scars that distorted his face said.

"A heavy purse," the sailor with green eyes added.

A full-bodied woman behind him at another table turned, waved a many-ringed hand, and said in a gentle, growly voice, "Nay. Not the heavy purse, but rather what that heavy purse can buy: thick walls and a sound roof."

"A willing woman," said a sallow faced man with a squint eye who looked as though it would take two purses to find such a woman.

"Food and firewood," called a man from a table on the other side of the room.

"A judge," another said. This brought much laughter.

"How do you buy a good husband?" A server laid a platter of bread on the table.

"Aye. There's a rare thing," the many-ringed woman said.

Rumshae at a far table joined in. "A good joke." They fluttered their long, upright ears, making the bells on them jingle.

"A good laugh."

"A good peace."

A human sailor said, "A good wind and good relations with Discoria."

A mellifluous voice said, "My children. Though they have grown and gone, I think about them every day."

Bowmark looked over. His eyes widened at the sight of a gray-skinned man with webbed fingers and slit nostrils above his large eyes. "Give me pardon." Bowmark rose and ignored the continuing serious and frivolous answers. "I see someone I must speak to."

With opposing emotions tumbling around his chest, Bowmark walked to the gray-skinned man. He looked up from his nearly finished meal of marinated sea insects.

"I have—" He thought of Scolla's anger. How could he say it so this seafolk would not explode in anger at how the Sea Predators had murdered seafolks seven years ago? "I have something that belongs—that belonged to one of your people. I thought if I gave this thing to you, you might be able to return it to his family. So they can know what happened."

The seafolk cocked his head and studied Bowmark with large, silvery-blue eyes. "What happened to him?"

How could he justify what his people had done? "There was a storm. A big one. We found him dead on the beach, with two almost adults."

The seafolk shook his head. "We are very hard to drown." He pushed away his plate. "Perhaps they were battered on rocks. Still . . ." He studied Bowmark again. "Not the eyes, not the hair, but something marks you as a sunfolk. Am I right?"

"Ah."

"The lack of body hair. The metallic skin. Those are the clues. Why travel thousands of miles to deliver this item? Why didn't you give it to the next seafolk in your port? I may not run across his family for decades."

"I, ah. We did not know your people existed until he, ah, showed up."

The seafolk sat up straighter. "Really? How can there be an inhabited island we haven't discovered?"

"I don't know."

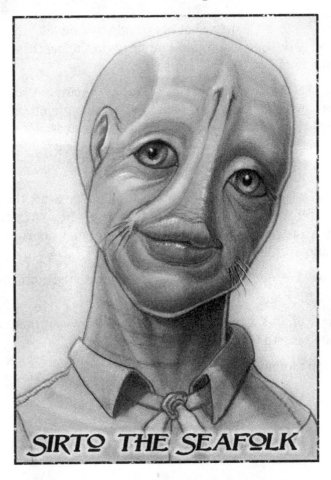

SIRTO THE SEAFOLK

The seafolk stood. "By all means, let us see this item. Only first, and you should find this interesting, let me call my traveling companion. Some of the East Islands sunfolks have a custom. Once a decade, they choose a boy about your age to travel the world for a year or two. He looks for Holy Books of some sort. They've been looking for centuries. They are a generous people who overcompensate us. They do all they can to make our lives a joy. We are happy to aid them on their quest."

He turned, then turned back. "Oh, my name is Sirto. My companion is PledgeKept. You two should truly enjoy one another. Perhaps you could share our room tonight. Wait here." The seafolk rushed up the stairs.

Bowmark gasped. A tsunami of hospitality had smashed over him. How could his people have murdered such a one? He was sorry to give up the Atlas, his guide to the world, but to give it to one such as this eased the loss. But why was he giving up the Atlas? After all, he was planning to dump Scolla and his disapproval of Bowmark owning an Atlas.

He sank into the chair vacated by Sirto and rubbed his wrist across his forehead. He had fallen into a game with unknown and indecipherable rules. Stupidity and shame sat on either shoulder.

Behind him, Sirto said, "And here he is, a lad from an unknown island."

Bowmark turned in the chair and looked up at a young man who looked like Sunrise's cousin from Vertical Drop. He looked into PledgeKept's golden brown eyes and at the three horizontal tattooed lines under his right eye. He should know what that meant.

PledgeKept frowned and looked at Bowmark's large spearhead tattoo on his left shoulder and then the arrowheads scarred and tattooed above his right eyebrow.

PledgeKept stepped back and pulled a knife the same time Bowmark knocked over the chair in his haste to grab a knife and assume a defensive posture. "My enemy!" they exclaimed together.

Other people stood and backed away.

"What is this?" Sirto cried.

PledgeKept's knife gently arced as he sought an opening.

"Not here," Bowmark said. "Innocent people could be hurt." Some men shouted, but what they said, Bowmark did not know. He kept his gaze on the Southil's eyes as he slowly, carefully backed toward the door.

PledgeKept followed, pulling out another knife and ignoring Sirto who clapped his hands in distress, saying, "Lads! Lads! This is unneeded. Stop!"

Bowmark's heel touched the closed door and he dared not drop his defense long enough to open it. The two crouched, their arms out, knives gleaming in their hands.

The patrons of the inn jammed against the walls.

"Lads! Listen! We can discuss this over a tankard. This is some misunderstanding."

"No misunderstanding," PledgeKept said as he kept every bit of attention on Bowmark's face. "Before you stands a cruel murderer. His people slaughter other people like animals. They tear out the hearts of their victims and stack them as offerings to the god of war, Vanquish All."

"Lies," Bowmark said. "We would never worship that Hag of Murder. It is your people that have pursued mine from island to island, staining the seas with our blood. It is you who wear capes of human skin."

"I beg you, lads, stop! PledgeKept's people are peaceful. PledgeKept! Put the knives away!"

"Not while this man breathes."

The seafolk man twisted. "Someone! Help me stop this!"

PledgeKept darted forward and swung his blade. Bowmark ducked, blocked, and slammed into the door.

PLEDGEKEPT

The many-ringed woman screamed.

The rusting hinges of the door gave way. Bowmark stumbled backward.

PledgeKept slashed forward.

Men rushed and grappled the two from behind.

PledgeKept struggled against two men gripping each arm and one with an arm around his neck.

Bowmark stood with hands clutching him all over, and not once did he cease watching PledgeKept and looking for an opening. Men wrenched his arms, but he did not let go of the knives. If PledgeKept's people learned that his still lived, they would scour the seas until they found StoneGrove and slaughtered everyone. Bowmark must not let PledgeKept return to the Southils. Bowmark's whole life had been training for this moment: this need to protect his people from the enemy.

Guards rushed in and tied their forearms behind their backs, hobbled their feet, set nooses about their necks, and pried the knives from their hands.

Sirto pushed himself in front of PledgeKept. "I will not have this violence brought aboard my ship. Find your own way home." He marched away.

PledgeKept made no reply and only made sure to keep Bowmark in view as they were prodded down the street accompanied by a growing crowd and then forced into a large black building with polished stone walls, and into a room that smelled strongly of wax, perfume, and sweat. They were shoved down an aisle to a wooden wall that reached to their shoulders. Atop the wall, a metal grid rose to the ceiling.

Behind PledgeKept and Bowmark, people from the inn and street filled up benches and talked loudly and excitedly with each other. Some captains with tassels of authority on their shoulders walked in and moved up front against a side wall and eyed the young men.

Guards palpated the islander's clothing and pulled out knives of varying sizes from Bowmark's boots and pants and shirt.

A corpulent man of pale hue, wearing a red robe and scarlet cylindrical cap, entered the room from a door behind the wall and mounted a raised chair where he could look down upon the men. "This disarming is taking too long," he growled. "Strip them."

When PledgeKept's arms were untied, he lashed out at the guards who were tugging off his shirt. They knocked him down, tightened his noose, and kicked him until he curled into an unresisting ball. They finished pulling off his clothes and jerked him upright.

Bowmark did not resist even though humiliation and rage heated his face and chest. The goal was killing PledgeKept, so he could not let himself be damaged by these guards.

Both of them had their hands retied together in the front and then tethered to their waists. Behind them, a woman cried, "Oh, Larinna, look at those beauties." Then followed a discourse of their various body parts. Bowmark clenched his teeth and kept his gaze steadfastly on PledgeKept.

The judge raised his hand, and a boy in the back of the room blew a strange curling metal trumpet. The people quieted. The man in red harrumphed. "I have a bed. I have a table. Why, I don't know. When I lie on one or sit at the other, I am called to come here. Once, I would like to finish a meal that is still warm. Strangers, I suppose you think you had a good reason to disturb the peace of Bysea. You with the black hair, what happened?"

PledgeKept said, "Master, this man is a spy for a blood-drinking people who will gladly steal all that is in Bysea and kill everyone here."

Bowmark could not restrain himself. "Lies! His people have sought mine for centuries in their quest to obliterate us."

"Quiet!" roared the judge. "I need three witnesses." A number of people in the room stood. "You, you, and you." Three stayed up while the rest sat. "Sailor, what did you see?"

The squint-eyed man said, "There I was in the Blue Banner, minding my own business and drinking fine rotgut, when this fellow with the black hair comes down the stairs with a seafolk captain. They walk over to this fellow with the red hair. They take one look at each other and shout, "You're my enemy!" Next thing they're waving knives and throwing furniture."

"Hold a moment. A seafolk was also in this fight?"

"No, your judgeship. He was trying to stop the fight."

"Go on."

"The redhead says he's innocent. They try to cut each other. The guards come and grab the red-head. Me and some of the others grab the black-haired one."

"Enough. You."

The blue-black man fiddled with his shirt buttons as he said, "The red-haired boy seemed friendly enough until he saw the black-haired one. They shouted something about enemies. The red-haired one said he was going to hurt some innocent people.

The black-haired boy talked about tearing out people's hearts. They both had a knife in each hand. There was a lot of talk about my people this, your people that. I don't think they live in Bysea."

"Hold. You two. Are either of you a resident of Bysea?"

"No," they replied in unison, both staring at each other.

"All right. You."

A dark brown man with yellow eyes and yellow hair said, "'Tis as the others said. I think one said something about using the other one's skin as a cape. It did not look like a scuffle for fun. I think they would have killed whoever got between them."

"Hold. Sergeant."

"A serving girl came running to us about a fight in the Blue Banner. We heard a scream. When we opened the door, that one fell into our arms. This one tried to stab him, but the patrons were able to grab him. They resisted arrest."

"Hold." The judge scowled down at the young men, who ignored him and only stared at each other. He raised his hand and the boy blew his trumpet again. "Here is my judgment. Bysea does not need, does not want, and will not have your wars brought here. We don't care if you kill each other in some wasteland, but we will not allow you to disturb our peace and endanger our citizens and trade. Your sentence: a flogging of ten strokes each, a night in captivity, and exile. Should you return and renew this feud within our borders, you shall be weighted with stones and thrown into the sea. Ship captains, I need one going north, one south."

The captains conferred with each other briefly and two stepped forward.

The judge thumped his desk. "You with the black hair, have you pay or ability?"

PledgeKept said in a quavering voice, "I know how to run the riggings on a two or three masted ship."

The judge said, "You'll sail south with that captain. You are indentured to him for six months. If you attempt to desert, he has the right to kill you." He shifted in his chair. "You with the big tattoo, have you any pay or ability to sail?"

Bowmark snorted. "I have some gems. I can sail my outrigger."

"Right. You'll pay this captain for a six-month tour north. Sergeant, check his belongings."

The guard squeezed the last of Bowmark's gems from the waistband and handed them to the ship's captain.

The judge slapped his hands on the arms of his chair. "Everybody go home." He climbed down and left.

CPSIA information can be obtained
at www.ICGtesting.com
Printed in the USA
LVHW111110061020
667983LV00018B/1728

9 781942 926030